ONE

FATAL

MISTAKE

TOM HUNT

ORION

An Orion paperback

First published in Great Britain in 2019 by Orion Fiction,
This paperback edition published in 2020 by Orion Fiction,
an imprint of The Orion Publishing Group Ltd.,
Carmelite House, 50 Victoria Embankment
London EC4Y 0DZ

An Hachette UK Company

1 3 5 7 9 10 8 6 4 2

Copyright © Andy Hunt 2019

Published by arrangement with **Berkley, an imprint of
Penguin Publishing Group, a division of Penguin Random House LLC**.
First published in the United States in 2018.

A CIP catalogue record for this book is
available from the British Library.

ISBN (Paperback) 978 1 4091 9232 9

Printed and bound in Great Britain by Clays Ltd, Elcograf S.p.A

www.orionbooks.co.uk

ONE FATAL MISTAKE

By Tom Hunt

A Killer Choice
One Fatal Mistake

To Hayley.
Thanks for the countless laughs
and memories over the years.

THURSDAY

THURSDAY

ONE

THE FRONT DOOR FLEW OPEN AND A SHADOWY FIGURE COVERED IN BLOOD stormed into the house. The living room was nearly pitch-black as Joshua Mayo ran across the room, down the hallway, into the bathroom. He flipped on the bathroom light and quickly stripped out of his bloody clothes—his winter coat, shirt, shoes, pants. He threw everything into a pile in the corner.

He walked over to the sink, gripped the sides of it, and closed his eyes. Paused for a moment. Breathed deeply, slowly. In and out. The past thirty minutes had happened at warp speed and he needed a moment to slow his racing heart, calm the roiling chaos in his mind.

Standing over the sink, his entire body shaking, he looked nothing like an eighteen-year-old honor-roll student. Deep shadows hollowed out his pale cheeks. His eyes were red and puffy from the crying he'd done earlier. His blond hair was spiky in some places, matted to his skull in others.

And then there was the blood. It was everywhere. Smudged all over his hands. Streaked in his hair. Splattered onto his face, vivid as war paint.

He took a final deep breath and stepped away from the sink. It was time to bury his emotions and focus. His mom would be home in the next half hour and there was so much to do before then.

He stepped into the shower and turned on the water. It washed over him, rinsing the blood down the drain—bright red, then pink, then clear.

THE SHOWER TOOK TWO MINUTES. WHEN HE FINISHED, HE TOWELED HIM-self dry and threw open the small door under the sink. He found a roll of garbage bags, tore one off, and put all his bloody clothes into the bag. After changing into a pair of sweatpants and a sweatshirt in his bedroom, he carried the bag out to the garage.

In the corner of the garage, he scanned an assortment of items stored on a large shelving unit—some of his mom's gardening tools, three half-inflated basketballs, a few cans of paint—and grabbed a red plastic gasoline can they used for fueling the lawn mower in the summer. He shook the can and heard some liquid slosh around inside.

He set down the can and garbage bag and ran back into the house. Rummaged around in a few drawers and cupboards until he found what he was looking for: a book of matches.

He carried everything out to the small wooden deck on the back side of the house. Even though he wasn't wearing a coat, Joshua barely noticed the biting early-February cold. All the deck furniture had been stored away for the winter, but the grill was still in the corner, a black protective cover draped over it. He pulled the cover off, lifted the lid, and dumped the contents of the garbage bag onto the grill—his coat, shirt, pants, shoes.

He looked out from the deck at the small backyard, the tranquil farmland that stretched forever, the night sky above. Silence was everywhere. Their closest neighbors were half a mile away in opposite directions—the Thompsons to the east, the Chamberlains to the west—and the lights in both of their homes were out. Far in the distance, six miles away, he could just barely see the outline of a few mid-rise buildings and houses in Cedar Rapids.

Joshua picked up the can and poured gas over the clothes on the grill, emptying the can. The fumes made his eyes water. Once the clothes were soaked, he wadded up the garbage bag and placed it on top of everything.

He grabbed the book of matches and tore one off. Tried to strike it once, twice, until the flame finally caught. He threw the match onto the grill and the clothes caught fire instantly.

FLAMES JUMPED AND RAGED FOR A FEW MINUTES, THEN DIED OUT. JOSHUA stepped closer to the grill and looked inside. The coat was a smoldering lump; the shoes had melted into a deformed blob of leather and plastic. Everything was charred but hadn't burned away entirely. Evidence would still remain.

He had to get rid of it all.

He ran inside and grabbed another garbage bag. Ran back out to the patio and threw the remains of his clothes into it. He hurried down to the lawn and found the loose board near the base of the patio, the board he had always moved to the side when he'd sneaked under the patio to play when he was younger.

He threw the bag of clothes under the patio and put the board back in place. Tomorrow—he'd figure out how to dispose of everything then. When things weren't so hectic.

He threw the cover back over the grill and took the gas can to the storage rack in the garage. Before going back into the house, he looked at his car, a white Nissan Altima, a hand-me-down from his mom. Earlier, he'd poured water over the car's hood and windshield to wash away the splatters of blood, but he looked it over once again to make sure he hadn't missed anything. Everything looked clean; no blood remained. The only evidence that the car had just been involved in a hit-and-run accident was the smashed grille and the crack that splintered through the middle of the windshield, but those could be explained away.

He exited the garage and walked through the house to his bedroom. He lay down in bed. He didn't think he'd be able to sleep, not with the way his body was humming like a low-voltage electrical wire, but there was always a chance. By some miracle, he might actually drift off and the worst night of his life would come to an end.

Before he closed his eyes, there was one final thing he needed to do. He grabbed his phone off the bedside table and pulled up his most recent text exchange. He typed out a message:

> *You there?*

A moment later, the response appeared onscreen:

> I'm here. Did you get back home?
> *Yeah. I washed up. Got rid of the clothes.*

What about your mom?

She's not home yet. I'm alone.

Joshua waited. Then he typed: I can't believe we're covering this up. The response came after a few seconds:

I feel bad, too. Sick to my stomach. But we could've been in deep trouble if we went to the police. We did what had to be done.

A moment later, another message appeared:

It will be our little secret. No one will ever know about this but us.

FRIDAY

TWO

AMBER YOUNGBLOOD PULLED A BLACK CAMRY INTO A STREET-SIDE PARK-
ing stall and killed the engine. She stared out at the downtown square
of Hastings, Nebraska. Dark storefronts. Empty sidewalks. Vacant
parking stalls lining the silent street. This early in the morning, there
was no activity in the small town—but that would soon change.

Her husband, Ross, sat in the passenger seat, statue still, no expression on his hawkish, weather-beaten face. Black jeans, black sweatshirt,
both tight against his thin, scrawny-strong frame. His long hair was
tied into a ponytail, a sprinkle of gray sharing space with the darker
hairs.

"So we're doing this," Ross said. "We're really doing this."

"Damn straight we are."

Ross turned and faced the man who'd just answered. His older
brother, Shane. The third and final member of their party. A massive,

stocky man squeezed into the car's small backseat like an elephant in a cartoon. He had a flat, unsmiling face. Unkempt beard. His lips were arranged into a scowl, his eyes emotionless. Late thirties, a few years older than Ross and Amber.

"Ain't getting cold feet, are you?" Shane said.

"Hell no," Ross answered. "I'm ready to go."

"Good." Shane looked at Amber. "You?"

"Yeah," Amber said. "I'm ready."

The discomfort in her stomach told a different story. She'd already puked once this morning because she was so nervous; she felt like she could again at any moment.

They stared out the car's tinted windows for a silent moment at the not-yet-open businesses lining the town square. A few restaurants, an insurance office, a barbershop. At the end of the block was a building they'd driven by repeatedly over the past week, committing every last detail to memory. It was a large building with a brick façade. HASTINGS STATE BANK, the sign above the door read. WHERE PEOPLE COME FIRST.

"There it is," Shane said. "The bank. About to take that bastard down."

"Let's review the plan," Ross said. "One last time."

"Review the plan? Shit, Ross. You should have the plan down cold by now."

"I do."

"Then why the hell you asking to review it again?"

"Just wanted something to talk about. I don't like the silence. Trust me, I know what to do when this goes down."

"You better. Focus, man. We gotta focus. Can't afford any mistakes here. You grabbed the baggie before we left, right?"

"Yeah, I got it," Ross said. He pulled a small baggie filled with about twenty pills from his pocket, a mix of white, blue, and yellow ones.

"Pop one," Shane said. "Time to get serious. And stick with the yellows. Don't need much. Just a quick hit."

Ross grabbed a yellow pill from the bag and put it into his mouth.

"Good," Shane said. "Now toss it back here."

Ross tossed the baggie toward the backseat. Shane pulled out a yellow pill and swallowed it.

"A little vitamin R," he said. "Just what the doctor ordered."

He threw the baggie back to the front seat. Ross grabbed it and put it into his pocket.

They waited. Amber glanced at the dashboard clock: 7:44. Just a few more minutes. She drummed her fingers against the steering wheel, wiped away the sweat on her forehead, chewed on her lip. She couldn't believe they were about to do this. Rob a bank. Like something out of a movie. She never thought things would actually reach this point; she figured a minor detail would fall through and they'd have to back out at the last minute. But here they were. Only moments away.

"Let's get ready," Shane said.

He grabbed a backpack resting next to him and pulled out three *Star Wars* masks—cheap plastic Halloween masks, the kind available from countless Web sites and novelty shops. He handed Yoda to Amber. Chewbacca to Ross. Kept Darth Vader for himself.

They put on their masks. The Yoda mask was hot and the eyeholes partially obstructed Amber's vision. Smelled, too—a musty, plasticky smell that hung in her nostrils. She turned and looked at Ross in his Chewbacca mask. His eyes were jumping around in the mask's eyeholes, going crazy, the same jittery gaze he always got whenever he was wired on Ritalin. But past that look, she could see the fear in his eyes. The nervous fear.

The look said everything. They'd been through a lot together. But nothing like this.

Shane pulled three black handguns from the backpack and handed them out.

"Should open any minute now," Shane said, staring out at the bank. "Only one thing left to say."

He chuckled dryly.

"May the force be with us."

///////////////////

The microwave beeped and Karen Mayo grabbed two bowls of instant oatmeal from inside. She carried the bowls over to the kitchen table and placed one at her seat, the other in front of her son. Joshua sat at the table, eyes glued to his smartphone, wearing pajama pants and the same faded blue MEN'S GOLF CONFERENCE CHAMPS T-shirt he wore to bed most every night.

"You know the rule," she said. "No phones at the table."

"I know. Just a second."

Karen took her seat. Joshua's eyes remained locked on his phone screen.

"So, what'd you do while I was out last night?" she asked. "Anything exciting?"

"Not really."

"Just a regular, boring old night?"

He glanced up at her. Back down at his phone.

"Yeah. Pretty much."

She already knew something had happened last night; she just didn't know what. She wanted to give Joshua the chance to come clean and be up front with her. But if he wasn't going to say anything . . .

"Actually, while you're on your phone, maybe you can do me a favor," she said. "Google 'How to fix a cracked car windshield' for me, will you?"

He looked up at her, his blue eyes wide with alarm.

"What?"

"Your car," Karen said. "I saw it this morning when I was in the garage. The cracked windshield, the broken grille. What in the world did you do to it last night?"

He lowered his eyes. Stared at his bowl of oatmeal. Busted. And he knew it.

"Sorry," he said.

"Doesn't answer my question. What happened, Joshua?"

He fidgeted in his seat. His eyes skittered around the room.

"Well?"

"Aaron came over to play some *Madden*," he said. "He was—"

"*Madden*? What is that?"

"Football. On PS4."

"PS4?"

"PlayStation 4. It's a video game. He scored a touchdown to beat me and was rubbing it in, joking around. I started chasing him around the house. He ran into the garage and tripped, knocked over that big shelf thing."

"Is he all right? Injured?"

"He's fine. But the shelf fell onto my car and slammed against the windshield."

She gave one of her long sighs, the type she reserved for Joshua anytime he did something that would end up costing her money. It was a reaction they were both familiar with by now. She couldn't even count the number of times he and his friends had broken something in her house while horsing around; they were like little Tasmanian Devils when they got together. Over the years, they'd shattered windows, put a gaping hole in a trampoline, left countless scuff marks and spills throughout the house. The basketball hoop she bought Joshua for his birthday last summer hadn't lasted even two weeks before one of his friends jumped off a chair to slam-dunk the ball and snapped the rim right off.

Now she could add his car grille and windshield to that list.

"This is wonderful," she said. "You'll look great, driving around in a car that looks like it was in a demolition derby."

"I'm sorry, Mom," he said. "It was a dumb mistake."

"You got the *dumb* part right."

"I feel bad. I do. I promise I'll pay for it all myself."

"With what money?"

"I don't know. I'll figure something out."

"I just wish you would be more responsible," she said. "I'm not angry. I'm—"

"Disappointed. I know. I really am sorry, Mom."

She decided not to press the issue. What was the point? All that would accomplish was starting the day out on a bad note, maybe even a minor argument. She didn't need that. Neither of them did.

FIFTEEN MINUTES LATER, KAREN BACKED OUT OF THE DRIVEWAY AND drove through a winding labyrinth of gravel roads, passing empty, frozen farmland and the occasional house until she arrived at the on-ramp for I-380. She eased onto the interstate and drove toward Cedar Rapids, six miles away.

In the passenger seat, Joshua was bundled up in a thick black winter coat, looking (of course) at his phone. She told him she didn't want him driving his car until that crack was fixed—she was probably being overcautious, but it looked unsafe.

"I forgot to ask you," Karen said. "Did you see that photo I posted to Facebook yesterday? The one for Throwback Thursday?"

"Yeah," Joshua said, not looking up from his phone. "Pretty funny."

She smiled. "I thought you'd like that one."

Every Thursday, she scoured her photo albums to find an old picture of Joshua to post to Facebook for Throwback Thursday. She had endless options to choose from; as he was growing up, few milestones in his life passed without her documenting them with a roll or two of film. She had album after album full of photos of him at various sporting events, photos commemorating a variety of firsts (his first haircut, the first time he lost a tooth, his first days of school), photos of him posing with spreads of the gifts he received for Christmases and birthdays over the years—action figures and Legos when he was younger, golf clubs and balls and tees when he got older.

Yesterday, she'd posted a photo from Halloween a decade ago. She was dressed in an oversize foam hot dog costume with only her face visible. Right next to her was Joshua, eight years old, dressed as a small ketchup bottle. "Here's two doggone cuties!" was the caption she'd added to the post.

"Okay, so it was a little corny, but that's what moms are for, right?" she said. "Oh, and I've got a good one lined up for next week, too. I found all the photos from your sixth birthday party. The one we had at Chuck E. Cheese."

Joshua cracked a small smile but kept his eyes on his phone. As she continued driving, Karen stole quick glances out of the corner of her eye at him. Something about him seemed . . . not quite right. As they drove down the interstate, she finally realized what it was.

"Your coat," she said. "Why are you wearing that old coat?"

He looked up from his phone. "What?"

"Why aren't you wearing your new coat?" she asked. "The one I got you for Christmas."

"I don't know. Just felt like wearing this one."

She shook her head. No use in even trying to make sense of that. He'd begged for a new coat for Christmas—the latest design from some fancy foreign company whose name she couldn't even pronounce, a big puffy thing with fake animal fur lining the hood. Looked like a coat designed for an Arctic explorer or something. She'd practically flipped when he told her the coat's four-hundred-dollar cost, but she saved up and bought him one for Christmas anyway.

And now, barely two months later, he'd gone back to the old coat.

She drove on down the interstate, slowly approaching Cedar Rapids, where she worked and Joshua attended school.

"I've got a good feeling about today," she said. "I think today might be the day."

"For what?"

"The day you find out if you got into Clemson. They said they'd get back to you by the end of the month, right? That's only a few days away. Wouldn't that be something? We've been waiting long enough."

No response. She glanced over at Joshua. His phone was gone; now he was blankly staring straight ahead, his thin body slouched in the seat, blond hair combed over his forehead. He looked so gloomy. Off in his own little world. He was about as alert as a zombie most mornings, but there seemed to be something more to it today, something sad and mechanical.

"You there?" she said, snapping her fingers. "What's going on with you? You're so out of it this morning."

He glanced toward her. "I'm fine. Just tired."

It was more than tiredness, she was sure. Probably had something to do with being eighteen years old and getting a ride to school from Mom. Or maybe it was girl problems. Last week, his girlfriend had broken up with him, and he'd been moping around the house since then. No way she was touching that subject; he'd already been very clear that discussing the breakup with his mother was the last thing in the world he was interested in. She suppressed a chuckle, recalling the look of horror that crossed his face a few days ago when she asked him if he wanted her advice on how to move on after the breakup.

The car was mostly silent for the rest of the drive. Twenty minutes after leaving their house in the country, she pulled into the parking lot of Jefferson High School.

"Have a good day," she said as Joshua exited the car.

"Yeah. You, too."

"Hey. Perk up, J-Bird."

He smiled. But like everything else about him this morning, something about it seemed just a little off.

///////////////

Head hanging, Joshua Mayo walked up to the entrance to Jefferson High School. He was surrounded by students bundled up in winter coats and hats, backpacks slung over their shoulders. Some in groups, some by themselves.

Inside, he went into the first men's bathroom he saw. It was empty, thank God. He locked himself in a stall and leaned his forehead against the door, closing his eyes.

He was exhausted; sleep had been impossible. All evening, the grisly, gruesome details of everything that had happened last night replayed in his mind, repeated endlessly, over and over again. He couldn't believe that he'd killed a man; it was such an incredible, harrowing thought.

This morning, he'd checked on his phone every local Web site he could think of, looking for any sort of news about a body being discovered, but there'd been nothing. It wasn't so surprising. The accident took place deep in the country. Out on a worn, little-traveled gravel path that cut through a wooded region named Hawkeye Wildlife Management Area. A massive twenty-square-mile stretch of forested land full of trees and lakes and not much else. The only reason people went out by the wildlife management area this time of year was to hunt or camp . . . but hunting season had ended months ago and it was far too cold to camp right now.

He guessed it would be days, maybe even a week or longer, before someone ventured out far enough to discover the body.

Eventually it would happen, though. And once the body was found, there'd be a police investigation. What would happen then? He truly didn't know. They'd cleaned up the scene and searched to make sure they didn't leave anything behind that could link them to the crime, but there was no way to be certain they'd found everything. The moment had been so frantic. He knew the police wouldn't need much. If they found a piece of fabric, a fingerprint, even something as minor as a footprint, they might be able to connect him to the dead body. And that would be it. His life would be over.

Joshua exited the stall and walked over to the sink. Washed his hands, splashed some water on his face. Before exiting the bathroom, he grabbed his phone from his pocket. Brought up the text exchange from last night. He typed out a message.

Rough morning. Couldn't sleep last night.

He waited a minute. The response appeared:

Me neither. Just remember, we did the right thing. It sounds horrible, but the guy was dead. No way to save him. Calling the police would've only gotten us in deep, deep trouble. We didn't have a choice.

Joshua stared at the phone. No matter how many times he heard that justification—*the guy was already dead; going to the police wouldn't have saved him*—it didn't make him feel any better about what had happened and the decision they'd made.

He typed: **It's just tough to handle. Really tough.**

I feel awful, too. Just hang in there. Try to act normal. We'll talk when I'm free. Later today.

Joshua texted: **K.**

He put his phone in his pocket and walked to the cafeteria. The room was packed with students sitting at tables, waiting for the school day to begin. Warbling, excited chatter was everywhere. He found his friends Freddy and Aaron at a table in the middle of the room and sat down beside them.

"Just in time," Aaron said. He was skinny with long, shaggy dark hair and an easy, full smile. "I was about to tell Freddy about this weekend. I'm going on a college visit. Visiting my older brother at Luther. It's gonna be wild."

He started talking about a kegger his brother was going to throw Saturday night, but Joshua could barely pay attention. He looked around the cafeteria, at the groups of students sitting and chatting with friends. Smiling faces and laughter everywhere, gossiping, talking about plans for the weekend. He wondered if he'd ever be able to forget about last night and feel that carefree again.

"My brother was telling me about this one girl," Aaron went on. "Monica. Total babe. Said he's gonna set me up with her."

He pulled his phone from his pocket.

"I found her on Instagram. Check it out."

He opened her profile and turned the screen toward them. He quickly scrolled through photos of a cute blond girl in various poses: dressed up for a night out, walking a dog, studying in the library.

"You're telling me your brother is setting you up with this girl?" Freddy said.

"Yeah."

"And you think you actually have a chance with her?"

"Yeah."

"Dude, this is a college chick. She's, like, way out of your league."

"My brother says I'm her type."

Freddy laughed. "Her type, sure. Twenty bucks says nothing happens with her."

"You're on."

Freddy and Aaron shook on their bet and continued talking. Joshua silently sat there, still thinking about last night. In bed, he'd come up with a story to explain the car damage, the story about Aaron knocking the shelving unit onto the windshield. Wasn't the best explanation, and there'd been something in his mom's reaction that told him she didn't quite believe him, but he hoped the story would hold up.

"What about your weekend, J?" Aaron asked. "You gonna meet up with Ashley?"

"No," Joshua said. "I told you. It's over."

Last week, when his girlfriend had broken up with him, it had been a hot topic of discussion between Freddy and Aaron, whether the breakup would be permanent or not.

"I still think you're gonna get back with her," Freddy said.

"I bet he won't," Aaron said.

"Twenty bucks?"

"You're on." They shook. Freddy turned to Joshua. "You're totally getting back with her. Just admit it."

Joshua tried to smile, but all he could force through was an uncomfortable wince.

THREE

"IT'S GAME TIME," SHANE SAID.

Staring at the bank entrance from half a block away, Amber watched as a skinny old man in a gray security guard uniform appeared behind the bank's glass entrance doors. Even with the Yoda mask partially obstructing her vision, she could see him pull a set of keys from his pocket, fit one into the door's keyhole, and unlock the door. He walked back to the bank floor.

"Open for business," Shane said. "Let's go."

Amber floored the accelerator for the half block to the bank and haphazardly pulled into one of the vacant stalls by the entrance. They barged out of the car and stormed inside—clad in black, their guns drawn—Darth leading, Chewbacca right behind him, Yoda bringing up the rear.

Inside, the bank layout was exactly like the photos Shane had taken earlier in the week, the photos he'd had them study constantly over the past few days. An open, spacious lobby with marble floors. A small standing desk for a security guard right inside the entrance. A waiting area and a counter with three teller windows off to the side. In the far back were a few doors leading to offices and the safe.

Per the plan, Ross went straight to the counter and Shane ran to the rear, their guns in the air. Amber went to the security guard standing by the entrance, the old-timer they'd seen unlock the door moments ago. He was a frail old guy in a gray uniform, a badge that didn't mean shit pinned to his chest.

"On the ground," she yelled, pointing her gun. "Down! Now!"

She lowered her voice to sound hard and edgy, like a seasoned pro, but it sounded ridiculous to her. Almost comical.

The security guard stared at her, unmoving. She wondered if he could tell, just from the sound of her voice and the way she held the gun, that he was dealing with a rank amateur who was probably more terrified than he was.

"I said down, Pops! Don't make me have to use this."

The security guard remained frozen. Just as Amber started to worry seriously—*God, am I actually going to have to* shoot *him?*—the security guard hit the ground as if his legs had stopped working.

Amber focused on the back of his head, her breath hot and heavy in the mask, that same musty scent every time she inhaled. Behind her, she could hear pure chaos.

A scream.

A yell.

Ross's voice: "Hands in the air!"

Someone crying.

Commotion.

Shane's voice: "Nobody fucking move."

He barked the words, commanding and authoritative. Just from the sound of his voice, anyone could've determined that the brutish man in the Darth Vader mask was the one in charge. The ringleader.

Amber kept the gun pointed at the motionless geezer on the ground and snuck a quick glance behind her. Saw Ross in his Yoda mask, standing in front of the counter, moving his gun between three tellers. Two women, one man—wearing nice button-up shirts and dress pants, all with their hands in the air, looks of openmouthed astonishment on their faces.

Ross threw a backpack on the counter, directly in front of one of the clerks. "Empty the drawers," he said. "No dye packs, no tracers."

The clerk lowered his hands and began shoveling stacks and assorted bills from his money drawer into the backpack.

In the rear of the bank, Shane walked a few feet behind two men in suits, his gun pointed at their backs. They disappeared through a thick black door.

Amber's eyes went back to the guard. He was still on the ground, facedown, hands splayed out from his body.

"Please, p-please don't hurt me," the guard said in a low voice. "I have a wife. And grandchildren."

"Shut up and you'll see them again," she said. Again, her lowered, toughened voice sounded absurd to her. An empty threat.

Seconds that felt like hours passed. She focused on the guard, her heartbeat rocking against her chest. Her face was drenched under the musty mask, sweat dripping into her eyes.

Ross's voice yelled out: "Coming your way!"

A backpack slid over on the ground and stopped a few feet from her. A moment later, Shane appeared from the back, holding another backpack in one hand, still pointing his gun at the two suited men in front of him. Shane slid it over to Amber and it came to a stop near the one Ross had sent over.

Two backpacks now.

Shane led the men in suits behind the counter, next to the clerks. He looked at his wristwatch, then pointed at Amber. He made a circular motion with his index finger.

It was time. She leaned down so her face was only inches from the back of the security guard's head. "Count to one hundred; then you can move," she said. "Don't try to be a hero."

She stuck her gun in the waistband of her pants and hurried over to the two bags on the ground. She grabbed one in each hand and ran past the entrance, back outside. On the town square, there was still no sign of activity; nothing had changed in the minutes they'd been inside.

She sprinted to the car and sat down in the front seat. Ripped off the Yoda mask and tossed it and the backpacks of money into the backseat. Fired up the engine.

Panting like she'd just run a marathon, she focused on the bank entrance. She brushed some strands of blond hair from her eyes.

She waited.

Waited some more.

And then the bank door flew open. Chewbacca stormed out, sprinting toward the car with Ross's long, lean movements. A few steps behind him, Darth Vader followed, Shane rumbling along.

Amber tensed up. Almost time.

Ross reached the car first. He threw open the passenger door and jumped inside, slamming the door shut behind him. A moment later, Darth reached the rear door. He pulled on the handle. The door didn't open. He started frantically yanking on the handle, but the door stayed shut.

"It's locked!" Shane screamed, pounding his fist on the window. "Unlock the fucking door!"

"Go," Ross said to Amber. "Floor it!"

Amber slammed her foot on the accelerator and the car sped out of the parking stall, leaving Shane behind. Looking in the rearview mirror, Amber watched Shane chase them for half a block, then give up. He stood in the middle of the road, staring at them from behind the Darth Vader mask, watching the car disappear. Perhaps he was just now realizing what had happened: he'd been double-crossed. Screwed out of the money.

Amber whipped the wheel to the left and the Camry took a turn without slowing. The tires screeched, cutting through the tranquil morning. She flew through an intersection. They sped past silent homes and empty streets.

Next to her, Ross tore off his Chewbacca mask. The ponytail he'd tied his hair in before the robbery had come undone and his long hair flowed like the mane of a wild animal.

"We did it!" he yelled. "Can't believe it. We did it!"

"Not over yet," Amber said. "We need to get out of here first."

"Then, book it, babe. Let's roll."

Amber sped through the sleepy town and took a left turn. Straight for a few blocks. After a minute, she passed a sign that read: THANKS FOR VISITING HASTINGS, NEBRASKA. Modest houses with small front yards immediately gave way to flat, frozen farmland.

They motored down a two-lane highway, Hastings disappearing behind them.

///////////////

After dropping off Joshua, Karen drove back across the city. Took Eighth Avenue SW over the Cedar River and arrived at Mercy Hospital, the biggest hospital in Cedar Rapids. After changing into scrubs, the day-shift nurses met the night shift for handoff. Then Karen's day began.

Fifty million places to be. Always on her feet. Medication to administer. Reports to write. Check-ins to update physicians. As a nurse in the intensive care unit, she spent her entire morning jumping between the patients under her care, making assessments of and adjustments to their treatment to keep them stable and hopefully move them closer to recovering from major surgery. One heart attack patient was diabetic, and she stopped by his room consistently to monitor his insulin levels. Another patient had spiked a fever—could mean a new infection—so she took a few samples to send to the lab.

When her break came in the midmorning, she went to the small room that served as the floor's kitchen / break room. A few of her co-workers sat at the table in the middle of the room. She poured a cup of coffee and sat down next to Carmella, a cute Hispanic girl with smooth olive skin and curly brown hair. She was in her mid-twenties, the youngest nurse on their floor, though she looked barely older than a teenager. Her green scrubs hung off her petite body like a tent.

"Just the person we wanted to see," Carmella said to her. "Tell us all about it. Right now."

"Tell you about what?" Karen said.

"Your date. We want to hear all about last night's date."

"That's right, your date," Peg said. She was a rail-thin nurse, a lifer who'd been a nurse for decades. "Was he cute?"

"In good shape?"

"What kind of car did he drive?"

"What about his butt? Nice butt?"

"Tell us all about the dinner, the conversation—"

"And don't leave out the part about the hot, steamy lovemaking," Carmella said.

"Oh, we definitely want to hear about that."

The ladies at the table began laughing. Karen couldn't hold back a smile. "There was nothing of the sort," she said.

"Details, baby—give us the details," Carmella said.

Her date. The reason she hadn't been home last night. Joshua hadn't asked her about the date this morning, and she'd held on to a glimmer of hope that her coworkers would forget to ask about it, too.

No such luck.

So she rehashed everything about the date. She'd been exchanging messages with him on one of the dating sites she was a member of, and they'd decided to finally meet up at a bar last night. Her date had arrived ten minutes late; while waiting for him, she'd sat at a table alone, surrounded by young, beautiful drunk people who all looked like high school students to her, like they should be classmates of Joshua's, not out drinking at a bar. Once her date finally showed up, he spent more time watching the basketball game on the TV than talking with her. The few times they did talk, it was clear from the look on his face that he was having difficulty hearing what she was saying. An unremarkable evening, just like every other date she'd been on recently.

It had been scarcely a month since she'd decided to start dating again. For years, she'd simply had no time to date. Between raising Joshua by herself, going back to college for her nursing degree once he got older, and attending his golf meets and other functions when he reached high school, she hardly had a moment to breathe, let alone start a relationship. Joshua's life was her life; there wasn't time for anything else.

But she knew that there'd soon be a huge void when Joshua left for college. It was something she could still hardly fathom, that in roughly six months she'd be in the house by herself, without him. And so came her New Year's resolution, made barely more than a month ago: start dating. Really try to find someone.

When she'd told her coworkers about her plans, the news had gone off like a bomb. All of them except for Carmella were married, and they'd thrown themselves into the task of finding her a man. Scouring online dating sites. E-mailing choices to her. Telling her about someone from church or a former coworker who'd be perfect for her.

"Long story short," Karen said, finishing up her recap, "I don't think there'll be a second date."

Carmella started talking about a doctor down on the third floor she wanted to set her up with. Karen politely nodded but barely paid attention. She'd heard it all before.

"What about this weekend, lovergirl?" Peg asked. "How many hot dates do you have lined up for this weekend?"

"None," Karen said. "I have the weekend off and I'll be relaxing. A nice, quiet weekend with nothing going on. Exactly what I need."

///////////////////

A bell rang, classroom doors flew open, and students swarmed into the hallways. Joshua worked his way through the mob. The day was just half over and, already, it had been grueling. He didn't know how he was going to make it through a few more hours.

When he got to his locker, it took three tries to enter his combination correctly. He grabbed his phone off a shelf and quickly checked the same local news sites he'd checked after every class so far.

No report of a body being found out by Hawkeye Wildlife Management Area.

Nothing about a missing person.

Joshua set his phone back in his locker. He closed his eyes, clenched and unclenched his hands. He'd hoped that the school day would provide a distraction, but it hadn't. That same nervous, uneasy feeling had eaten away at him all day, just as it had every moment since last night.

Right as he was about to close his locker, his phone chimed with a new message. He tensed up and grabbed it. The message onscreen was from the number he'd texted earlier:

You there?

Joshua typed out: **Yeah. Here.**

How you doing?
   Not good.
Me, either. Just know, we're in this together. You and me.
You're not alone.
   I know. It's still tough. Can't stop thinking about everything
   that happened.

A bell rang, signaling one minute until next period began.

Gotta go, Joshua typed.

Me, too. I love you. Never forget that. I love you more than anything in the world.

    K. Love you, too.

Stay strong. Talk soon.

Joshua set his phone in his locker and shut the door.

THE REST OF THE SCHOOL DAY WAS JUST AS DIFFICULT AS THE MORNING.
Every class dragged by. Every hour was a struggle. After school, Joshua went to an indoor driving range across town with a few golf teammates. Around twenty golfers were lined up, spaced out a few feet apart, swinging mechanically, the boys' team in a row on one half, the girls on the other. At the far end of the row his ex-girlfriend, Ashley, swung away, wearing a polo and a pair of khakis, her brunette hair pulled into a tight ponytail.

The only sound in the cavernous room was the smack of golf clubs and the occasional mumbled chatter.

Joshua set a ball down, adjusted his grip on the club, and swung. The ball soared for a bit and sharply sliced to the right before it was caught in the netting set up at the edge of the room. He set another ball down and hit it. Another slice.

"Gotta stop thinking about Ashley, man," Aaron said from the tee box next to him.

"I'm not."

"Sure you are. Better not get back with her. I'll be pissed if you cost me twenty bucks."

Aaron laughed. Joshua didn't react. He continued to hit drive after drive, most of them shanks. Twenty minutes in, the feeling suddenly hit him: a discomfort in his stomach, a feeling like he was totally overwhelmed. He ran to the bathroom. Once he was alone in a stall, he was certain he'd start vomiting. Or crying. But nothing happened. He stood in the bathroom, alone, staring down at the toilet.

He returned to the driving range and continued hitting golf balls, his swing steady as a pendulum. The entire time, all he could think of was the body out in Hawkeye Wildlife Management Area. The body that was slowly rotting away.

The body that was out there because of him.

FOUR

TWO HUNDRED MILES OUTSIDE OF HASTINGS, AMBER PULLED UP TO A
roadside convenience store in the middle of nowhere. Looked like
a place that time forgot, like something straight out of the 1950s:
a rickety, ramshackle building with a nonelectric Shell sign out
front and, nailed to the walls, sun-faded tin sheets advertising car
brands.

"Why we stopping?" Ross asked.

"Low on gas. Less than a quarter tank."

Amber parked next to one of the gas pumps. She stepped outside
and put the nozzle in the tank. She stared at the counter as it ticked
upward, the numbers passing in a blur. The bank robbery had happened four hours ago, but everything still lingered—the nerves, the
jackhammering of her heart, the rush of the escape. After leaving
Hastings, they'd driven through flat countryside interrupted by the

occasional small town. The entire drive, she'd tried to calm herself, but she just couldn't ditch that uneasy, anxious feeling.

She looked at Ross, still slouched in the passenger seat. He blankly stared out the windshield, his mouth a straight line, forearms crossed over his slender chest.

She walked around the car and tapped the window. Ross lowered it and she leaned in.

"You doing all right?" she asked.

"Yeah," he said. He ran a hand through his long hair. "I just . . . I can't believe we did it. I can't believe we screwed Shane over."

"I can't, either. But it had to be done. You know that."

Ross continued to stare out the windshield, at the flat farmland that stretched forever beyond the gas station. He looked so sad. She knew it had to be difficult for him, the way they'd double-crossed Shane. Shane was his older brother. They'd grown up together, shared a lifetime of memories, had a bond that was almost as tight as the one she and Ross had.

"Cheer up, baby," she said to him. "Everything went exactly like we planned it. We're rich."

That made Ross smile, which seemed to take ten years off his hardened face. Once they were safely away from Hastings, Ross had counted the money from both backpacks. Took him nearly half an hour. When he finished, he'd counted almost forty thousand dollars between the two bags, some loose bills, some stacks of money. The number blew Amber away. Shane had mentioned that the bank they'd targeted was some sort of shipping facility for other banks in nearby small towns, but going into the robbery she didn't think they'd get anything near forty thousand dollars.

Ross consolidated the money into one backpack and, for almost half an hour, he'd stared at all that money crammed inside, admired it, picked up handfuls of it, and dropped it back into the backpack. He'd talked about all the things they could buy with the money, speaking so excitedly that his words slurred together—and when Amber looked at him a few minutes later, he was asleep. Just like that, he'd crashed. Sudden, sharp crashes like that were common when he was coming off a high from drugs.

"Forty thousand dollars," she said to him now. "We can do anything with that kind of money. Go anywhere."

"I know," Ross said. "But I just can't stop thinking about Shane. Been through a lot with him. Tough to believe that it's all over." He turned to her. "Think he got picked up?"

"Probably. Don't know where he would've escaped to."

The backpack with the money was resting in Ross's lap. Amber reached in and grabbed a handful of bills from inside, held them up for Ross to see.

"You know what this money represents," she said. "A new life for us. A better life. A life away from Shane, away from all the other distractions."

She stared out at the endless, empty land surrounding them.

"Just you and me," she said. "You and me against the world. That's the way it'll be from now on."

ONCE THE GAS TANK WAS FULL, AMBER WENT INSIDE TO PAY. EVEN THOUGH the gas station was outdated, there was a display of disposable cell phones right inside the door. She bought one. She and Ross hadn't packed clothes or any personal belongings before the robbery. They didn't want Shane to get suspicious if he saw a suitcase. They hadn't even brought their phones. They were starting over in every sense of the term. Nothing but their wallets and the clothes on their backs.

Ross insisted he was fine to drive after his nap, and they switched seats. Despite her nerves, Amber fell asleep almost instantly.

When she awoke, they were on a gravel road, kicking up dust and dirt behind them. Ross had an arm around her, one hand on the steering wheel. She was curled up, leaning into his body. There was a forest to their left, large trees rising into the sky. Flat farmland to their right. It was like the road was a divider between two completely different worlds.

The radio was on low. Willie Nelson. Ross was singing along in the husky voice she'd heard belt out thousands of songs over the years. His voice was low and deep, barely more than a mumble.

. . . on the road again . . .

She silently sat there in his embrace for a moment, listening to him sing. The song was one of her favorites. He'd sung it on the night they met. Eighteen years ago, that had been. With Ross's low voice sounding in the car, she stared out the window and thought back to that night, back to when it all began.

Her life up to the point she met Ross was mostly unspectacular. She left home a few weeks after graduating high school in Tennessee. Traveled around, crashed on some couches. Worked as a waitress at nearly every townie bar and greasy spoon in the state. Before she realized it, a few years had flown by.

The night she met Ross, she was doing what she did most every night she didn't have to work: sitting alone at a bar, peeling the label off a beer bottle, wondering if she'd ever figure out her life.

Two men carrying guitars walked onto the small stage at the front of the bar. They introduced themselves as Ross and Shane Youngblood. The Blood Brothers. They couldn't have looked more different. Shane was a giant in every sense, tall and overweight, a bushy beard covering the lower half of his face. Ross was slender, with hair down to his shoulders. He wore a cowboy hat and a button-up tucked into a pair of jeans.

The Blood Brothers sat on small stools onstage. Ross adjusted the microphone and began singing, one old country-western song after another. His voice was deep and throaty, smooth as honey. Shane played guitar in the background, occasionally providing backup vocals, but it was like he wasn't even there.

She kept her eyes locked on Ross as they played. He was ruggedly handsome, had that true cowboy look to him, but she felt more than physical attraction. It was like they shared something between them. It was a spark. A connection. The bar was half-full, but to her it felt like it was just the two of them, him serenading her.

After the set was over, she nearly melted when Ross walked up and offered to buy her a drink.

They talked all night. Exchanged life stories. Ross had lost his parents when he was fifteen, and Shane, his older brother by a few years, had become his legal guardian. Ross dropped out of school and spent his days working with Shane at the car repair shop they inherited from their father. Spent their nights playing guitar together. After a few years, they decided to sell the car shop and go all in on chasing their music dream. Since then, they'd toured all over Tennessee, booking gigs at any bar or festival that would take them, hoping that their big break was just around the corner.

Amber gave Ross her number. After only a few weeks of hanging out, she quit her job and joined Ross and Shane as they toured around to different bars throughout Tennessee in Shane's old conversion van. Life became nonstop. Late nights. Constant partying. A different town every night. The three of them were inseparable, she and the Blood Brothers. One bar to the next. One performance after another.

It was crazy, constant fun. Ross and Shane were forces of nature, identical in everything but appearance. Two hard-driving, hard-partying good ol' country boys. Seemed like they had only two speeds: fast and faster.

Her relationship with Ross moved just as quickly. Being with him was a trip, a wild ride; the spark hadn't died out. They started living together. Got married after a few years, a small affair at a local courthouse with Shane as the only attendee.

The late nights became later, the wild nights even wilder . . . and then things started getting a little too wild. Shane began using amphetamines. Ritalin, Adderall. The pills transformed him. He'd already had a short temper—every week or two, a night out would end with Shane getting in a fistfight—but the amphetamines made it worse. It was like he actively looked for a reason to start trouble. All it would take was a minor perceived slight to set him off. Someone looking at him wrong or cutting in front of him in line at the bar.

Every night soon started following the same pattern. Ross and Shane would play music at that night's bar for a few hours. The three of them would party afterward, throwing back drinks. Around his third or fourth drink, Shane would pop a few pills. And the night would go straight downhill. He'd become aggressive and hostile. He'd take a few more pills, start mouthing off. More often than not, the night would end with Shane getting in a fight, sometimes taking on two or three people, before Amber and Ross hurriedly ushered him out of the bar.

All of a sudden, it wasn't fun any longer. She was in her late twenties—the all-night parties had lost their appeal. The travel had, too. And Shane was starting to truly worry her; it was only a matter of time before he did something to get himself arrested, maybe even worse.

She asked Ross to leave Shane and break up the Blood Brothers, maybe get a normal job and settle down, but he insisted that he couldn't abandon Shane. Family, he told her. He couldn't turn his back on family. Not after how Shane had been there for him when their parents died. Not after all they'd been through together.

But there was more to it than that; she could tell. The more time she spent around them, the more she realized that Ross was just plain scared of Shane. Unable to stand up to him. Part of it was size, with Shane being taller and twice as big as Ross, but part of it was attitude. Shane was flat-out intimidating. Outspoken. Loud. Bossy.

Amber started waitressing again, staying home and working while Ross and Shane traveled. She felt Ross slipping away from her. Felt a divide she'd never felt in their marriage before. Whenever she'd ask Ross to leave Shane, the response was always the same as before: family—he couldn't turn his back on family.

The phone call that shattered everything came on a Tuesday morning. The police, calling to tell her that Ross had been arrested and charged with drug possession. And intent to distribute.

She drove to jail and listened to Ross explain everything. Shane had started selling drugs to people who attended their concerts, usually slipped into the cases of their CDs. He convinced Ross to join him. The wrong person found out and they were busted.

Ross begged Amber to forgive him, to stand by his side, to give him another chance, but she'd had enough. She shook her head, stood up, and told Ross she never wanted to see him again. She walked out of the jail, leaving Ross behind, and—

The car jerked forward. Ross's singing was interrupted by a loud grating noise from the underside of the car. Amber sat up in her seat.

"What the hell?" Ross said.

The car jolted and lurched and began violently shaking. Ross pulled to the side of the gravel road and came to a stop on the shoulder. He stepped outside and popped the hood. After a minute of looking at the engine, he slammed the hood shut.

"Connecting rod is broken," he said. He kicked the driver's-side door a few times, hard enough to leave a dent. "Christ. You gotta be kidding me."

"Can we still drive it?"

"Hell no. It busted a hole in the crankcase. Engine's shot."

"What are we gonna do?"

Ross looked around. The forest was to their left, flat farmland to their right. Not much else.

"We're out in the middle of nowhere," he said. He shook his head and kicked the door again. "I'll drive this piece of junk into those woods over there. Hide it a little. Make sure no one sees it if they drive by."

"Then what?"

"Walk through the forest, I guess. Hope it leads somewhere."

Amber checked the disposable phone for a map. No service. She put it in her pocket.

Ross sat back down in the driver's seat. The car started with a loud noise. It shook and rocked as he slowly drove it into the woods. He stopped the car a couple of hundred feet into the forest and grabbed the backpack filled with money. Ross slung it over his shoulder and they exited the car and started walking. Right on the edge of the woods, they passed a worn metal sign littered with buckshot.

HAWKEYE WILDLIFE MANAGEMENT AREA, it read.

/////////////////////

The day continued for Karen. She jumped from one room to the next, alternating between one task and another. A constant stream of things to do.

A few hours from the end of her shift, she was filling out a chart when she looked over at the storage room on their floor. Through the small window on the door, she saw Carmella standing in the room, her back to the door. She was alone.

Karen figured she was grabbing supplies for one of her patients, but when she looked up a few minutes later, Carmella was still there. Alone in the corner of the room.

Karen walked over and stuck her head into the room. She heard a light whimpering noise—it took her a moment to realize that Carmella was crying.

"What's wrong?" Karen said.

Carmella turned around. There were tearstains under her eyes.

"I didn't hear you come in," she said. "You startled me."

Karen stepped into the room and shut the door behind her.

"What is it? What's wrong?"

"Nothing."

"So you're crying in the middle of the day for no reason?" Karen said. "Come on, honey. What is it?"

Carmella shook her head. She dabbed at her eyes with the sleeve of her scrubs. A small patch of green cloth darkened.

"It was Mrs. Johnson," she said.

"Oh dear. Did something happen?"

"No, she's fine. It was just . . . earlier, when I was in her room, she told me one of her jokes. It was a cheesy, corny joke but I couldn't stop laughing. After I left her room, I pulled out my phone to text the joke to my mom . . . and for just that moment, when I was holding my phone, I forgot. Forgot about the funeral, forgot that she was gone, forgot about it all."

"I'm sorry, sweetie."

"That's happened a few times since my mom passed. I'll hear a joke or see something and I'll pull out my phone to text her about it. Then I remember, and it hurts. It hurts a lot."

"The same thing happened to me when my mother passed," Karen said. "Day by day. That's how you get through it. Sometimes you have setbacks but you keep going on."

Carmella smiled at her. She dabbed her eyes again.

"Thanks," she said.

"Of course. Anytime you—"

"I'm not thanking you for the advice. Well, I am. I appreciate that. But everything else you did when my mom was sick—that's what I'm thanking you for."

"You've already thanked me. Plenty of times."

"It can never be enough," she said. "I mean it."

Karen nodded, thinking back. Two months ago, they'd been leaving the hospital together after a shift when Carmella dropped her purse. The contents spilled everywhere—a makeup compact, her keys, a few credit cards . . . and a vial of Dilaudid. An opioid ten times stronger than morphine. A drug commonly used on the street.

Karen picked up the vial and stared at it—stunned, in total shock. She couldn't believe it: Carmella was stealing medication from their floor. When Karen finally found her voice, she managed a single word. *Why?*

Carmella explained that the medication wasn't for her; it was for her mother, who was bedridden at home with a terminal illness. The painkillers she'd been given weren't having much of an effect, and doctors wouldn't prescribe anything stronger. And so, for weeks, Carmella had been stealing leftover vials of Dilaudid from their floor. After she administered a portion to a patient, she'd pocket the vial instead of disposing of it in the waste bin, then smuggle it back home for her mother.

Tears in her eyes, Carmella begged Karen not to turn her in. She claimed that she just wanted to help give her mother a softer landing. Insisted that she couldn't bear to see her mother suffer for the final few weeks of her life without doing something.

What happened next was all up to Karen. Turn Carmella in, and Carmella would be fired. She'd lose her license, probably go to jail. Had Carmella been stealing the drugs for an addiction or to sell on the street, the decision would've been a no-brainer. Karen would've reported her in a heartbeat.

But this situation was different. Could she ruin Carmella's life for wanting to help the person who'd raised her? Karen had debated that question for a long time. A few sleepless nights, plenty of back-and-forth. In the end, she decided not to turn Carmella in. The decision weighed on her heavily. Had anyone found out what she'd done, she would've lost her job, her livelihood, everything.

But she just couldn't bring herself to ruin Carmella's life. Turning her in would've been the right thing, but Karen would've felt so guilty, so horrible.

For a few weeks, Karen had looked the other way as Carmella stole partially used vials of Dilaudid during her shifts. And then one day she didn't need them anymore.

"I know I've already thanked you, but I want to do it again," Carmella said. "It made the ending so much easier for my mom."

"I'm glad it helped. Let's leave it at that. Now, come on. We better get back to work."

Carmella wiped her eyes a final time. They walked out to the floor.

"By the way," Karen said, "what was the joke?"

"The joke?"

"Yeah. The joke Mrs. Johnson told you. Your mother might not be around to hear it, but you can share it with me."

"You sure? It's cheesy. I'm talking really, really cheesy."

"Come on. Tell it to me."

"Okay. How many doctors does it take to screw in a lightbulb?"

"How many?"

"Depends on whether it has health insurance or not."

Karen smiled.

"You're right," she said. "Good Lord, that's terrible."

WHEN THE DAY FINALLY ENDED FOR KAREN, SHE CHANGED AND LEFT THE hospital. Took a different route than she had that morning and pulled into a small parking lot next to a Chevy dealership. She walked inside and found the man she was looking for in an office right past the entrance. He was sitting at a desk, wearing khakis and a button-up with the dealership logo on the front.

"Teddy," she said.

He looked over. Seemed to take him a moment to recognize her. "Oh. Hey."

"I had a quick question," she said. "Figured you might be able to help me."

"Just gimme a second."

He pecked away at his keyboard. She stood at the edge of the room and watched him. It never ceased to amaze her how much Joshua looked like his father. Teddy's face was fuller, but he had the same jawline and nose as Joshua, the same blue eyes. More than anything, it was the hair that made them look so similar——Teddy and Joshua had identical shades of hair, so blond it looked white.

It was impossible for her to look at Teddy and not think that she was looking at a forty-two-year-old version of Joshua. Only difference was that Teddy was a good thirty pounds heavier than Joshua was, with the bump of a beer gut hanging over his waistband.

He tapped a final few keys and swiveled around in his chair.

"What's going on?" he asked.

"Joshua. His car windshield is all busted up. He claims he was horsing around and his friend fell onto it. I was wondering, could I get the crack fixed here? In the dealership garage? The sooner the better. I figure I'll pay for it and he can reimburse me."

"You could get it fixed here, but you'd probably get laughed out of the place if you pulled in with that old beater. And the cost would be double. I'll text you the numbers of a few people who could help. Independent garages."

"Any idea how much it will run me?"

"No clue. I only sell the cars. Don't know the first thing about fixing them."

They made small talk for a bit. As far as exes went, they had a pretty good relationship. Not really friends, but not scorched-earth enemies. They chatted when they ran into each other at Joshua's golf meets, occasionally texted back and forth about him. She'd even bought her current car from Teddy a few years back.

A coworker dropped into Teddy's office and asked to speak with him. Teddy stepped out into the hallway and Karen waited in the small office. Teddy's desk was littered with various framed pictures of Joshua. One of him and Joshua standing on a golf green, both wearing polos and sunglasses. Another photo of Joshua when he was just a child, probably five or six, holding up a set of Fisher-Price plastic golf clubs. Taped to a file cabinet was a cutout newspaper article about Joshua's high school golf team winning their conference tournament last year. The sentences that mentioned Joshua were highlighted in yellow marker.

Other golf decorations hung from the wall. IT'S TEE TIME SOME-WHERE, read a sticker. I'D RATHER BE DRIVING A TITLEIST, read another, accompanied by a picture of a cartoon character swinging a golf club.

Teddy stuck his head back into the office.

"Looks like I'm needed. I'll have to text you those phone numbers of mechanics when I find them."

"Sure," she said. She walked out into the hallway.

"I meant to ask you—how is he?" Teddy said.

"Who? Joshua?"

"Yeah. He seemed down last time I saw him. Wanted to make sure he's doing all right."

"He was a little out of it this morning. Distracted. Not that that is anything new. Girl problems, school problems—could be anything. He's a teenager."

Teddy disappeared through an open door and she walked back out to her car.

TWENTY MINUTES AFTER LEAVING THE CAR DEALERSHIP, SHE ARRIVED back home. She and Joshua lived in the same house she'd grown up in, a beige ranch house in the country with an American flag and a wooden WELCOME sign next to the front door. A narrow driveway led from the gravel road to a two-car garage.

When she was younger, she never imagined she'd end up living in the house she grew up in. But here she was. After Joshua was born, she moved back home so her parents could help raise him, and she'd never moved out, even after she inherited the house when they passed away more than a decade ago. There was something comforting about having spent a majority of her life living in the same house. She figured there was plenty out there she'd never gotten to experience or see—a whole world, really—but she didn't really feel like she was missing out. There was no sense of emptiness or regret.

She parked her car in the garage and walked across the yard. Outside the front door, she checked the mailbox before going inside. There were three letters.

The first was their energy bill.

The second was a Walgreens ad.

The third was a letter that nearly made her collapse.

* * *

"SO, WHAT WAS THE HIGHLIGHT OF YOUR DAY?"

Karen stared across the kitchen table at Joshua. She could tell that whatever had been bugging him this morning was still bugging him. He hadn't so much as cracked a smile since his friend Freddy dropped him off after golf practice an hour ago, but the real reason she knew something was up was the burger on the plate in front of him. The burger was from the Map Room, their favorite local burger spot. Joshua normally wolfed down his burger in the time it took her to swallow her first bite. Tonight, the monstrous burger sitting on the plate in front of him was missing only a few nibbles.

"Well?" she said. "What's your highlight?"

"Nothing, really," Joshua said.

"Come on. You know how to play the game. You can't respond with *nothing*. What's the best thing that happened to you all day?"

They did this every night during dinner, sharing the highlight of their day with each other. She'd done the same thing with her parents growing up.

"Okay, I'll go first," Karen said after a nonresponse from Joshua. "Mrs. Wellington, that nice old lady who's been my patient for a few weeks? She had a checkup today. She's improved so much that she was released this morning. Her family was overjoyed."

"That's cool," he said.

"Yeah. It is."

She took a few bites from her burger and carried her plate to the counter. She wrapped up half of it for lunch tomorrow, then washed her plate under the faucet. She grabbed a manila envelope off the counter and carried it back over to the table.

"Think of a highlight yet?" she asked.

"Not really."

She set the envelope on the table in front of Joshua.

"I'll help you out, then. That envelope was in the mailbox when I got home from work. That, right there, is the highlight of your day. Probably the highlight of your year."

He picked up the envelope. The corner was stamped with a logo: Clemson University. She'd been tempted to tear it open when she found it in the mail earlier but resisted. She had a pretty good idea of what was inside. An envelope that big could mean only one thing.

Joshua opened the envelope and pulled a letter from inside. He scanned it.

"I got in," he said.

Karen was unable to hold back a beaming smile. "Congrats, sweetie."

For a year now, Joshua had had one goal for college. Get into the Landscape Architecture program at Clemson. A highly competitive program that was one of the best in the nation. He liked to draw and he loved to golf, and he combined the two into his dream of designing golf courses for a living someday. Getting into a landscape architecture program was the first step toward that.

They'd devoted endless hours to studying for college entry exams and putting together his application. He'd submitted an entire portfolio of drawings, some of golf courses, some of random things he'd drawn over the years. They'd spent countless late nights worrying about when they'd finally hear back. And all of those endless hours had been leading up to this one moment.

As she'd been waiting for him to arrive home, she'd envisioned how he'd react when he saw the letter. She'd pictured him laughing, crying, hugging her, overwhelmed with the euphoria of seeing his college dream come true.

Instead, he sat there. Stared at the letter. Barely any emotion on his face.

"Feel free to react," she said.

"This is awesome," he said. "Really awesome."

"You've been waiting for this letter for months. I figured you'd be dancing on the roof when you read it."

She reached over and took the letter from his hand. Placed it on the table.

"What's going on?" she said. "You've been acting so blue all day."

"It's nothing."

"Don't worry about Ashley. You'll find another girl. Any girl would be lucky to—"

"It's not my girlfriend, Mom."

"Well, something's going on," she said. "Just know if you want to talk, I'm here. You know that. If you need anything, I'm here."

"Thanks. But I'll be fine."

Joshua grabbed the letter off the table and carried it to his room, leaving his barely touched burger on the plate.

JOSHUA SAT AT THE SMALL DESK IN HIS ROOM, HOLDING THE ACCEPTANCE letter in his hand. He read it and reread it, over and over again.

A dream come true, the letter was, but reading it brought no joy, not even a shred of happiness. He had too many other things to worry about.

He set the letter off to the side and stood up from the desk. He looked around his room. His backpack was in the corner, underneath a shelf with a few bobbleheads of Cubs players. Below the shelf were golfing trophies and mementos—ribbons and medals; his trophy for finishing fourth at regionals last year; a small plaque commemorating the only hole in one he'd ever gotten in his life, out at Brown Deer a few years ago. There was a small pushpin board covered in ticket stubs from concerts and movies he and his friends had gone to.

On top of his dresser was a small television with his PlayStation 4 hooked up to it. Maybe a video game or two would help take his mind off everything. He inserted a disc and played *Madden* against the computer for a while. He could barely concentrate.

There was a knock on the door and his mom stuck her head in. She looked at the television.

"You get accepted to college, so you figure you don't have to do homework anymore, huh?" she said.

"It's already done."

"Not sure if I believe that one or not." She smiled. "I just wanted to tell you good night before I went to bed. Promise me you won't stay up late?"

"Promise," Joshua said.

She walked into the room. "Pause it for a second," she said. After he'd paused the game, she reached down and hugged him.

"Congrats again," she said. "It's amazing you got in. How many times did I tell you all that hard work would pay off? I'm so proud of you."

"Thanks, Mom."

She kissed him on the cheek. "Have a good night."

She left the room. Once she was gone, he quit the *Madden* game. Lay back down in bed. Stared at the ceiling. Brought up Netflix on his iPad and endlessly scrolled through movies and TV shows. Couldn't find anything to watch. He wasn't in the mood to laugh, wasn't in the mood to watch something that would depress him further. Really, he wasn't in any sort of mood. He felt only that constant, dull gloominess.

KAREN LAY IN BED, HEAD RESTING ON THE PILLOW, THE ROOM PITCH- black. She closed her eyes but she couldn't sleep. She was still wired from that Clemson letter. It was something incredible, seeing Joshua's dream come true—but it was a little bittersweet, too. The acceptance letter made it real: he'd be leaving soon, for a college that was halfway across the country, hundreds of miles away.

Hard to believe how the past eighteen years had flown by. She still remembered how she thought her life was over, so many years ago when she found out she was pregnant by Teddy Watson, a guy she'd been dating for only a few months. Both in their early twenties, neither ready for the news. Teddy had been more concerned with his golf handicap than with growing up. She was focused on figuring out what to do with the communications degree she'd graduated with two years earlier. Their relationship had been mostly about fun. They were both young. He was irresponsible, a little bit of a goofball, but that was all she was looking for at the time.

Then came the bombshell news. After Joshua was born, life became chaotic. Late nights. Endless work. No sleep or social life, even less when she went back to school for her nursing degree a few years after his birth. Her parents had helped her raise Joshua for the first seven years, until her mother passed away and her father was admitted to a nursing home a few months later.

And Teddy . . . Well, he did his best. He tried. He'd still never really figured his life out and hadn't changed much from the early-twenties guy she dated (the car salesman job was the latest in a series of jobs he'd held over the years), but he truly cared about Joshua. That counted for something—counted for a lot, actually—but he was more of a friend to Joshua than a father. Golf was the bond that linked them. In the summer, they'd go to the golf course for entire days, sunup to sundown. They went on a road trip to a few golf courses last summer. They met up and watched all the professional tournaments together.

Teddy cared about Joshua, but she'd been the one who raised him, devoted her life to him. And now it was coming to an end. Joshua was about to leave. She supposed it was just that time, that juncture in life, but it still broke her heart.

She thought about everything for a long time until, finally, she fell asleep.

SATURDAY

SATURDAY

FIVE

AT NEARLY THREE IN THE MORNING, ONCE HE WAS SURE THAT HIS MOM
was asleep, Joshua left his bedroom. He crept down the hallway and
walked out into the cold, still night. In the backyard, he grabbed the
bag of clothes he'd stored underneath the deck Thursday night.

It was time to get rid of them. He couldn't keep them here at
the house, and the ground was too frozen to bury them. He'd have to
find a river to throw them into. All the nearby, smaller rivers were
frozen over, but he hoped the Cedar River wasn't. It was a larger river
that cut through Cedar Rapids and the surrounding rural areas. If he
drove out far enough, he could toss the clothes in the river without
anyone spotting him. The river was big enough and deep enough that
they'd never be found.

Before leaving, he set the bag on the ground and opened it. A smoky smell wafted up. He took a final look inside to make sure there was nothing he'd overlooked.

One by one, he lifted the items out.

His jeans, charred and blackened. He checked the pockets. Nothing inside.

His half-melted shoes.

His socks.

His coat. The expensive coat he'd gotten for Christmas. It was made of heavy-duty Gore-Tex and the flames had done little damage to it. A few sections were burned but the coat was mostly intact. He searched the coat's pockets and found a glove.

He froze.

A glove. *One* glove. He looked through the pockets again, but there wasn't another one. He looked back in the bag. Nothing was left inside.

His hurried into the garage and threw open his car door. Looked under the seats, in the backseat, even in the glove compartment. No glove.

He sneaked back inside, moving quickly, quietly. He looked everywhere in his room, in the bathroom, in the living room.

No glove anywhere.

The second glove was missing.

He grabbed his phone and pulled up the number from earlier.

Still awake? he texted.

The response came almost instantly: **Yeah. Can't sleep.**

I can't find one of my gloves. Did you grab it last night?

What? No.

Joshua thought back to the frantic moments after the accident and everything else that happened. He vaguely remembered throwing the gloves into his coat pocket. One of them must have fallen out at some point. That was the only explanation he could think of. They'd searched the scene before leaving and found nothing, but they must've somehow overlooked the glove.

His phone chimed again. **What's going on? Starting to get worried here.**

Joshua stared at the screen. He could fix this. There'd been nothing on the news about the body yet. It hadn't been found. If the glove was out there, he could grab it, get rid of it, and everything would be fine. No—not fine. Not fine at all. But it would be a bullet dodged. A potential disaster averted.

It's nothing, Joshua texted back. **False alarm. Going to bed now.**

He put his phone in his pocket and went back outside. He threw the bloody clothes back into the garbage bag and hid it under the deck in the same spot as earlier.

He walked into the garage and hit the button for the automatic garage opener. It clattered open. He was worried the noise would wake his mom, but it didn't. Thank God for that—he was far too shell-shocked to come up with a rational explanation for why he had a sudden desire to leave the house at three in the morning.

He got in his car, pulled onto the gravel road, and headed toward Hawkeye Wildlife Management Area.

JOSHUA STARED OUT PAST HIS CAR'S CRACKED WINDSHIELD, HIS HEAD-lights cutting through the darkness of the night and illuminating the gravel road in front of him. The houses appeared less and less frequently as he drove farther into the deep maze of the country—a house every half mile, then every mile. None had lights on; many had been abandoned for years. He reached Hawkeye Wildlife Management Area and turned onto one of the paths that led through the forest. This was the true boonies. Acre after acre of endless woods, bushes, trees.

He drove on. The forest swallowed him. Large trees bordered his path on both sides, rising into the starry night sky. There was little organization to the paths that cut through the forest. Roads that went this way and that. Some that abruptly stopped. Trees and bare, frozen ground everywhere. It all looked so identical. No buildings, no landmarks, nothing distinguishing.

He turned onto a dirt path. Drove for a while. Ran into a dead end. Turned around.

More driving. Another path. Another dead end.

It didn't take long to realize he had no idea where he was going. He thought he remembered how to get to the site of the accident, but everything looked so similar.

Up one road, down another. He looked at the dashboard clock and realized it had been nearly an hour since he left the house.

He started to imagine the worst-case scenario. Someone had already found the body. An investigation was currently happening. Or maybe the person hadn't been dead, only unconscious. He'd walked away from the scene and reported everything to the police. But no, the person he'd hit was definitely dead. No doubt about it.

He drove on, eyes scanning the road, the surrounding land, so nervous and scared he was practically shaking. He felt like—

There it was.

The body.

He slammed on the brakes and his car skidded to a stop. A huddled dark mass was in the ditch a few feet off the road. The black coat and dark pants made the body blend in with the shadows. Had he been driving a little faster, he probably would've passed right by.

He killed the engine and stepped outside, taking in a deep breath of the frigid night air.

He had to find the glove and get out of here.

It was time to hurry.

HE HIT THE BUTTON TO POP THE TRUNK AND WALKED OVER. HE RUMMAGED through the trunk contents—a blanket, some jumper cables, his golf clubs—until he found what he was looking for. A small cardboard box with EMERGENCY written on the outside.

Inside were a couple of granola bars, a flashlight, some tools. He grabbed the flashlight and turned it on. He could see the body in his peripheral vision, only a few feet away from his car. He was nearly standing right on top of it. He kept his head turned, refusing to look directly at the body. He didn't know if he could handle seeing it up close.

He scanned the ground with the flashlight beam, sweeping it back and forth as he slowly walked away from the car and the body, the beam passing over pine needles, frozen dirt, patches of dead grass, trees with thick trunks and skeletal branches.

No glove.

He slowly walked farther and farther away from the car, moving the flashlight back and forth like a searchlight.

Still, no glove.

The cold air stung his lungs. Plumes of fog every time he exhaled. His heart started beating faster, faster.

He walked for a minute and stopped. The night of the accident, they hadn't gone this far away from the body; the glove wouldn't be all the way out here. He walked back toward the body, sweeping the flashlight across the ground as he continued searching.

//////////////////////

Amber trudged through the forest, following Ross. More accurately, following the beam from Ross's flashlight. They'd found it in a pouch on the backpack a few hours ago and thank God for that—without the flashlight, the darkness would have been impossible to navigate.

She walked on. Everything hurt. Her stomach, from hunger. Her legs and feet, from the endless walking. Her chest, from breathing lungful after lungful of cold air.

It felt like they'd been wandering around the forest forever. The disposable phone she'd bought at the gas station earlier turned out to be junk—the reception was spotty and the battery died after barely twenty minutes of trying to find a signal—which made it impossible to tell which direction they were heading. They'd simply started trekking around after leaving the car in the woods. They'd now been wandering for so long, she was certain they must be walking in circles. Everything looked so similar. Just trees and grass. They'd found a few worn roads they walked on for a while, but none had led anywhere.

It was so dark that she could just barely see Ross, fifteen feet in front of her, the backpack slung over his shoulder.

"Would you hurry the hell up?" he said.

"I'm trying."

Ross walked in the sped-up, jerky way he always walked when he was riding high from drugs. He'd taken at least three or four pills over the past few hours, his mood fluctuating between loudly grumbling and complaining and a silent, sulking anger. She listened to him, not saying much. When Ross got like this, it was best to remain quiet. Didn't take much to set him off.

Everything seemed close to hopeless now, but she still believed that somehow, someway, it would all work out. They'd come too far and been through too much to give up now. As they trudged through the forest, she thought back to all the events that had led up to this point.

After Ross was locked up in jail, she left Tennessee and moved to Nebraska to escape everything. She tried to start over and had the worst year of her life. She was sad. Lonely. Depressed. Bored. She found a job at a tire factory and threw herself into it, working fifty, sixty hours a week to distract herself from the boredom.

Almost a year after he'd been arrested, Ross showed up on her doorstep. The first thing he did when he was released, he said, was track her down. He begged her to take him back. Promised that he was a changed man. Insisted that he was through with the wild and crazy nights, through with travel and the music scene, and that he only wanted to be with her.

She had missed him so much, more and more with every lonely month that passed, that she told Ross she'd give him another chance. Ross moved in, and for a while, life in Nebraska was good. They both turned thirty. Ross started working a construction job and their lives became shockingly normal and routine—instead of endless tours around Tennessee and partying all night afterward, they worked nine-to-five jobs and spent every evening together. They moved into a nicer apartment. Started having money for groceries, setting aside a little for the future. At one juncture, their lives reached a point of such normality that they started spending their Saturdays focusing on different weekend projects—painting the bathroom, laying down new living room carpet, finding cheap furniture on Craigslist.

Then Shane showed up. He'd gotten in a few fights in jail and hadn't been released early for good behavior like Ross had. He tracked Ross down and came to him when he was released. Claimed he needed a place to stay. Had nowhere to go.

The last thing she wanted was him reentering their lives when things were better than they'd ever been, but Ross insisted. He said that he had to help Shane get back on his feet, couldn't turn his back on his brother.

Shane started sleeping on their couch, and soon, he and Ross fell back into their previous lives. Late nights. Shady characters. Ross lost his job. He and Shane started disappearing for hours at a time.

She asked Ross to leave Shane, and the response came back same as before: family. He couldn't turn his back on family. It was like he was blind to the fact that Shane was dragging him down—that, or he just didn't care. It was that old inability to stand up to Shane. Like he was scared of him.

At some point, Ross started using amphetamines like Shane. He became more irritable. Snapping at her more often. Staying up for entire days at a time, then crashing. It was like he was transforming into someone totally different, someone out of control.

The nights became later; the people Ross and Shane hung out with were shadier. Drugs became an everyday habit. Before long, they weren't even hiding their drug use. It was more than pills. Sometimes they would inhale household cleaning products and huff spray paint for a quick high. Other times, they would smash pills and snort the powder while she was a few feet away.

Time and time again, she thought about leaving Ross, but she always stuck by him. She believed in him, because she knew that, deep down, there was a good person inside Ross. Somewhere in there was the person he had been right after he was released from jail, before Shane showed up. The one she'd spent every weekend with, doing household projects and snuggling on the couch. The person who occasionally sang to her at night. The person who had a softer side. Shane was evil, a nasty person who'd always been that way, but Ross was different. The drugs transformed him and made him lose control, but there was more to him than that. He was worth fighting for.

If she could somehow get him away from Shane, she could save him. She just had to make her move before the late nights and drugs and whatever else they were involved in ruined Ross's life for good. Around that time, Shane came to them with a plan. He got a tip-off about a bank in a small town named Hastings, Nebraska. Some sort of area shipping facility. A major payday. He needed a third person for the job and asked Amber. Hold the security guard at bay and drive him and Ross away—that's all she'd have to do.

Shane had seen it as an opportunity to pull off something big, but Amber had seen it as something entirely different. She'd seen it as an opportunity to purge Shane from their lives and have enough money to start anew. The money was key; they were completely wiped out. Had nowhere near what they needed to begin a new life. The money she'd saved when Ross had been in jail had disappeared.

She sat down with Ross one night when Shane was gone and told him about her idea to ditch Shane after robbing the bank. She put her foot down: her or Shane, she said; he had to choose one or the other. Either he agreed to double-cross Shane and disappear with her, or she would leave him for good. This was their chance, probably would be the only chance they'd get, to escape Shane and have the money to start over, anywhere they wanted. Either they take that chance, or their relationship was over. She refused to stand by his side as he threw his life down the drain with Shane.

Ross chose her. She knew it hadn't been easy for him to decide to double-cross his brother. As bossy and brash as Shane was, Ross genuinely loved him. Looked up to him. But it seemed like he'd finally seen the writing on the wall, that he'd end up back in jail if he continued on the same path with Shane.

She and Ross put together a plan and executed it to perfection on the morning of the bank robbery. They had the money. They'd left Shane behind. And now, here they were. If they could somehow get out of this forest and get back on the road, maybe everything could work out.

They walked on.

SIX

STILL WEARING HER BATHROBE, KAREN SAT AT THE KITCHEN TABLE, STAR-ing at her phone, willing it to ring. After a minute of silence, she tapped the screen a few times and brought up Joshua's number. Called it. Got the same result as she had with the previous three calls she'd placed to him over the past fifteen minutes: a few rings, then voice mail.

This is Joshua. Leave a message.

"It's me," Karen said. "Again. Just . . . call me when you get this. Let me know you're okay."

She set the phone on the table. Paced around the kitchen. Filled a glass with water and took a drink. Stared out the window. Anything to distract herself from the unease eating away inside her.

Calm down, she told herself.

Fifteen minutes ago, just before four in the morning, she woke up to go to the bathroom and found the door to Joshua's room open a crack. When she went to close it, she saw that his bed was empty. She started to worry after she couldn't find him anywhere in the house. Started to panic once she got no response to a call and a text. And now, after a few more calls and texts had gone unanswered, her panic had escalated to something more. Something close to hysteria.

She walked down the hallway, back into Joshua's room. Checked in his closet—nothing but clothes. Checked under his bed—an old golf bag with no clubs in it, some plastic storage bins, a few random socks. He wasn't here, not that she expected to find him. Did she really think he'd be hiding in his room like he did when they played hide-and-go-seek when he was young?

Karen went back to the kitchen. Paced. She sat down again and ran her hands through her hair. She remembered how distant Joshua had acted yesterday. Was there something more to it than normal teenager problems? Was the story about the damage to his—

She tensed up in her chair. His car. She hadn't checked to see if his car was still there.

She hurried out to the garage. Her Chevy Malibu was inside. His Altima wasn't. So he'd gone somewhere—where? Why didn't he leave her a message? And why wasn't he answering his phone?

She went back to the kitchen. Called Joshua again. Sent another text. No response to either.

Call his friends—that was her next step. Maybe he'd sneaked out of the house to meet up with them. It was a Friday night, after all—well, Saturday morning now. But something still felt off. Instinct, intuition, whatever you wanted to call it.

Maybe Teddy knew something. He and Joshua were supposed to watch some golf tournament on TV together this weekend. Maybe

Joshua couldn't sleep, went over to his father's house early. That didn't make much sense, but there was always a chance.

She grabbed her phone to call Teddy—and then it hit her.

The phone. Not her phone. Joshua's phone.

She could check the location.

Last year, when Joshua's grades started to drop, she'd given him an ultimatum: he couldn't do anything until he finished his homework—no hanging out with his girlfriend at the time, no golfing, no going to his friends' houses. To make sure he stuck to it, she installed a tracking program on his phone so she could check his location on her computer. The whole thing felt a little weird to her—it was so invasive—and when his grades improved almost immediately, she stopped using the program.

But she hadn't deleted it.

Right now, she could see where he was.

She sprang up from the couch and hurried to her bedroom. She sat down at the small computer desk in the corner. Opened her laptop and entered her password. Practically broke the mouse button as she clicked around to access the phone tracker app.

The program opened. A map appeared onscreen. Right in the middle, there it was: a red dot.

Joshua's phone.

The dot was about fifteen miles south of Cedar Rapids, down in the middle of Hawkeye Wildlife Management Area.

What was he doing all the way out there? A party? Doubtful. It was freezing. And he always said something to her if he had late-night plans; that was their agreement.

She looked at the dot onscreen. She didn't know what was going on. Didn't know if he was safe. Didn't know anything, only that she was too nervous and worried to sit still.

She printed out the map, then threw off her bathrobe, changed into a sweatshirt and jeans, and hurried out to the garage.

She backed down the driveway and started driving along the gravel road, heading toward the red dot.

////////////////

Joshua scanned the ground, his eyes following the flashlight beam as it swept back and forth across the terrain. The hand holding the flashlight was trembling. The longer he searched, the less likely it seemed that the glove was out here. It was a horrifying thought. He had no idea where else the glove could be.

He'd been searching throughout the forest for twenty minutes—Thirty? Forty? He had no concept of time—sweeping the flashlight back and forth, back and forth, all across the ground. He'd almost given up but had continued on.

It was so spooky and isolated here. The forest was quiet and still, but he'd heard noises as he searched. An animal howling in the distance. Branches rustling in the wind. At one point, he thought he'd heard a noise coming from inside his car. Sounded like a ringing or beeping—his phone, maybe? He searched his pockets and realized he'd left it in the car. He'd check it later; his phone wasn't his focus now. Didn't make sense that someone would be calling him this late at night, anyway.

He kept searching, focused on the ground, feeling more and more worried with every passing second—and then finally, unbelievably, there it was.

The glove.

It was a good fifty feet from the body, right beside a cluster of pine needles and small shrubs, which partially camouflaged it. He had no idea how it had gotten so far from the body. He didn't remember walking in this area after the accident—but then again, he'd been so overwhelmed that he didn't remember much of anything that happened that night.

He picked the glove up off the ground and stuffed it in his coat pocket. He walked over to his car. Grabbed the door handle.

And then he stopped. He shone his flashlight down and looked at the body. He couldn't resist. It was like he didn't have a choice, like he was being pulled to it by an invisible force.

For the first time since he arrived, he got a good look at it. The body was facedown, so he could see only the back of the dead man's head. Dark hair. Black coat and pants. One arm was splayed out at an awkward angle. A pair of earbuds dangled by a thin white wire from his jacket pocket. He'd been listening to music right before the accident. Probably hadn't heard the car approaching.

Joshua walked over and looked down at the body. Close-up, he could just barely see the blood covering the ground, soaked into the dirt around the body.

He nudged the body with his foot, flopping it onto its back, and got a close-up look at the aftermath of Thursday night.

The cold weather had slowed decomposition, but the body was still grotesque, nothing more than a bloated, decaying corpse. Dried blood everywhere. His expression was frozen, mouth open, empty, unblinking eyes staring up at the sky. His nose was a crooked mess and there was a nasty gash on the right side of his head, just above an area where his skull was partially caved in.

The sight of the body brought back every memory from Thursday night. The crunch of the car hitting the man, the thud of the body smashing into the windshield, the frantic moments after the accident, when he'd realized the man wasn't dead and—

Joshua's stomach turned as he thought back to what happened then. A wave of emotion nearly knocked him over. In some ways, this moment right now was worse than the accident. After the accident, everything had happened so quickly that it had felt like an out-of-body experience. Like it wasn't real. But not tonight. Right now, he was calm. Composed. Everything was slowed down, not going a million miles an hour.

Looking at the body, he thought about going to the police. This instant, calling them up and telling them everything. Doing the right thing. He hadn't been thinking straight Thursday night; everything had been so frantic. But right now, he could go to the police. Clear his conscience. Maybe he—

A light glinted in the corner of his eye. He snapped his head toward it. Every muscle in his body froze.

A pair of headlights was approaching on the road, heading straight toward him. The car pulled behind his and stopped. This close, he recognized the car instantly.

It was his mom's car.

//////////////////////

Karen saw Joshua's car, parked on the side of the road, then saw Joshua a few feet away, holding a flashlight, standing over something on the ground. A dark, shadowy shape.

She pulled her car up behind his and killed the engine.

"What in the world are you doing out here?" she said, stepping out of the car. She walked toward him.

"Mom, I—"

"It's the middle of the night and—"

She stopped. Up close, even in the darkness, she could see the object Joshua was standing over. The shadowy shape was . . . a person.

Face a ghostly white.

Covered in blood.

Not moving.

"What . . ." she said. "What . . . happened?"

Joshua stared back, silent.

"Is he . . . dead?"

Joshua nodded. "Yeah. I hit him with my car and . . ." He shook his head. "It's complicated."

She looked at his car. Glanced back down at the body. Looked back at Joshua.

"You hit him . . . and killed him?"

"Yeah. But there's more to it than that."

"How? What?"

"It happened on—"

"Hold on," she said. Karen felt a low, throbbing pressure behind her eyes. She walked over to Joshua's car and sat down on the hood. She didn't know if her legs could support her much longer.

"It happened the other night, on Thursday," Joshua said, speaking slowly, his voice so low she could barely hear it. "Me and Dad were out here. There's this ledge we come to sometimes to hit golf balls. It's high above this long field of bushes and trees. A friend gave him some range balls and he called me to see if I wanted to come out and hit them."

The throbbing behind Karen's eyes was deepening, becoming an insistent pounding. Teddy was involved in this, too?

"So I picked him up and we drove out here. It was fun, cold but not too cold, hitting the balls and watching them soar. When we went through the entire bucket, I started driving back, through the forest. And then it happened. I drove over this small hill and a man was on the other side of it. He was just . . . there in the middle of the road, all of a sudden. I hit the brakes but it was too late. The car slammed into the guy. Sent him into the windshield and over the roof."

Karen lifted her hand to her mouth.

"We both jumped out of the car and ran over to him," Joshua continued. "It was . . . bad. The guy's face was all smashed up. Blood was pouring out of his nose, everywhere. But he wasn't dead. He was only hurt."

Joshua slowly shook his head. His eyes had started to water and he wiped away a tear. He sniffled.

"We were about to call an ambulance and then the guy just snapped. He stood up and started screaming at me. He shoved me a few times, kept cursing and yelling. Dad tried to get the guy to calm down and they started yelling back and forth. The guy tackled him and pinned Dad to the ground. Dad tried to fight back but the guy was big and strong, way stronger than either of us. He had his hands around Dad's throat. Dad was making this choking noise like he couldn't breathe. I thought the guy was going to kill him. There wasn't time to think or anything. I grabbed this big rock off the ground and smashed it against the side of the guy's head. He flopped to the ground. Stopped moving. He wasn't breathing. I ran over and started pounding on his chest, trying to . . . I don't know . . . save him or something. His blood was splattering all over me. But it was no use. He was dead."

Karen stared down at her hands. Her son had killed a man. She understood and comprehended every word Joshua had said, but it wouldn't sink in. The words slipped straight off the surface of her mind.

She tried to talk. Didn't have a voice. Finally found it.

"Teddy? You were with your dad?"

Joshua nodded. "After we realized the guy was dead, we just stood there. Barely able to move. Both of us were in shock."

"Why didn't you go to the police?"

"Dad was worried how the police would look at things. Or how a jury would. I could've tackled the guy, or shoved him. Instead I hit him with a rock and killed him. Maybe they would look at the rock as a deadly weapon or something. Dad kept talking about a case from a few years ago that was similar to this. Some politician's son."

She remembered the case. Pretty big story at the time. The son of a city council member had been out with friends, they had an argument with some people, and a fight broke out. A video camera captured him grabbing a beer bottle and striking someone over the head. A fatal blow. He'd pled self-defense at his trial but the jury hadn't bought it. They'd charged him with involuntary manslaughter. Ten years in jail.

"Dad kept saying he didn't want that to be me," Joshua said. "Said he didn't want me to spend the next few years in jail. It sounded crazy, but he thought we should just leave. Not report what happened. Not take the risk that I could get in trouble."

"And you agreed to this? You thought it was a good idea to leave the scene?"

"No. I don't know. Everything was happening so quickly. It's like I wasn't myself. I could barely think."

"What happened next?"

"We took the rock I hit the guy with and threw it deep into the woods. Far away from the body. Then I dropped Dad off at his place and went home."

She thought she was going to be sick. Or start crying. Or scream at the top of her lungs. She looked down at the body and, as gruesome as it was, stared without blinking for a long moment.

"This took place the other night?" she asked.

Joshua nodded.

"Why are you here now, then?"

"I lost a glove out here. I came back to get it."

She took a breath. A slow-boil anger was starting to break through her confusion. Teddy. How could he possibly think it was a good idea to leave the body out here? Had he really thought that not reporting something so awful was the right thing to do? She couldn't believe that he had done something so stupid. She was furious with him—but she was angry at Joshua, too. He was eighteen years old. He wasn't a kid. He knew the difference between right and wrong.

"We have to go to the police," she said.

Joshua blankly stared back. Nodded.

"Right now, we'll call them. Tell them you made a mistake. Explain that you were in shock—"

She stopped. Squinted. Focused on something in the distance.

"Oh my God," she said.

About one hundred feet away was the beam of a flashlight, headed straight toward them.

//////////////

Amber and Ross walked on. She felt so tired that she could barely continue. Her feet were dragging. Her eyelids were starting to close.

Her stomach was growling. She struggled to keep up with Ross; his movements were so jumpy and sped up.

She looked up ahead at Ross, trudging along, grumbling to himself. The longer they were out here, the more he'd started cursing and complaining about how angry he was, how hungry he was. He kept popping pills, too. They made him even more short-tempered and irritable. Earlier, he'd gotten so mad that he yanked open the backpack and started sifting through everything frantically. Not much was inside—the money, the *Star Wars* masks, and her gun, which she'd put in the backpack after the robbery. Whatever Ross was looking for inside, he hadn't found it. He grumbled a curse word and yanked the zipper shut with such a forceful motion that he broke the zipper. Since then he'd carried the bag in one hand instead of strapping it onto his back. Occasionally, a loose bill would flutter out of the opening in the backpack and be swept away in the light breeze.

Amber honestly didn't know how much more she could take. She was just too tired. She didn't know how much more Ross could take, either. He seemed like he was going to overheat or something soon. It was—

Ross stopped walking. It was so dark she nearly walked right into him.

"I'll be damned," he said, staring ahead. "People. And they got a couple cars with them."

She saw it all. Roughly a quarter mile in front of them was a car with its interior light on. Two people were barely visible outside the car. A second car was parked a few feet away.

For the first time in hours, Ross smiled.

"Might be our lucky day," he said.

SEVEN

JOSHUA LOOKED AT THE APPROACHING FLASHLIGHT. IT WAS TOO DARK TO see who was behind it. A park ranger? An off-season hunter? A police officer? It didn't really matter. Regardless of who it was, this was going to be it.

"Just stay calm," his mom said. "Whoever this is, when they see the body, we'll be honest, tell them everything. And then we'll call the police. Tell them you made a mistake. A terrible decision. And we'll hope they understand."

Maybe that was for the best. Go to the police, even if an entire day had passed. Just end this right now.

The flashlight was only thirty feet away. Twenty. His heart thundered as he waited for the person behind it to arrive. He looked at the body on the ground. It was on the opposite side of the car from the approaching flashlight. The car hid the body, but it was still impossible to miss. Right out in the open.

He looked at his mom. She stared back, gave him a weak smile.

The flashlight finally reached them, and the person holding it stopped walking on the other side of the car, a few feet away. The light shone directly into his eyes and blinded him for a second. When his vision cleared, he could see there were two people behind the flashlight, not one. Both wore black sweatshirts. A man was on the left—tall and skinny, long hair, rough features, shivering from the cold, carrying a backpack in one hand. And a woman, standing beside him, looking so tired she could barely stand.

"WHATCHA DOING ALL THE WAY OUT HERE?" THE MAN ASKED. HE SET HIS backpack on the ground next to him—the top of the bag was open but Karen couldn't see what was inside. He shone the flashlight at Joshua, then at Karen. She squinted and raised her hand to shield her eyes.

"Nothing," she said.

"Nothing, huh? Came out to the middle of nowhere for the hell of it?"

"We're just . . . camping," she said.

"Where's your tent?"

She pointed out at the forest. "Out there. My husband's there."

She didn't know who these two people were, but she didn't want them to know she and Joshua were out here alone. She had a bad feeling about the situation. The man was moving in the herky-jerky way of someone on amphetamines. When she first saw him, she thought he was shivering from the cold. That wasn't it, though. His body was shaking because he was under the influence of something.

"Your husband, you say?" the man said.

She nodded. He shone the light down at her hand. "Don't see no ring."

"I'm not wearing it."

The edge of his mouth curled into a sneer. "You're a shit liar, you know that?"

The guy moved the light over to Joshua's Altima, then to her Malibu. The hand holding the flashlight was trembling. She glanced down at the body. These two people still hadn't seen it. They stood on the other side of Joshua's car, looking at Karen and Joshua over the hood. The car blocked the body from being in their line of sight.

"Two pretty slick rides," the man said. "They both yours?"

She nodded.

"Let's see here." He pointed back and forth between them. "Eeny, meeny, miny, mo."

He kept his finger pointed at her car.

"We'll take the Malibu."

"Take it?"

"Yeah. Hand over the keys. Unless you got a problem with that." The man reached down and lifted the hem of his hoodie. Even with the light partially blinding her, Karen could clearly see what was tucked into the waistband of his pants: a handgun. A big, black, nasty handgun.

Her breath caught in her throat.

"J-just take it," she said, trying to keep her voice calm. She grabbed her keys from her pocket.

He turned to the woman.

"Go grab the keys, babe."

The woman walked over to Karen.

"We don't want any trouble," she said. It was the first time she'd spoken. Her voice was quiet and frail, sounded like she was totally exhausted. She walked around the front of the car to grab the keys. She saw the body and froze. Stared down at it for a moment, focusing on it, then let out a startled yelp and backed away.

"What's your problem?" the man said.

"There's a . . . a body."

The man walked around the car and shone his flashlight down at the body.

"What the . . ." He looked up at Karen. "What's going on here?"

She and Joshua were silent. The man pulled the gun from his waistband.

"Answer me."

"There was a car accident," Joshua said.

"Fuck." He shone the light down at the body. He kept shaking. Karen got a good look at his eyes and saw that his pupils were dilated. They were jumping around like crazy.

"Let's go, Ross," the woman said. "Let's—"

"Don't say my name," he yelled.

"Let's get out of here." She grabbed the keys from Karen.

"I'm putting the bag in the car," the woman said to the man— Ross. "Then we'll leave."

Ross was silent. He stared at the body, looked up at Karen and Joshua. The woman grabbed the backpack off the ground and carried it to Karen's car. She placed it in the backseat.

"Let's get out of here," she said.

"Hold up," Ross said. "We gotta do something about these two."

Ross motioned the woman over to the side. They walked a few feet away from Karen and Joshua. Ross turned back and looked at them.

"Stay right there," he said. "Don't move."

"Just leave," Karen said. "We already reported the accident to the police. They're on their way."

He glared at her. "Already told you, you're a shit liar. Stay there and shut up."

/////////////////

Amber took a deep breath; she couldn't believe any of this. She looked over at the two people. Must be a mom and her kid. She and Ross had moved a few feet away from them, out of their earshot. The body was still there, resting on the ground beside them. She was still rattled from seeing it. She'd never seen a dead body so close.

Ross was right beside her, pacing and mumbling to himself, everything at a faster speed than usual: cursing, sighing, twitching. His eyes were wide and frenzied. Nervous, fidgety movements. It was like his entire body was hypercharged.

"Let's leave," Amber said. "Now."

"What about those two?" Ross said.

"We'll leave them. Just forget them."

"They know my name," Ross said. His words were starting to slur. "They know what we look like."

"Doesn't matter. They don't know where we're heading. We'll be long gone by the time they get to the police."

"Bastards'll probably try to blame us for the dead body." He turned his head toward them. "Be much easier if we kill them."

"Kill them?"

"Yeah. Kill them, we don't have to worry about them describing us to the police, giving them my name, nothing like that."

Ross reached into his pocket and grabbed the baggie of pills. She reached out and squeezed his hand before he could grasp one.

"Don't," she said. He was already wired. She didn't want him clouding his judgment even more right now.

He yanked his hand out of hers. Grabbed a pill and popped it. Shoved the baggie back in his pocket.

"You can't murder them, Ross," she said.

"Watch me."

She thought—hoped—the way Ross was talking was all an act. Hard talk. She wanted to believe that he was incapable of something so awful, but the drugs changed him, altered his personality. Turned him into someone who was colder, angrier.

She'd forgiven him for plenty over the years, but she couldn't look past something like murder. That was just too much. If he crossed that line, she'd give up on him.

"Just calm down," she said. "Just slow down for—"

"I'm gonna kill them."

"No. Calm down. Just think about this."

///////////////

Karen and Joshua were a few feet away but she could hear the occasional word from Ross; his voice would rise to a near yell at times. *Kill them*—she'd heard that phrase a few times. As terrifying as the words were, it was the wild, unpredictable look in Ross's eyes that truly scared her.

Kill them—he repeated the phrase.

"Mom," Joshua whispered.

She looked at him, right beside her. He held his keys in his hand. He gestured to his car. About ten feet away from them.

"Let's run," he whispered.

She looked over at Ross. He was talking to the woman, gesturing wildly, the gun still in his hand. It looked like the woman was trying to calm him down. Ross grabbed a baggie of pills from his pocket and popped one. He kept talking in a raised voice, his words slurred.

The way he was talking and moving, she was positive if they stuck around there, he would kill them.

Karen looked at Joshua's car, down at the keys in his hand.

No time to think. No time to debate.

She locked eyes with Joshua and held up three fingers.

Three.

She looked at Ross and the woman. They were still talking. Their backs weren't fully turned to her and Joshua, but they were at an angle, she and Joshua not in their line of sight.

Two.

Karen tensed the muscles in her legs.

One.

They both sprinted to his car, covering the distance in only a few seconds. She threw open the passenger door and collapsed into the front seat. Joshua ran around the car, tumbled into the driver's seat, and fired up the engine.

She heard Ross yell out: "Shit!"

He sprinted over to the car, arms pumping, still holding the gun. Ross jumped onto the hood just as the car started reversing.

He yelled at them through the windshield.

Karen screamed.

Joshua yanked the steering wheel to the right, to the left, trying to throw him off the hood. The car swerved and veered but Ross stayed on, one hand gripping the edge of the hood, the other holding the gun.

The crack of a gunshot rang out.

Karen screamed again.

More gunshots. One right after another they came, three or four shots in the span of a few seconds. As Ross shot the gun, Joshua kept swerving and reversing, causing the gun to fire waywardly, off to the side and into the air.

And then Ross pointed the gun downward and fired. The car rocked to one side and started wobbling and shaking, slowing down.

The tire—he'd shot out the tire.

Ross braced himself on the hood and pointed the gun right at Joshua through the windshield. Joshua slammed on the brakes and the car stopped reversing. Ross jumped off the hood.

"Out of the car!" he screamed.

Karen and Joshua stepped outside. Her heart was thundering.

Ross's eyes, wild and frantic, moved between them. He moved the gun to Joshua, pointed it back at her.

"Calm down," Karen yelled.

Ross pointed the gun at her, at Joshua. He screamed something that was so jumbled it was incomprehensible.

Before anything more happened, a barely there voice spoke.

"Help."

/////////////

It took Amber a moment to realize she'd been shot.

Standing off to the side, she'd watched Ross run over, jump onto the car, and start shooting, the arm holding the gun flailing around as he tried to balance himself on the hood as the car swerved. A moment later, she felt it in her stomach. Not pain, really. Just a warm sensation, a low-burn heat.

She looked down and saw that her black sweatshirt was damp. She patted her stomach and looked at her hand. It was covered in blood.

Right then, the pain hit. It was sharp and sudden. She fell to her knees. Opened her mouth but no words came.

Everything started to spin. Through her hazy vision, she saw the car come to a stop. Ross jumped off the hood. The car doors opened and the kid and the mom got out.

Everyone began yelling. Ross waved the gun around, moving it between the two of them.

Amber opened her mouth again. This time, she spoke a single word.

"Help."

////////////////

Karen watched Ross sprint over to the wounded woman. He dropped to his knees and held her in his arms. He brought his face close to hers and started speaking in a low voice.

"What is it?" he said.

"Sh-shot," she said.

"What?"

"Shot. Stomach."

He brushed his hand against her sweatshirt. Blood smudged onto his hand.

He held her in his arms and continued talking in a low voice, barely above a whisper; his words were so quick and jumbled Karen couldn't tell what he was saying.

She looked at Joshua. Standing on the other side of his car. The front of the car sagged to the right from the flat tire.

Ross suddenly went silent. He snapped his head toward them and his eyes locked on Joshua. He stood up and took a step toward them.

"You asshole," he said.

"Stop!" Karen said.

"You stupid asshole."

She screamed for him to stop again, but he ignored her. Another step. His eyes, burning, intense, stayed on Joshua. The hand holding the gun was shaking and trembling.

"I'm a nurse," Karen said. "I can help her."

Ross looked over.

"If I can slow the bleeding, I can help her. But you need to calm down. Please."

He nodded to her. Karen ran over to the woman and dropped to her knees. The woman's eyes were closed. Karen lifted her sweatshirt. There was a gunshot wound just to the left of her stomach. Blood was everywhere. Karen applied pressure. The woman's eyes stayed closed but she winced. A reaction.

From behind her, Ross's rough voice: "Does it hurt?"

Karen turned and looked at him.

"You have to call nine-one-one," she said.

"No," Ross said. "No cops."

"Then take her to a hospital. Leave with her. She has to get this looked at right away."

"So you can call the cops when we leave? No way."

"No, we—"

"Shut up."

Ross ran his hands through his hair. Shook his head. Mumbled to himself. There was a look of wild desperation in his eyes. He glanced at Joshua's car, leaning to the side from the flat tire. He glanced at her Malibu, thirty feet or so from Joshua's car.

"You take her," he said to Karen.

"What? No. I'm not leaving my son here. I can't—"

"Take her—now!" he screamed. He gestured toward Joshua with the gun. "He's staying here. You try anything, he gets a bullet. My wife dies, he gets a bullet. You go to the cops or tell anyone, he gets a bullet. I'm not fucking around here."

He bent over the woman and fished inside her pants pockets. He grabbed a set of keys from inside. The keys to Karen's car.

He threw them at Karen and they landed at her feet. "The keys to that car," he said, pointing at her car. "Put her inside and go."

Karen's ears were ringing. She felt like she was trying to process a million things at once. Everything was happening so quickly.

"Go!" he yelled. "Now!"

She grabbed the keys and walked over to the injured woman. She wrapped a hand around her back and helped her stand up and walk over to her car. She opened the rear door and laid her down in the backseat. She ran around the car and sat in the driver's seat. Ross ran over and leaned into the backseat.

"Babe, you're going to be fine," he said, squeezing her shoulders. His voice was calmer now, not as frantic. Almost soothing.

The woman weakly nodded.

"This nurse here, she's taking you to the hospital. If I showed up with you in a stolen car, they'd have questions. I wouldn't have answers. We'd both get arrested. We can't have that."

He kissed her forehead.

"You'll be fine. Just hang on. You can do this."

He slammed the door shut and looked at Karen.

"Go," he said. "Make up a story for why she's hurt. And don't try nothing cute." He gestured toward Joshua with the gun. "She doesn't make it, and he'll pay."

Karen put the car in reverse, turned around, and started driving back through the forest.

EIGHT

KAREN PUSHED SEVENTY AS SHE DROVE DOWN THE HIGHWAY. EVERY second was precious. Behind her, the woman who'd been shot lay on her back, her hand over her stomach. Blood oozed onto her arm, smudging onto the leather seat.

"What's your name?" Karen said.

The woman mumbled a response.

"What was that?"

"Amber."

"Amber, great. You're going to be fine. Just hang in there. Okay?"

She nodded. Karen kept her eyes focused on the highway. She'd nearly gotten lost finding her way out of the forest, but, thank God, her phone got reception and she found the path leading out.

"That wound might look bad, but it's not," Karen said. "The bullet missed your vital organs."

She had no clue whether that was the truth but it sounded good, hopefully kept Amber calm.

"What about that man you were with? Is that your husband?"

"Y-yeah."

"Did you say his name was Ross?"

"Uh-huh. Ross."

Karen continued to ask her questions as she drove down the highway, Cedar Rapids just a few miles away in the distance. She was headed to Mercy Hospital, where she worked. There might've been another hospital that was closer, maybe in Solon, but there hadn't been time to look up directions or an address on her phone. She'd gotten in her car and booked.

After white-knuckling it through the city, she arrived at Mercy. She pulled up right outside the entrance to the emergency room, rushed inside, and told them that she had a patient.

A few workers ran out to her car. They lifted Amber from the backseat, put her on a stretcher, and wheeled her into the hospital.

Karen watched them disappear past a set of double doors, into the hospital.

////////////////

Fifteen minutes after arriving at the hospital, Karen sat in the waiting area by herself, staring at the magazines piled on the table in front of her. There were a million things to worry about, but all she could think of was Joshua.

She called his phone. No answer. She pulled up her phone's keypad and hit three digits: 911. She stared at her screen for a moment, then deleted the number without placing the call. It was just too risky to call the police right now. There was no telling what would happen if she told them everything and they showed up in the forest. Ross had seemed so irrational, so angry. He'd threatened to kill Joshua if she involved the police, and she feared it wasn't an empty threat.

An older nurse with long, dark hair appeared and sat down next to Karen. She set a disposable cup on the table.

"Coffee," she said. "I'll apologize in advance for the taste. But it's all we have."

"I know all about the coffee here," Karen said. "I actually work up on the ICU floor. I'm a nurse."

"No kidding." She gestured to the double doors Amber had disappeared through when they arrived. "So, what in the world happened?"

"I was out driving," Karen began. She knew people would have questions, and she'd come up with a story to explain everything as she waited. "And suddenly, I saw a person lying on the side of the road. I walked over. She was alive but I could tell she was hurt. Badly. At first, I thought she must've been hit by a car, but then I looked at her injury and saw it was a gunshot. I loaded her into my backseat and drove here."

The nurse brought a hand to her chest. "Goodness. Where did this happen?"

"Off of Highway Thirty. West of the city."

Both the story and the location were made-up; she'd figure it out later if pressed for details. Main thing was, the location was nowhere near the Hawkeye Wildlife Management Area. She didn't want anyone going near there right now.

"Will she live?" Karen asked.

"Too early to tell. She lost a lot of blood. She's in surgery now and we'll hope for the best."

"Do you know who she is?"

"Right now, she's a Jane Doe. She didn't have any ID on her."

"Am I free to leave? I don't think there's much more I can do here."

"You'll have to stick around for a while," she said. "The police will be here shortly. We reported the gunshot wound to them. They'll need to get your statement."

//////////////////////

Joshua sat on the ground, the same place he'd been since his mom left. The sun had started to rise—the surrounding forest was brighter but still gloomy, just bare trees and discolored grass.

"Oh Jesus . . . If I lose her . . ."

Ross had said little during the past fifteen minutes, but when he did speak, it was usually something along those lines. Mumbling curse words and partial phrases, a few threats. Joshua kept thinking about doing something—attempting to run and disappear in the forest, screaming for help, escaping to his car—but it all seemed too risky or pointless. If he tried to run away, he'd be lucky to get a few feet before Ross started shooting. Screaming for help wouldn't accomplish anything; there wasn't anyone for miles. And the flat tire made his car worthless.

"Your mom better not try nothing," Ross said, turning to Joshua. "She goes to the cops, she tells anyone about this, I'll take you out. This place'll be a bloodbath."

Ross thrust a hand into his jeans pocket. Felt around for a couple of seconds. Pulled out his baggie of pills. He took one, hands shaking. Around ten pills were left.

He paced, ran his hand through his hair, bit his lower lip, the same nervous mannerisms he'd been doing for the past few minutes. In the distance, an animal howled. Ross looked in the direction of the noise. He shook his head. He glanced over at the dead body. Stared at it for a second. Shook his head again.

"How far's your house, kid?" he said to Joshua.

"My house?"

"Yeah."

"Ten, fifteen miles."

"Anyone home right now?"

"No."

"Your dad? Brothers or sisters?"

"No. It's just me and my mom."

He looked past the body, at Joshua's car. It was still there. The driver's-side door was open and the interior light was on.

"The keys. Hand 'em over," Ross said.

"They're still in the ignition."

Ross walked over to the car and leaned into the driver's seat. He grabbed the keys out of the ignition and popped the trunk. He leaned inside and moved some things around, stealing glances at Joshua.

"You know how to change a tire?"

Joshua shook his head.

"I'll do it, then. Don't try nothing."

Ross rolled the spare tire to the front of the car and began to change out the flat. Flashlight in mouth, he concentrated and stole the occasional glance at Joshua as he worked. It took him a few minutes to finish.

"Let's go," he said, standing up.

"Go?" Joshua said. "Where?"

"Your house. Creepy as hell, being all the way out here with that body. And I'm starving. So hurry it up. Let's get the hell out of here."

NINE

"AND RIGHT ON THE EDGE OF THE ROAD, I SAW A BODY. BLOOD WAS everywhere."

Karen slowly shook her head as she told the story. Carmella and three other nurses from her floor sat across from her, each wearing green scrubs. They leaned forward in their seats, eyes locked on Karen. Somehow, word had spread up to the ICU bay about her arrival in the emergency room and a few of her coworkers had come down to get the scoop.

She told them the same story she'd told the ER nurse earlier. She spoke slowly, distractedly, her thoughts still on Joshua. When she finished, her coworkers stared at her for a silent moment.

"What a story," one of the nurses finally said.

"And I thought I was having an exciting day."

"You're Wonder Woman," Carmella said. "Only blond. And old."

There were a few chuckles. Karen tried to smile. Not much of one came.

She glanced over at the double doors, a few feet away. "I just hope she'll make it," she said.

Still no update. She didn't even want to imagine what would happen if Amber didn't pull through.

Her coworkers continued talking, asking her questions. Karen halfheartedly answered, but she could barely concentrate. After a few questions, the ER nurse she'd talked to earlier walked into the waiting area.

"I'll need a moment of your time," she said to Karen. "A police detective is here to speak with you."

A MAN WHO LOOKED TO BE IN HIS FORTIES WALKED INTO THE WAITING area and stood next to the nurse. Dark hair, just a little gray. Strong jawline. A light blue button-up tucked into a pair of jeans.

"I'm Detective Francis," he said. "Call me Franny, though. Everyone does."

Karen's coworkers stood up. They passed by her as they walked to the door.

"Good luck," Carmella said. She lowered her voice to a whisper: "Oh, and he's not wearing a ring."

Carmella smiled. Karen didn't even attempt to return it. She was too nervous. It was one thing to make up the story for a nurse or her coworkers. A different matter entirely to lie to a police detective.

"Sounds like you had quite the morning," Detective Francis—Franny—said. He sat next to her and took out a notepad.

Karen nodded.

"Go ahead and tell me everything that happened. Take your time."

"There's not much to tell, honestly," she began. She repeated her made-up story about finding Amber on the side of the highway, putting her in the backseat, and driving her to the hospital.

"Quite the story," Franny said once she finished. "Now, you found her off of Highway Thirty?"

"Yes. That's right."

"East or west of the city?"

"West."

"How far out? Was there any sort of landmark nearby?"

She paused for a moment. Thought. Tried to picture Highway 30.

"It was a good ten miles outside of the city," she said, "only a few feet past the turnoff for Atkins. I remember that."

Once Detective Franny went out there, he'd find no blood or any other sort of evidence that a person had been shot nearby. She didn't know what would happen after that—maybe he'd have more questions; maybe he'd even start to suspect she was lying—but that was something to worry about later. Right now, all she wanted to do was end this interrogation. Get Franny out of there so she could return to Joshua.

"The Atkins turnoff—I know the area," Franny said. "Why were you all the way out there this early?"

"Couldn't sleep. Decided to drive around. I like how peaceful the roads are in the early mornings. And then I saw the body, right there on the edge of the road."

"When you found her, was there anyone else in the area? Any cars driving away?"

"Not that I saw."

"Why didn't you call nine-one-one?"

"Instinct, I guess. I saw her there and I was so shocked by the sight. Saving her—that was the only thing on my mind. I'm a nurse; I know how seconds can matter in situations like this. By the time I thought about calling nine-one-one, I was halfway to the hospital. Figured it was quicker to drive her here myself."

"Did she say much on her way here?"

"Amber—she told me her name. That was about it."

"Well, that's a start. We'll take her fingerprints and run those to see if there's a match."

Franny asked her a few more questions. When he finished, he gave her a polite, brief smile.

"You probably can't wait to head home," he said. "Heck of a start to the day."

"You can say that again."

"Just one final thing and you can go. I'd like to take a look at your car. The car you picked her up in."

"The car?"

"Yeah. Just a quick look. Maybe an item fell out of her pocket, something like that. You never know. Won't take but a second."

"Of course," she said.

They stood up from their chairs and she slipped on her coat. They exited the hospital and approached her car, the only one in the small emergency room parking lot.

Franny pulled out his notebook and looked over his notes as they walked.

"Just so I'm clear on this," he said. "For my report. You were driving all the way out there on Highway Thirty at four this morning because you couldn't sleep?"

"Yes," Karen said.

Franny didn't say anything in response. She could practically hear the gears turning in his head, thinking about the story. How had she not realized how ridiculous the story was? Driving around at four in the morning? Because she couldn't sleep?

"Sometimes I just enjoy driving," Karen said. "That's how I relax. I had some things to think about. My son is getting ready to graduate. I think I'm more nervous about what the future holds than he is. It's weird, knowing he'll be gone."

They reached the car. Franny walked around to the side of the car. He cupped his hands over the passenger window and looked in at the front seat.

"I know the feeling," he said. "My two daughters live with me. Twin girls. Can't even imagine what the house will be like when they're gone."

Franny opened the passenger door and leaned into the front seat. He looked around the car's interior. He leaned past the front seat and looked at the bloodstained backseat.

"They're only thirteen, but college seems like it's just around the corner," he said. "They're a handful but I can't imagine life without them. Even the weekends they're with their mother, the house feels empty and—*Jesus*."

Franny practically screamed the word. He stepped away from the car and turned to her. He stared at her, eyes hard, mouth half-open. He glanced over at the car again and turned back to her, the same confused, slightly alarmed expression on his face.

A reaction like that could mean only one thing: he'd found something.

TEN

DETECTIVE FRANNY REACHED INTO THE BACKSEAT AND EMERGED WITH A black backpack in his hand. He set it on the ground. The top of the bag was unzipped—piles and stacks of money were inside, more money than Karen had ever seen in her life.

"Oh my God," she said. She stared at the backpack. Amber had thrown it into the backseat earlier, in the forest. In the chaos of everything that had happened, Karen had forgotten about that.

"I found this in the backseat," Franny said. "Looks like the zipper's broken, and I glanced inside. Saw the money. What is going on?"

"Amber—she had it with her when I found her."

"She did? Why didn't you mention this earlier?"

"I completely forgot. I'm sorry."

Franny silently stared at her. Seemed like there was a slightly different look in his eyes, a change in his demeanor.

"Everything was so frantic," Karen said. "But, yes. She was definitely wearing this bag when I found her. Strapped to her back. She must've taken it off when she was in the backseat."

"You didn't see her do that? Or notice that it was filled with money?"

"I was barely paying attention to anything. I was focused on getting to the hospital." She looked down at the open bag. "I had no idea this money was inside. . . . I can't believe it."

Franny kept his eyes on her, then leaned down and sifted through the money in the bag. He grabbed two items that were crumpled in the corner of the bag. He held the items in the air—one green, one brown.

"Masks," he said. "Looks like . . . Yoda and Chewbacca. From *Star Wars*. Something else in there, too."

He pointed at a dark metallic object in the corner of the bag.

"Is that . . ."

"A gun," Franny said. "Looks like our friend has some explaining to do."

Franny told her he was going to call in and report everything. He stepped a few feet away and started talking on his phone. Karen stared down at the open backpack, at all of that money. The masks. The gun. She took a few deep, slow breaths, tried to calm herself.

After talking into the phone for a few moments, Franny ended the call.

"Turns out there was a bank robbery, people in *Star Wars* masks, over in Nebraska the other day. Made off with a pretty nice haul, sounds like. Reports say there were three people who pulled off the robbery."

He looked back down at the backpack.

"So what happened to the other two?" he said. "If this woman Amber was one of the robbers, where are the other two right now?"

//////////////////

Joshua gripped the steering wheel with both hands and stared out his car's cracked windshield. Ross was in the backseat, behind him.

"The gun's pointed right at you, big man," Ross said. "Don't try nothing. Just drive."

Joshua drove on, back through the forest. He caught Ross's reflection in the rearview mirror. He was just as restless and jumpy as he'd been in the forest. His head was on a swivel, constantly scanning the road, glancing out the window, looking at Joshua. His loud, heavy breathing was the only sound in the car.

"House better be empty," Ross said.

"It will be."

"Could get ugly if it ain't."

The car's dashboard clock read just after six, which meant not even an hour had passed since the gunshots in the forest. It felt like another lifetime.

"The phone in the cup holder, that yours?"

Joshua glanced down. His phone was still in the center console cup holder, where he'd put it when he arrived at the forest.

"Yeah. It's mine."

"Throw it back here."

Joshua grabbed the phone and tossed it over his shoulder. Ross grabbed it off the seat and put it in his pocket.

When they reached the house, Joshua slowed and pulled into the driveway. He parked the car outside the garage. He exited the car and walked across the front lawn, Ross a few feet behind him with the gun. They walked through the front door into the living room.

"Where's the kitchen?" Ross said.

"The kitchen?"

"Yeah."

"Why?"

"Just answer the damn question. Where is it?"

"Next room over."

"Stay here. Don't talk. Don't move. Don't do nothing but breathe."

Ross hurried past the doorway. Joshua heard a few drawers being opened in the kitchen. A moment later, Ross returned carrying a box of plastic zip ties.

"That door right there," he said, gesturing to a door just off the hallway. "Where's it lead?"

"A storage room."

"Any chairs in there?"

"A few."

"Okay. Go in there."

They walked down the hallway, past the door, into the storage room. Shelving racks lining the walls held a variety of items, mostly Joshua's old toys and school projects. There were stacks of Tupperware containers with different labels on the outside: FIFTH GRADE, DRAWINGS, LEGOS. A plastic set of Fisher-Price golf clubs was balanced against the wall, underneath a shelf with all of his old Transformers figures lined up.

"Where the chairs at?"

"In the closet."

Ross threw open the closet door and grabbed a metal folding chair. He set it up in the middle of the room.

"Sit down," he said.

Joshua sat down. Ross zip-tied his hands behind him, secured them to a support beam on the back side of the chair, then zip-tied his ankles to the chair legs. Joshua could barely move.

Ross set the gun on a table to the side and pulled a phone from his pocket.

"Your phone," Ross said to him. "What's the code to unlock it?"

Joshua told him. Ross tapped the screen a few times. He was biting his lower lip, chewing it like it was a piece of gum, his jaw clenching and unclenching.

"Your mom, what's her cell number?" Ross asked.

"It's saved in there. Under 'Mom.'"

Ross tapped the screen.

"Want you to call her, see how Amber's doing," he said.

He held the phone to Joshua's ear and the line rang.

/////////////////

A police cruiser pulled into the ER parking lot and two uniformed officers stepped out. Karen had gone back inside the hospital to escape the cold while she waited, and she watched through the window as the officers approached Franny and began talking. The three of them walked to her car and looked at the backpack filled with money on the ground, then examined the exterior of her car, leaned in, and looked inside. Franny gestured in her direction and the officers glanced over. There was more talking, a few more glances toward her. One of the officers made a call. The other scribbled in a notepad.

They suspected something. She was positive they knew there was more to the story she'd told earlier. It only made sense. She figured

Franny could tell she was lying just by looking at her eyes or listening to the tone of her voice when she answered his questions. He probably had special training on how to spot when people weren't telling the truth, something like that. Right now, she figured he was talking to the two officers about—

Her phone rang, startling her. She grabbed it from her purse.

Joshua's name was displayed. All of the air left her body in a rush.

"Are you fine?" she answered.

"Yeah. We're at the house now. He—"

"What? Our house?"

"He made me come here. We—"

"How is she?" Ross's gruff voice interrupted Joshua.

"What—"

"Answer me. How is she? Is she gonna live?"

"She'll be fine," Karen said.

Earlier, a nurse had told Karen that doctors had removed the bullet from Amber. It was still early, but the outlook was good. They'd soon transfer her to the ICU ward—Karen's own floor. At noon, they'd take her in for additional scans to learn more.

"She's going to be fine?" Ross said into the phone. "You're sure?"

"It sounds like it."

"Okay, get back here."

"I'm still at the hospital. I will as soon as I can. Just, please, don't do anything."

The line went dead. Karen put her phone back in her purse. They were at the house. She couldn't decide if that was good or bad. It wasn't as secluded as the forest, but it was still so far out in the country. Anything could happen.

"Who was on the phone?"

She turned around. Franny stood behind her.

"My son was calling," she said. "He's not feeling well. Could I head home and check on him?"

"In a minute," he said. "First, I need you to show me where you found the woman. The exact location. We'll need to examine the scene. See if she dropped an item, left something behind, that sort of thing."

"It was by the turnoff for Atkins, on—"

"Yeah, you said that. But that's a pretty big area. Be much easier if you show us. Won't take long. Then you can drive back home."

"That's fine," Karen said. Get this over with and get back home; that was all she cared about.

"We're finished with your car, so you can drive there yourself," Franny said. "I'll follow you."

//////////////////

Twenty minutes later, Karen stood on the gravel shoulder next to Highway 30, hands buried in her coat pockets, lightly shivering, her breath fogging the air. A few feet away, Franny stood in front of his parked black Crown Victoria, near a small green sign that read MILE 242. The two uniformed officers stood off to the side. Occasionally, a car would pass, but the highway was mostly empty.

"Could you take me through it again?" Franny asked. "Tell me exactly what happened."

"I was driving on the highway," Karen said. "I saw a huddled object on the side of the road. I slowed down and realized it was a person. She was injured. I helped her into my car and took her straight to the hospital."

"And she had a backpack with her?"

"Right."

Franny stared at the ground. "So where's the blood? If this lady was lying on the edge of the road after getting shot, there should be blood everywhere out here. But there's nothing. It's not raining or snowing. Wouldn't have been washed away."

"I don't know," Karen said. "Maybe she was shot right before I found her. Maybe there wasn't time for her to bleed everywhere."

"Could be." He looked around—nothing in any direction but trees and flatland. "You're sure you didn't see anyone in the area, maybe running from the scene? No car or vehicle, anything like that?"

"No. Not that I noticed."

"And you're sure this is the correct area?"

"Yes. I remember passing the turnoff for Atkins. And that tree— I remember that, too."

She pointed to a somewhat distinctive twisted tree on the side of the road. Franny glanced at the tree. He paced around the side of the highway, head down.

"Whole thing is weird," he said. "The money. That's what really bothers me. Whoever shot her, why would they leave the money behind? I bet there was at least twenty, thirty thousand dollars in that backpack. Probably more."

Karen shrugged. "Maybe the person who shot her didn't know the money was in there. Or maybe I scared off whoever shot her. They saw my car approaching and disappeared before I could see them. There wasn't time for them to grab the backpack."

"There's a chance." Franny paced some more, occasionally kicking at the ground and scattering rocks on the shoulder. He walked over to the two uniformed officers and they briefly talked, low voices, out of her earshot. The conversation seemed to last forever. They looked over at her, looked at her car, looked at the ground.

Finally, Franny broke away and slowly walked back over to her.

"This is a weird one; that's for sure," he said. "Anything else we should know?"

This was her chance, maybe her final chance, to involve the police . . . but she just couldn't bring herself to say anything. There were too many uncertainties. If the police showed up and surprised Ross, there was no telling what might happen. Maybe there'd be a negotiation, a standoff, a shoot-out. There were a million ways something like that could end.

"No, I've told you everything," she said.

//////////////

Franny said he'd contact her with further questions. Told her she was free to go. She returned to her car and drove away.

Once she was a few miles from the scene, she pulled onto a gravel road and drove until she was far from the highway. No houses nearby. No other cars around. Just flat, bare farmland. She stopped her car and gripped the steering wheel with both hands, leaning forward and lightly tapping her forehead against it, resisting the urge to scream at the top of her lungs.

She still couldn't believe she'd survived everything. So many close calls. Maybe she'd made a mistake, not telling the truth to the police, but there was no time to dwell on that. She needed to get back home, back to Joshua, back to whatever awaited her.

She kept her eyes closed, forehead leaning against the steering wheel, for a brief moment. Just to calm herself. To slow everything down. It felt like she was being buried under a million things at once and she needed to pause before it became too overwhelming.

She opened her eyes and sat up in her seat. She had to get back to Joshua.

She pulled back onto the highway and headed for home.

ELEVEN

FIFTEEN MINUTES LATER, KAREN ARRIVED AT THEIR HOUSE. THE BLINDS were pulled in a few windows, but other than that, nothing looked different or out of place. She parked beside Joshua's car in the driveway, walked up to the front door, and rang the doorbell.

"You alone?" Ross's gruff voice said from the other side of the door.

"Yes."

"Come in."

She opened the door and stepped into the living room. The sunlight creeping past the blinds allowed her to see Ross standing a few feet in front of her with the gun in his hand. It was pointed to the floor, but that didn't put her at ease. Not at all.

"Got your phone on you?" he asked.

"In my pocket."

"Grab it. Throw it on the ground." Karen did. "Now put your hands up."

She raised her hands.

"Walk down the hallway," he said. "Into the door that's open. I'll be right behind you."

She walked across the living room. Down the hallway. The door to the storage room was open. She entered. Joshua sat in a chair right inside the door, his arms bound behind him, legs secured to the chair.

The moment she stepped into the room, she ran over and hugged him.

"You're fine?" she asked.

He nodded. She kept her arms around him, squeezing hard.

"That's enough," Ross said. "Take a seat."

He took a chair from the corner of the room and placed it in front of her. It was a plastic chair with armrests, slightly different from the folding chair Joshua sat in. Ross grabbed a box of zip ties resting on the table and secured her wrists to the armrests and her ankles to the chair legs. The ties were so tight they felt like they were cutting off the circulation to her hands and feet.

Ross stared down at her, his body lightly twitching, clenching and unclenching his jaw. "Tell me everything. She's gonna live?"

"Yes, it sounds like it," Karen said.

A relieved look crossed Ross's face for a second.

"What'd you tell them?" he asked. "What was your story?"

"I said I was out driving alone and found her on the side of the road, injured."

"They believed you?"

"I think so. I work at the hospital I took her to, so I think they trusted me. The police had questions about—"

"The police!" he screamed, tensing up. "What the hell?"

"Gunshot wounds have to be reported to the authorities. It's the law. After the hospital notified the police, a detective came and asked me questions. I told him the same story about finding her on the side of the road."

"The police, Jesus." Ross shook his head. "You're sure they didn't suspect nothing?"

"I don't think so. But when they finished asking questions, they wanted to search the car. I had to let them. I didn't want to make them suspicious. When they looked in the backseat, they found—"

"Shit, the money."

Karen nodded. "Yeah. They found the money. The masks and a gun, too."

Ross grimaced and slammed a clenched fist against the wall.

"So the money's gone?" he said.

She nodded. Ross started pacing around the room. As he walked, he constantly made nervous, fidgety movements: running a hand through his hair, shaking his head, blinking a few times in rapid succession.

"Do they know who she is?" he asked.

"No. They're checking her fingerprints, though.

"But they know she robbed a bank?"

Karen nodded.

"What's gonna happen next, then? When they release her from the hospital, what'll happen?"

"I don't know," Karen said.

"Jail, right? She'll go straight to jail."

"Probably. Yeah."

Ross stopped pacing. Stared off. Shook his head.

"That can't happen," he mumbled. "My baby's not going to jail. No way."

ROSS STORMED OUT OF THE ROOM. KAREN COULD HEAR HIS FOOTSTEPS through the walls as he stomped down the hallway into the living room.

The room was silent for a moment after he left. She looked at Joshua. They sat right next to each other, Joshua with his hands tied behind his back, Karen with her hands secured to the chair armrests, both of them with their feet tied to the chair legs.

"What are we going to do?" Joshua asked.

"Keep your voice down," she said. "He's only in the next room. These walls are thin."

She struggled in her chair. She wasn't slipping free of the zip ties. They were on too tight.

"Can you get free?" she asked.

Joshua wiggled his body in the chair and struggled against the zip ties binding his wrists together. He shook his head. Even if one of them could get free, what were they going to do? Ross had a gun. They'd need some sort of weapon to even have a chance.

From down the hallway came the sound of Ross opening doors. Rummaging around. Clattering and clanging.

"What is he doing?" Joshua asked.

"I don't know," she said. "We just need to stay calm."

There was more clattering and clanging. The garage, Karen realized—he was in the garage.

"Maybe we can talk our way out of this," she said. "Convince him to leave. Stay calm and hope we can end this."

* * *

A FEW MINUTES LATER, THE NOISES FROM THE GARAGE STOPPED. ROSS returned to the room. He carried a can of red spray paint and a small paper bag in one hand.

He sat down at the table and sprayed some paint into the bag, stuck his nose inside, and inhaled deeply. He started mumbling to himself. Karen could just barely hear every third or fourth word. Mostly curse words.

Karen cleared her throat.

"We can end this, right now," Karen said.

He looked over.

"What?"

"We can end this. I'll give you my keys. You can take the car and leave. I won't even report it missing."

"I'm not going anywhere without my wife."

"You'll have to," she said. "If you don't leave here, things are going to get out of control soon. People will start wondering where we are. Joshua's friends. My coworkers. They'll start looking, calling around, when they can't reach us. They might even get the police involved. I don't want that. You don't, either. So just take my car. Disappear from here and just leave us alone."

Right now, that was her main focus. Getting him to leave before the situation became volatile. The pills Ross was taking, the paint he was huffing—it would all only make him more unpredictable. The longer he was around, the more likely something bad would happen. And she'd meant what she said about the police. If they showed up to the house and discovered what was going on, there was no telling what could happen.

"I can tell you're in over your head," she said.

"I'm not."

"It's fine if you are. Please, just take my keys. Leave. It's your only way out of this. You can—"

"Listen, I'm not abandoning my wife. So drop it."

He stood up from the table. Paced. Shook his head.

"Please, just—"

"Shut the hell up," Ross said. "Be quiet. I need to think."

THE ROOM WAS SILENT FOR A LONG TIME. ROSS CONTINUED TO PACE around the room, past the rows of shelves. Occasionally, he would spray some paint into the paper bag and deeply inhale. His chin and cheeks were smudged with dried red spray paint. The few times she tried to say something, Ross cut her off with a wave of his hand.

"Think I got an idea," Ross said, his voice cutting through the silence in the room. He stared at Karen. "This hospital Amber's at, you work there, you said. Right?"

Karen nodded.

"You know the layout, all that stuff?"

"Mostly, yes."

"Okay, so here's what's gonna happen," Ross said. "I want you to go there and break Amber out of her room. Help her escape from the hospital."

"What?"

"You go to the hospital. Use your ID badge to access the doors, everything like that. You help her escape from her room, bring her back here, and me and her will leave."

Karen felt like rolling her eyes. Or sighing. There was so much stupidity in Ross's idea, she didn't even know where to begin.

"That'd be impossible," she said.

"Why?"

"There are a million reasons. I can't just walk into her room undetected. The bay she's in is small. People will see me. And there are security cameras everywhere. I mean everywhere."

"So wear a disguise. One of those masks that doctors wear, put one of those over your face."

"It's not that easy. She's probably handcuffed to the bed. Good chance that a security guard or even a police officer is watching her room. She might not even be strong enough to walk. I'm telling you, it'd be impossible to get into her room and leave with her."

"There's gotta be a way."

"There isn't."

"Well, figure something out."

"Take the car and leave. That's the only way to end this. You can—"

"No, dammit!" Ross yelled. Some spittle flew from his mouth. He sprayed some paint into the bag and took another pull. He glared down at Karen.

"Listen to me. You ain't calling the shots around here," he said. "I am."

He pulled the gun from the waistband of his pants. Karen's heart jumped in her chest.

"Okay, okay. Just calm down."

"You don't think I'm serious, is that it?" Ross said.

"No, no, I don't—"

"You think I'm a punk?"

"No. Just calm down and—"

He lifted the gun and pointed it at Joshua. The muscles in his forearms were tight, like coiled hemp ropes. His grip was steady and firm holding the gun, only a slight tremble.

Joshua closed his eyes. Every muscle in Karen's body froze.

"No, please!" she screamed.

"I'm no punk," Ross said. "I'm not messing around here."

Karen opened her mouth to scream, but she was too late. With the gun pointed at Joshua, Ross pulled the trigger. A gunshot like a cannon blast exploded from the barrel.

TWELVE

THE SUDDEN, SHARP CRACK OF THE GUNSHOT MADE KAREN JUMP IN HER seat. Her ears rang. Her head spun.

And then she saw Joshua. His eyes were closed, jaw clenched, and he was bracing himself in the chair. Just behind him, a bullet hole had been ripped in the wall.

The smell of gunpowder filled the room. Ross stood in front of Joshua, the gun still extended. He slowly turned his head toward Karen. Nothing but clear, lucid intensity in his eyes, like he was a completely different person.

"Six inches," he said. "I aim six inches lower, and there'd be a big, big mess to clean up."

Karen was silent. Her ears continued to ring. The paralyzing fear that gripped her after the gunshot still lingered. For a brief, horrifying second, she'd truly thought Joshua had been shot, right in front of her.

"You're right, you know," Ross said, eyes never leaving Karen. "I'm scared as shit. All I want to do is get the hell out of here. But I'm not leaving alone. Amber is all that matters to me. Whatever it takes, I'm getting her back."

He lowered the gun.

"Next time I shoot, I'm not missing," he said. "So lemme ask the question again: You gonna break my wife out or not?"

"Yes," she said. The word was barely audible. She cleared her throat. "I will."

"Good. How you gonna do it? What's your plan?"

"I don't know," she said. She could barely think straight. "I need some time."

"Fine. Think. Have an answer when I get back."

Ross left the room. Karen's entire body was shaking. Her heart had stopped beating in the moments after the gunshot, but it was roaring now, hammering away.

She looked over at Joshua. He'd finally opened his eyes. His lips were drawn, his expression distant, dazed.

"Are you all right?" she said.

Joshua nodded. But he didn't look all right.

"We'll be fine," she said. "Just calm down. Take a few breaths."

She took her own advice, but the breaths did nothing to calm her.

SHE THOUGHT.

Her mind was so disoriented, it was difficult even to picture the place where she'd worked for the past decade. She couldn't recall the layout of the floor, the surrounding area, anything. But she concentrated. Thought about the endless precautions in place to protect patients, to keep them safe. She tried to think of any way she could bypass all of that and break Amber out of the hospital without being seen.

Eventually, she had something. A seed, then an idea, then a plan.

There was a chance it might succeed. Probably an even better chance it would fail. A million things could go wrong. It was a risk—but not doing anything was an even greater risk.

"YOU GOT AN ANSWER?"

Ross stared at Karen. He stood at the edge of the room, slouching against the doorframe, the can of spray paint in his hand.

"Well? You got a plan or not?"

Karen nodded. "I think so."

"What is it?"

For the next few minutes, she spoke in a quiet, calm voice as she told Ross her plan to break Amber out of the hospital.

"You think this'll work?" Ross asked when she finished.

"It could. If everything happens like I hope, it might."

He nodded. "Okay. Let's go, then."

"It has to happen later. At noon."

"Later? Why?"

"She's being taken in for tests at noon. That's what they told me earlier. That's my chance to break her out."

He looked at the clock on the wall. Just after nine thirty a.m.

"I'll help you," Karen said. "I'll do everything I can to break her out. But I want you to do me a favor. I want you to let my son go."

"No."

"Please. I just want him to be safe. I want you to let him go."

"So he can run to the cops? Tell them everything? Hell no. He's staying right here."

"He won't go to the police. Please. Do this for me."

"No chance," Ross said.

And he left the room.

KAREN AND JOSHUA SAT IN THEIR CHAIRS, NOT SPEAKING, NOT MOVING. It was like the events from the morning were just too much to handle and they couldn't do anything until they shut down and let their bodies decompress.

Joshua looked so gloomy and defeated. His face was pasty and colorless, looked like he was about to get sick. She imagined she probably looked the same.

"Doing all right, J-Bird?" she asked.

He did something with his head that wasn't really a nod, wasn't really a shake.

"We'll be fine," she said. "No need to worry."

He didn't respond. She didn't expect him to. The words didn't even sound convincing to her.

"Your plan," he said. "Your plan to break the woman out. You think it will work?"

"I don't know."

"What if it doesn't?"

"Same answer. I don't know." She shook her head. "I don't even want to think about that."

The room faded back to silence. She blankly looked at the shelves surrounding her. This room always brought a smile to her face, coming in here and looking at Joshua's things. There was a little bit of everything in the room. A milk crate overflowing with his old G.I. Joe toys, shoeboxes crammed with baseball cards, Tupperware containers full of Legos. One shelf held a stack of books—sports biographies, those Hardy Boys books he used to read, a few books about prepping for college entry exams. Balanced against the edge of the shelves was a set of plastic Fisher-Price golf clubs.

Every shelf held a memory, but looking at it all brought no smile now. It was mind-blowing that so much could happen in a single morning. And the morning wasn't even over. She could only imagine what surprises were in store for later. Space aliens landing in their front lawn, maybe.

And to think, this had all started because of a car accident. Out in the middle of the forest.

"The accident," she said to Joshua. "Tell me about the accident and everything that happened after."

"I already told you about it."

"There has to be more to it. I still don't understand why you didn't go to the police. Were you up to something you shouldn't have been?"

"No. We were just hitting golf balls. I don't know. . . . When it happened, everything was so frantic. It was like a million things were happening at once. The guy was screaming at me, at Dad. Then he was shoving us, and he was so strong and powerful. The next thing I knew, he had Dad pinned to the ground. I really thought he might kill him. And then I saw the rock on the ground. About the size of a baseball. I grabbed it and smashed it against the guy's head. The guy dropped to the ground. When I saw he wasn't breathing or moving, I went over and started pounding his chest. Trying to bring him back. But he was dead."

He shook his head.

"And then it was like I hit a wall. I couldn't move or think. It was like I wasn't even there. We stood in silence for a long time; then Dad started talking. Said he didn't think we should go to the police. Kept talking about that case from a few years ago, said he didn't want that to be me. Going to the police wouldn't bring the guy back to life. He kept saying that. All it would do was maybe get me in big trouble. And . . . I don't know. . . . I was so blown away that I agreed. I wasn't thinking right; maybe he wasn't, either. It was just so much happening at once. And we were so far out there. The body probably won't be found for days, weeks even.

"Then the next day came. And I really thought about going to the police. I felt terrible. But it seemed like it was too late to go to the police at that point. Like I really would be in trouble if I went to them a day later and told them we left the body out there."

"Do you know who this person was?" she said. "Do you know why he was all the way out there?"

"I have no idea. It's weird. This time of year, there's never anyone in the forest. No clue why he would've been there."

"Were you going to say anything to me?"

"Probably, yeah. At some point. I don't know."

Joshua went silent and blankly stared off some more. She was angry at him—and Teddy; she had so many questions for him—but she couldn't let her emotion get the best of her. She had to focus on their current situation. That was all that mattered now.

She turned back to the shelves and stared at all the toys and assorted items. She tried to focus on the happy memories that each item held, those bright moments of Joshua's life, but she couldn't concentrate at all, not when she had so many questions about what would happen next.

THIRTEEN

AMBER'S HEAD WAS FLOATING FROM WHATEVER DRUGS THEY'D GIVEN HER. She'd drifted in and out of sleep for the past few hours (hours? days? how long had it been?), able to recall only bits and pieces from everything that had happened since she was shot. She remembered being taken into the ER, remembered a few meetings with nurses and doctors after surgery, remembered being told that they expected her to survive the injury.

There'd also been a visit from a police detective. That had been the shocker of the day. Thinnish, middle-aged guy. He told her that he searched the car she arrived in and found the backpack full of money. Found the *Star Wars* masks, too. Those stupid masks. Shane had thought it'd be so funny to wear them for the robbery, but now those masks had made it easy to link them to the robbery in Nebraska.

The detective asked her questions. Questions about the bank robbery, questions about the people who'd helped her, nonstop questions, one after another. She hadn't answered them, partially because she was so groggy from the medication, partially because she was still in shock from everything that had happened.

Right before he left, the detective said something to her that she'd been thinking about constantly: fifteen to twenty years. That's what she was looking at for armed robbery.

She slowly moved her head and looked down at her wrist. She was handcuffed to one of the rails on the bed. First time she'd ever been handcuffed in her life. Staring down at the handcuffs, she almost started crying but caught herself before the tears came.

She wanted Ross. She felt so alone without him, here in this cold, empty room. Why had they ever left Nebraska? In retrospect, it was such a foolish idea. Their life in Nebraska might not have been perfect, but at least they'd had each other. Screw over Shane, take the money, and just start a new life—how had she not realized how ludicrous and poorly thought out that plan was? Predictably, it had ended in disaster.

She was shot.

She had no idea where Ross was.

The money was gone.

She was looking at twenty years in jail.

Suddenly, the tears broke through. Hot, streaming tears rolled down her cheeks. She cried because of the hopelessness. She cried because of the sad, lonely room around her. But more than anything, she cried because she missed Ross.

She just wanted him by her side.

////////////////

An hour passed. Karen and Joshua mostly sat in silence. She was alternately wired and exhausted. She'd closed her eyes a few times but she knew there was no way she would sleep. It was incredible how quickly all of this had happened. Just last night, she'd been finishing up dinner with Joshua, still on a high from his college acceptance. She'd been looking forward to a weekend doing nothing. And now, here she was. Tied up. A prisoner in her own home. About to break a patient out of the hospital.

She wondered if someone might try to reach her this morning, get suspicious when she didn't respond, maybe even come to the house to investigate. But she doubted it. It was the weekend—she wasn't scheduled to work and Joshua didn't have school. Neither of them had any plans. Their neighbors wouldn't be stopping by; they mostly kept to themselves. Truthfully, she didn't think she wanted anyone to stop by. There was no telling how Ross would react.

As they waited, Ross would walk by the room every couple of minutes and look in on them. After a while, he entered the room carrying her laptop computer. Must've grabbed it from her room. He set it on the table and sat down.

"What's the password?"

She told him. He entered it and clicked the trackpad, pecked away at a few keys. She could just barely see the screen. The Internet was up and an article about a bank robbery was displayed. She figured it was the robbery they were a part of.

"Well, shit," Ross said, staring at the screen.

"What?"

"Nothing."

He closed the computer.

"Can we check our phones?" she asked. "See if anyone is trying to contact us."

"No."

"Someone might be trying to call and—"

"You're not checking your phones. So shut the hell up."

Ross left the room. There was more sitting, more waiting, more silence.

Half an hour later, Ross returned to the room carrying one of her kitchen knives.

"Almost time, right?" he said.

She nodded. Ross cut through the zip ties securing her wrists to the chair arms. Blood rushed to her hands the moment she was free, her fingers tingling with a low pain. He cut the zip ties around her ankles. Same tingling feeling in her feet.

"You ready?" Ross said.

She almost laughed. Of course she wasn't ready. How could she be ready for this, for any of it? She wasn't even at the hospital yet, and already she was nervous. Deep in her stomach, she felt raw, fluttering panic, like a bird trapped in a cage.

"Same plan you talked about before?" Ross asked. "Nothing's changed?"

"Same plan."

"Okay. I'll stay here. Me and the kid. You break Amber out, bring her back here, and we'll leave. Let's go."

She stood up from the chair. Her knees popped like dull firecrackers. Slight cramps in her legs.

She took a few steps toward the door and stopped.

"Wait," she said. "Can I kiss my son?"

Ross looked over at Joshua, a few feet away.

"Make it quick," he said.

Karen walked over and kissed the top of Joshua's head. She placed her hand on his knee and squeezed. He looked so helpless and vulnerable, slumped in the chair, hands tied behind him, feet bound to the chair legs. A lump formed in her throat and her vision clouded with tears. She dried her eyes with the sleeve of her shirt.

"Everything will be fine," she said. "I'll break Amber out, just like I talked about. And this will all be over."

"Okay. Love you, Mom."

"Love you, too."

She kissed him a final time and crossed the room. She walked down the hallway, Ross a few steps behind her. In the living room, Ross grabbed a sheet of paper off a small end table next to the couch. He folded the sheet into thirds and handed it to her.

"Take this," he said. "It's a letter. Give it to Amber before everything happens."

Karen put the letter in her pocket. Ross opened the door for her. Before she stepped outside, he reached out and grabbed her arm.

"Just you remember one thing," Ross said. "We both want this to be over. You show up here with my wife, we go on our way. You don't show up with her, you make a call to the police, you try to pull something fast, and it'll be ugly."

His eyes stayed on her.

"I will kill the kid if I have to," he said. "Don't really want to, but if I have to, I will. I mean every word of that."

Karen stared back at Ross. *You won't hurt my baby,* she thought. *So help me God, if you harm Joshua, I will rip your head off.*

* * *

JOSHUA HEARD HIS MOM'S CAR PULL AWAY, THE TIRES CRUNCHING ON the driveway. A moment later, Ross walked into the room carrying a handful of Slim Jim beef sticks. He unwrapped one and threw the plastic wrapper on the floor. He took a big bite and chewed loudly. He looked even worse now than he had earlier. Eyes bloodshot, face nearly drained of color, spray paint smudged around his mouth.

"Can I have one of those?" Joshua asked.

"No," Ross said.

"I'm starving."

"You're not getting nothing until my wife is back here."

Even if that happened, Joshua didn't know what to expect. He doubted they would all go on their happy ways if his mom broke Amber out.

He'd find out soon enough. There was nothing to do but wait until then.

Karen drove the route she took every day for her morning commute. Same roads and turnoffs. As she neared the hospital, she drove past the turn for the employee parking garage she usually parked in. She drove around the hospital complex and found a side street with metered parking stalls a few blocks away. She pulled into an open stall.

Resting on the seat next to her was a box of two dozen doughnuts. She grabbed the box and stepped out of the car. Fed the meter. Walked to the hospital entrance. Through the front doors, down the hallways.

In her ICU bay, she walked into the small break area. Their floor manager, Peg, was inside, all alone. A few coworkers were out on the floor, scurrying around.

"What in the world are you doing here?" Peg asked her. "You're not scheduled to work this weekend."

"I was in the neighborhood. Wanted to check in after this morning's craziness. See how the woman I brought in was doing."

Karen set the box of doughnuts on the table.

"Figured I'd bring you doughnuts. Make the weekend shift a little easier to handle."

Peg opened the box and grabbed a glazed. Two of the doughnuts were already missing; on the drive there, Karen had devoured them.

"So how is she?" Karen asked. "The woman I brought in earlier."

"Sounds like she was pretty lucky," Peg said. "Bullet went in and out but left a nasty wound. A lot of swelling but that's starting to go down some. We're taking her in for a few scans to learn more, see how soon she can be released."

"Still planning on taking her in at noon? That's what I heard this morning."

"Yep. Noon. She's Crystal's patient."

Word about the doughnuts quickly spread throughout the floor, and a few nurses walked into the room. Carmella was with them.

"Save any lives on the way here, Karen?" she asked, smiling.

"Even better—I brought doughnuts."

"Doughnuts, saving lives—is there anything you can't do?"

Carmella grabbed a chocolate one from the box and took a bite.

"So, did he ask for your phone number?" she asked. "The cute guy, the cop, from earlier."

"Is that all you think about? Finding me a man? And no, he didn't ask for my number. Someone was shot—he was focused on that."

A few other nurses wandered into the break room. They made small talk, which consisted mostly of asking Karen questions about everything that had happened earlier.

"What room is she in?" Karen asked. "I'd like to go check on her. See if she's awake. Try to talk with her. I feel a bit of a connection, you know."

"Sure, of course. She's over there. Room seven."

Karen glanced over at room seven and saw a security guard named Brian sitting on a folding chair in front of the door. He was a young guy, even younger than Carmella. Small and scrawny with short hair. Wearing a uniform two sizes too big.

Karen walked over to him. When Brian saw her, his beady eyes lit up.

"It's Supergirl," he said. He extended his arms from his body, imitating Superman flying.

"Very funny," she said. "I'm going to drop into the room. Say hi to the girl I brought in yesterday."

"Sure, go for it."

"There are doughnuts in the kitchen. Help yourself."

"Don't have to tell me twice." He walked over to the break room, leaving Karen by herself. She pushed open the door and walked inside. Amber was in bed. Asleep, the sheet pulled over the top half of her body. She looked so serene, so calm. Paler than earlier. A little rough around the edges.

Karen glanced over her shoulder, out at the break room. Her co-workers were still inside, standing over the doughnut box, looking over the selection, talking with one another.

She stepped toward the bed and lightly shook Amber's arm.

"Wake up," she said. "Wake up. Wake up."

"WAKE UP. . . . WAKE UP. . . . WAKE UP."

The voice drifted in, barely there at first, distant, then louder.

"Wake up. . . ."

Amber's eyes fluttered open. Her vision was cloudy. Pressure behind her eyes, a burning in her stomach.

Bit by bit, the person standing at the side of her bed came into focus. A woman. Middle-aged. Blond hair. She looked familiar somehow.

"Can you talk?" she asked.

Amber stared back.

"Can you talk?" she repeated.

"Yes," Amber croaked.

"I'm Karen," she said. "I brought you here. In my car. After you were shot. Remember?"

Amber nodded weakly. She could recall only bits and pieces of the drive to the hospital, but she recognized Karen now.

"Listen to me carefully," she said. "I am going to break you out of here. At noon, you're being taken in for some tests. I'll break you out then. When it happens, don't make any noise. Don't scream or draw attention to yourself. Just remain calm. And trust me. Okay?"

"I-I don't understand."

"Your husband, Ross. After you were shot, he took my son and me hostage. He's making me break you out before you're released and the police arrest you."

Karen set a sheet of folded-up paper in Amber's lap.

"He wanted me to give you this," she said.

Amber reached down and unfolded the sheet of paper. She held it close to her face and started reading. A note was written in Ross's jagged, chicken-scratch handwriting.

> *Babe,*
>
> *We're caught up in a mess. But everything will be fine. This lady is going to break you out. Do what she says. You have to fight for me. Stay strong. I'm not gonna be next to you but I'll be with you.*
>
> *You're all I have in this world. All I care about. I sometimes feel like my life is one big failure. Seems like all I do is lose. But I have you so I feel like a winner. You're all I need. I love you more than anything.*
>
> *It's you and me against the world. We either get out of this or we go down together. I'd rather lose with you than win with anyone else.*
>
> *See you in a few, Buckaroo.*

Amber felt something rise within her chest. She thought she was going to cry but the moment passed. She wished Ross were standing beside her right now, so she could tell him that she felt the same way, that she loved him, that all she needed was him.

She treasured moments like this, when Ross would reveal his tender, soft side—the good person buried underneath the roughened, toughened exterior. These moments didn't happen often, but when they did, she was always reminded that she was doing the right thing, that Ross was worth fighting for, that deep down he was a good person.

Amber sniffled a few times and looked back up at Karen.

"Remember, this will happen at noon," Karen said. "In about an hour. Can you do this?"

Amber nodded. "Yeah. I can."

OUTSIDE AMBER'S ROOM, KAREN SCANNED THE ICU FLOOR UNTIL SHE spotted Carmella. She was at the nurses' station, looking at a form. All around her were people in motion, moving from one room to the next, to and from the hallway, scurrying all over.

For a moment, Karen stared at Carmella. She was biting her lower lip as she looked at the form. A small smudge of chocolate icing was on her scrubs.

Karen took a deep breath. It made her sick, what she was about to do. She walked over to the nurses' station and stood across from Carmella. "I need to talk to you," she said.

"Sure. Now? I'm a little busy with—"

"It's important. I only need a minute. Let's find somewhere quiet."

They walked to the storage room on the edge of the bay. The same room she'd seen Carmella crying in the other day. Karen shut the door behind them.

"What's going on?" Carmella asked.

"I need your help," Karen said.

"Sure, absolutely. What is it?"

"The patient I brought in. Amber. I need you to take her to her scans this morning. At noon."

"She's Crystal's patient, not mine."

"I know. I want you to make up a story. Tell Crystal you're already heading that way and you can drop her off, something like that. Figure it out."

"I suppose I could. Why does it matter?"

"It just does. And there's more. Much more. When you move her, I'm going to take her from you. We're going to make it look like you were ambushed."

Carmella's eyes narrowed. "What do you mean?"

"It sounds unbelievable. I know. Just know that I'm being forced to do this. Some things have happened, things that I can't tell you about. All that matters is that I have to break this woman out of the hospital. And I need you to help me."

"Karen, you can't be serious."

"I'm serious. You have no idea how serious I am."

"I don't understand. What is going on?"

"The less you know, the better."

"This is—"

"It's crazy, I know. But I don't have a choice."

Carmella's eyes stayed on Karen. She leaned a few inches closer and lowered her voice.

"I can call the police if you want me—"

"No," Karen said. "No police."

"Why not? You're freaking me out."

"We just can't. No police."

"Well, I'm not doing this. This is ridiculous."

Karen cleared her throat. She looked out the small window on the door, out at the bay. Still alive with the usual hustle and bustle. Any moment now, someone could come into the storage room and interrupt them.

"Listen, I hate doing this," Karen said, "but if you don't help me, I'll turn you in for taking the drugs. The drugs you stole for your mother."

"You're blackmailing me?" Carmella said.

"I guess I am. I'm sorry. If you don't help me, I'll tell hospital administration exactly what I've seen over the past few months. I don't have any evidence, but if people dug deep enough, I'm sure they could find something. They know where to look. There has to be security footage, something like that. You'd lose your job. Go to jail."

Carmella's face slowly crumbled to a hurt, pained expression. It killed Karen, seeing that look.

"It makes me sick, doing this," Karen said. "Threatening you. But that's how serious things are."

"You'd be in trouble, too," Carmella said. "You saw me take the drugs and didn't report it. If you turned me in, you'd be in trouble, too."

"I know. But that's nothing compared to the trouble I'm in now."

She grabbed Carmella's hand and squeezed.

"All you have to do is go through the new hospital wing when you move Amber," Karen said. "The one that's under construction. I'll be waiting and I'll lock you in a room. When people find you, tell them a lanky guy, longer hair, rough voice, mid-thirties, ambushed you and took Amber. That's it. You won't get in trouble. And you'll be doing me the biggest favor of my life."

She closed her hand even tighter around Carmella's.

"Please, sweetie. Do this as a favor for me."

"Fine," Carmella said.

"You'll help?"

Carmella nodded.

"Thank you. Thank you so much."

"You know that when I move her, I won't be alone," Carmella said. "Hospital policy. If she's in trouble with the law, security will be with me."

"I know."

"So what are you going to do?"

"Let me worry about that."

FOURTEEN

THE NEW WING OF THE HOSPITAL WASN'T OFFICIALLY OPEN YET, BUT CON-
struction was mostly finished. The carpet was laid down, the walls
were painted, and the nurses' station was fully built. The only thing
the floor was missing was electrical equipment. Which meant no com-
puters, no bedside machines . . . and no security cameras. That was
what interested Karen.

She crouched down behind the nurses' station, waiting. The nearly
complete bay surrounded her, silent except for the noise of her deep,
labored breathing. Her hands were warm with nervous perspiration;
she constantly wiped them on her pants to dry them.

Even though the floor wasn't officially open, nurses occasionally
moved patients through the new wing of the hospital to save time.
Their department was on floor four; Radiology was on floor four.
Instead of taking the elevator down one floor, crossing over to the

other wing, and taking the elevator up, they sometimes just cut through the new wing.

Karen waited for twenty agonizing minutes until she heard a noise. From the other end of the floor, out of sight, she heard a door open, then latch shut. She peeked out from behind the nurses' station and saw Carmella pushing Amber in a wheelchair. Even from a couple of hundred feet away, Karen recognized Brian walking next to them, in his security uniform. He was talking to Carmella, but Karen was too far away to hear the discussion.

Karen crawled out from behind the nurses' station and hurried down a nearby hallway. Doors to vacant patient rooms lined both sides of the hallway, all of them open.

Karen slammed one of the doors as she passed, the noise as loud as a gunshot in the deserted bay. She ran into the room directly across the hallway. She grabbed the pillow off the bed and tore off the pillowcase, then jumped behind a small dresser just inside the door.

She stared at the closed door across the hallway, winded from the sprint, her breaths quick and erratic. She was—

"Hello?"

Brian's voice. She could hear his footsteps tapping on the tiled floor, approaching.

"Hello?" he said again, a little louder. "Is someone there? This floor isn't open."

Her breaths were coming so quickly that Karen was practically choking on them. Brian appeared in front of her, right across the hallway, just a few feet away. He stared at the closed door, his back to her. He knocked on it. Waited a moment. "Anyone there?"

No response. He inched open the door and stuck his head inside.

"Hello?" He walked past the open door, into the room. Once he was a few feet inside, she stepped out from behind the dresser and crept into the hallway. She hurried over to the room door and slammed it shut. From inside the room, Brian yelled out.

Karen quickly looped one end of the pillowcase around the door handle. Waist-high railing was mounted on the hallway walls to help patients with walking, and she looped the other end of the pillowcase around the railing. She pulled tight so there was no give and tied the pillowcase into a knot.

Brian tried to pull the door open from the other side, but the pillowcase held; the door opened an inch and the pillowcase cinched tight, preventing the door from opening farther. He yelled and continued pulling the door.

Karen ran over to Carmella, standing at the edge of the hallway. Amber was right next to her in her wheelchair.

"We have to hurry," Karen said. There was no telling how much time they had. She grabbed Carmella's arm and guided her over to a nearby patient room.

"I'll lock you in here," Karen said. "Won't take but a few minutes for someone to investigate and find you. By that time, we'll be gone. Hopefully. Do you remember your story? What you'll tell people?"

"A man, skinny, long brown hair, stopped me as I was moving Amber. Mid-thirties. He had a gun. He forced me into a room and took her."

"Good." Karen ran into the room and tore the pillowcase off the bed. She carried it back to the hallway. Before closing the room door, she stared in at Carmella.

"I'm sorry," Karen said. "I'm so sorry. I'll explain everything later."

Karen shut the door. She tied the pillowcase around the door handle and railing, same as with Brian's door. Down the hallway, he was no longer pulling at his door. She could hear him talking, probably into his walkie-talkie, calling for help.

KAREN HURRIED BACK OVER TO AMBER.

"We've got to be quick, okay?" she said. "Can you walk?"

Amber wasn't even looking at Karen. She stared off, slumped in her wheelchair, her eyes half-open, her gaze empty. Whatever painkillers she was on were doing their job.

"Please, we have to hurry," Karen said, lightly shaking her arm. "Can you walk?"

"I'll try."

"We'll walk to the ground floor and leave through a side exit. My car's parked a few blocks from here. You can do this."

Amber mumbled something.

"What was that?"

"H-handcuffs."

Amber lifted her hand. Her wrist was handcuffed to a metal bar on the wheelchair.

"We'll fold up the chair, drag it down the stairs. I'll push you to the car."

Karen pushed the wheelchair over to a door at the end of the hallway. FIRE ESCAPE—CAUTION. ALARM WILL SOUND, read the red bar secured to the middle of the door. Yellow construction tape was tied in front of the door. Karen ripped it away.

"The stairs are past here," she said to Amber. "The other stairways have cameras, but the fire escape doesn't."

At least, she was almost positive there weren't any. A few years ago, a patient had wandered from his room and taken the fire escape stairwell out of the hospital. The search for him had been complicated because there was no security footage to study. She didn't think security cameras had been installed since then, but she wasn't positive.

Karen helped Amber out of the wheelchair. She folded up the wheelchair; it was still bulky but was thinner and not as cumbersome. She kept one hand draped behind Amber's back to support her, and they walked over to the fire door, Amber dragging behind her the wheelchair, still handcuffed to her wrist. With her free hand, Karen reached out and gripped the metal bar on the door.

"Three flights, all right?" she said to Amber. "You can do this."

Amber nodded. Karen took a deep breath and pushed against the metal bar. The door flew open and the alarm wailed and screeched. Past the door was a stairwell with a flight going up and a flight going down. They shuffled over to the stairs heading down. Step by step, they descended, Karen with one arm wrapped around Amber, helping her navigate the stairs, Amber dragging the wheelchair behind her. The alarm screamed, earsplittingly loud as they walked down.

It took only a few seconds to reach the landing for the third floor.

"Two flights to go," Karen said.

They continued down another flight of stairs, Karen descending a step, helping Amber take the step, then doing the same for the next step. She tried to listen for voices or footsteps approaching but she couldn't hear anything over the sound of the alarm. It was so loud she was getting a headache. She was—

Amber stumbled and lurched forward. Karen held on tight but Amber kept leaning forward . . . forward . . . forward, like a building about to topple. She tried to pull Amber back but she was just too heavy. Amber stumbled down a step and her momentum carried her forward. She fell down and tumbled end over end down the stairwell, her body clanging against the metal steps, the wheelchair clattering down alongside her. At the bottom of the stairwell, she slammed onto the flat landing area at the base of the stairs. She writhed on the ground, face locked in a pained expression.

Then she started screaming.

KAREN RAN DOWN THE STAIRS. AT THE BOTTOM OF THE STAIRWELL, SHE leaned over Amber, still huddled on the ground, still screaming. The wheelchair was a few feet away.

"Are you all right?" Karen asked.

"H-hurts."

Karen could barely hear her over the alarm. She looked down at Amber's stomach and saw blood staining the front of her hospital robe. She moved the robe to the side. The dressing covering her wound was soaked in blood. Karen peeled the dressing away and saw that Amber's stitches had been ripped out during the fall. The wound was reopened; blood poured from the hole in her stomach.

Karen placed the dressing back over the wound. She grabbed Amber's hand and squeezed.

"I know it hurts," Karen said. "But we have to get out of here. We have to hurry."

She helped Amber onto her feet. They took a few steps; then Amber fell to her knees, grimacing and holding her stomach.

"Come on. You can do this," Karen said.

Karen helped her to her feet again. With Karen's arm around Amber's back, they walked down the staircase, dragging the wheelchair behind them. Grunting and groaning, they reached the landing for the second floor.

One more flight to go.

Karen dragged Amber down the last flight of stairs. The alarm continued to wail. When they finally reached the ground floor, Karen pushed open the exit door. A blast of cold air hit them at once. She squinted; even with the sun hidden behind clouds, the outside sky was so much brighter than the dark stairwell.

She unfolded the wheelchair and set Amber in it.

"A few blocks; then we'll be at my car," Karen said.

She started pushing Amber down a walkway, moving as fast as she could without looking suspicious. After a couple of minutes, she reached the side street she'd parked on. She helped Amber out of the wheelchair and tried to cram it into the front seat. It wouldn't fit. Even when folded up, it was too big. She looked around, down at her car, then helped lower Amber so she was sitting on the ground next to the curb, a few feet to the right of the car. Karen moved the folded-up wheelchair so it was directly in front of her car and checked to make sure that Amber's handcuffed wrist was far enough away from the car tire to avoid injury.

"Don't move," she said to Amber. "Just stay right there."

She ran around the car and jumped inside. Pulled forward a few feet and heard the crunch of the car tires running over the wheelchair.

She stopped and jumped out of the car. The wheelchair was ruined, broken into pieces and shards of metal. The support beam Amber's handcuffs were attached to had snapped in two. She slipped the handcuffs off the wheelchair and helped Amber into the passenger seat.

Karen sprinted around the car and sat down in the driver's seat. She fired up the engine and sped away.

////////////////

Seated in the passenger seat of the car, Amber felt like she was floating. Or flying. She was cold and clammy. Her hospital robe had done nothing to protect her from the freezing air as they'd hurried to the car.

She closed her eyes. Clenched her teeth. Tried to ignore the burning in her stomach.

After she'd fallen in the stairwell, she'd nearly just given up. The pain had been so agonizing that she wanted to curl into a ball. Stay in the stairwell. Admit defeat and stop fighting.

But then she thought of Ross's letter. Thought of seeing him again. That was what pushed her to continue on. That was what helped her through the pain.

She placed her hand over her hospital gown and applied pressure to her stomach. She winced at the sharp dagger of pain. Blood gushed onto the already soaked front of her gown.

Ross. She thought about Ross. Thought about being with him again, starting over together.

As long as it was just the two of them, everything would be fine.

FIFTEEN

KAREN TURNED OFF THE GRAVEL ROAD AND PULLED INTO THE DRIVEWAY.
She parked next to Joshua's car. Amber sat next to her, pale and sweating, her breath coming in quick pants. Her hospital gown had gotten even bloodier during the drive; the entire middle of it was nearly covered.

Right as Karen turned off the car, Ross stormed out of the house and sprinted to them.

"Out of the car," he yelled to Karen. He gestured to an area in the middle of the front lawn. "Go over there."

Karen opened the car door and walked over. From a few feet away, she watched as Ross ran around the car and threw open the passenger door. He leaned inside and hugged Amber.

"I knew you'd make it, baby," he said. He cupped the sides of her face with his hands. "I knew it all along."

He kissed her, hugged her again. It reminded Karen of those videos of returning soldiers being greeted by their families—there was pure happiness, pure love, in his embrace.

"Careful," Karen said. "Her stitches were torn. Don't make it worse."

Ross looked at the blood on the front of Amber's hospital robe. He kissed her forehead and walked over to Karen.

"Anybody see you when you escaped?"

"No. I don't think so."

Ross gestured to Amber. "What happened to her?"

"We fell when we were leaving. Her wound got ripped open."

"So how bad is she?"

"I'm not a doctor."

"Didn't ask if you were. Just gimme your opinion."

"She's in bad shape," Karen said. "She needs to get back to a hospital."

"A hospital?"

"Yes. And soon."

Ross scratched the back of his neck, stared off for a moment.

"How's that supposed to work?" he asked. "Can't exactly show up to a hospital an hour after someone looking just like her escaped from one. Same injury and all."

"You'll have to go far away. Get to another state. Missouri's only a few hours from here. Illinois, too."

Right now, she just wanted them to leave. End this, right here, right now—that was her focus. Get them away from the house and far, far away.

"The keys are still in the ignition," Karen said. "I won't call the police. Just take my car and go."

"Listen, I'm no fool," Ross said. "That won't work. I know there's alerts and stuff that go out. I show up to a hospital with her, they'll look up her records, see that she escaped, and that will be it. She'll be arrested. Doesn't matter if the hospital's in another state."

"You'll have to take that risk. If her wound gets infected, she might not make it."

Ross bit his lower lip and stared at Amber, in the front seat.

"I gotta think about this," he said.

"You don't have time," Karen said.

"Won't take long. I think I got an idea. Just need to make a few phone calls."

He walked back over to the car.

"Meantime, I'm bringing her inside."

"What? No."

Ross nodded.

"You're a nurse. And you got a bed inside. We'll set her up there for now."

///////////////

Karen tried to protest, but Ross waved her off. He lifted Amber from the front seat and wrapped a steadying hand around her waist, helping her walk from the driveway up to the front door.

"Open that for me," he said to Karen. "And don't try nothing. The gun's in my waistband. Won't take but a second to grab it."

She opened the door and stepped into the living room. Ross and Amber entered a few feet behind her.

"Go down the hallway," Ross said to Karen. "I saw a bedroom earlier. We'll go there."

Karen walked down the hallway. In her bedroom, she stood off to one side and watched as Ross gently laid Amber in bed.

"You're going to be all right," Ross said, kissing her forehead. "Trust me, baby."

Ross motioned Karen out to the hallway. They left the bedroom and walked back to the storage room. Inside, Joshua was tied up in the same position he'd been in earlier. Ross sat Karen down in her chair and zip-tied her hands to the armrests and her feet to the chair legs.

"You need to listen to me. She's at serious risk," Karen said. "If the wound gets infected, there's nothing I can do here. I don't have the antibiotics she needs. You need to get her back to a hospital."

"I believe you. I just need to make a couple phone calls. Won't take long."

Ross walked out of the room. Karen closed her eyes. The rush of adrenaline she'd felt at the hospital had passed. It was only the afternoon but she felt so tired, so beaten down.

"Mom, what happened?" Joshua asked.

Karen sighed heavily. She told him a quick version of the events at the hospital.

"She's in my bedroom now," Karen said. "I don't know what's going to happen next. I'm hoping that this will be it."

She didn't know how much more she could take. She prayed that this was almost over. Ross had said he wouldn't harm them if she broke Amber out; she could only hope he meant it.

But if he went back on his word, she had a plan. She looked down at her leg. Right there, tucked away in her sock, she could just barely see the handle of the scalpel she had taken from the hospital.

////////////////////

Lying on her back, Amber winced. The pain in her stomach was sharp, not a stabbing sensation as much as a steady, constant throb. She reached down and pulled the gown to the side. The dressing covering her wound was soaked in deep crimson. She winced and peeled the dressing off. The stomach wound was almost an inch wide, a bright shade of red, the surrounding skin inflamed. Blood had started to coagulate and dry over it.

She looked away and glanced around the bedroom, searching for something to focus on, some way to distract herself from the pain. There wasn't much; bedrooms didn't get much more plain and ordinary than this one. The walls were covered in light blue wallpaper, the curtains and carpet a matching beige color. The only decorations were a few framed photographs resting on top of a dresser. There was one of the lady (what was her name? Karen) and a few friends, sitting at a restaurant table, smiling into the camera and holding margarita glasses in the air. A few other random photos, most of her kid. Some of him when he was younger: one at Disney World wearing a floppy hat with Goofy ears, another of him stepping off a school bus, a few of him holding golf clubs.

Ross entered the room. He carried a coffee mug in one hand. Flakes of red were smudged around his chin and lips. Even in her dazed state, she could see that he'd been huffing paint.

"Does it hurt?" he said. He sat down on the edge of the bed and ran his hand through her hair.

She gritted her teeth and nodded.

"You'll be fine," he said.

He held up a mug and rotated it to show her the characters printed on the side—Ernie, Bert, Grover, Oscar, Big Bird.

"Found this in the cupboard and thought you'd like it," he said. "Remember *Sesame Street*? How we used to always watch it?"

"Yeah," she said. After Ross was released from prison and they were living in Nebraska, they got only one channel on the small, outdated television in their apartment: the local PBS affiliate. Almost every morning, they'd been forced to watch *Sesame Street* during breakfast because they had no other options. It had been a running joke between them since then.

Ross cradled her head with one hand and lifted the coffee mug to her lips. His hands were slightly shaking.

"Here, drink some water."

He tilted the cup and some of the water spilled out and dribbled down her chin. He wiped it away with the back of his hand.

For the next minute, he held her in his arms and helped her drink. Here was the Ross she loved. The man she knew was worth fighting for and risking everything for. The good person who was still somewhere in there, deep down.

"That enough?" he asked her.

She nodded. Ross leaned over and kissed the top of her head. He grabbed her hand and held it in his.

"Listen, we can't stay here for long. We need to get you looked at and fixed up. Can't check you in to a hospital, though. Police know who you are now. They'll be looking for you. Can't let you get arrested."

Ross pulled a phone from his pocket—must've been the kid's phone, she figured.

"I got an idea," he said. "I think I know what we can do. Just gotta make one quick phone call first."

"Wh-who?" she asked.

"We're desperate, babe. Gotta call up the only guy who I think can help us. I'm calling up Shane."

SIXTEEN

"NO."

That was the only word Amber could get out. No strength to say anything beyond that, though she wanted to yell, scream at the top of her lungs.

"Yes, babe." Ross stroked her hair. "I gotta make the call. I don't know what else to do."

He scooted closer to her on the bed.

"He hasn't been picked up. I saw an article about the robbery earlier. He's still out there."

Amber shook her head.

"Yeah. I think he can help us. You remember that time I came home with my arm all stitched up, back when Shane and I were touring?"

She remembered. Years ago, that was. Late one night, Ross had shown up at their apartment after a performance with a nasty stitched-up wound on his arm. He told her he'd fallen off the stage while performing.

"Probably don't have to tell you this, but I didn't fall off the stage. Some guy thought we were shortchanging him on product, a fight broke out, and next thing I knew, he pulled out a knife and stabbed me."

At the time, his explanation for the injury had seemed odd, but she hadn't really suspected anything. It had happened before Ross was arrested, back when she thought that Ross and Shane were struggling singers chasing a dream, back before she had any idea they were selling drugs on the side.

"Point is, when I got stabbed, Shane insisted that we not call nine-one-one. He didn't want the attention. So he called up a friend, some doctor. This guy came over and stitched me right up, no questions asked. Turns out Shane had this doctor in his pocket because he sold him drugs, did some work on the side for him.

"So what I'm thinking is, if Shane calls up this doctor, he could help you out. Stitch you up. Give you whatever medication and stuff you need."

"No. No Shane."

"He's gonna be pissed. I know. But I think I can make a deal with him. Work something out. We're still brothers. The Blood Brothers. That counts for something."

Amber tried to speak but she couldn't. Her light-headedness was back, worse than before. She was floating, barely able to concentrate.

"We gotta get you stitched up," Ross said. He leaned down and ran a finger along her forearm. "Wish there was another way, but there isn't. Getting you fixed up, that's the focus right now. I just gotta convince Shane to help us."

Ross tapped the phone screen a few times. He put it on speaker and the line rang.

"Yeah?" a voice answered.

The speakerphone was slightly warbled, but Amber still recognized Shane's rough, throaty voice.

"It's Ross."

A few seconds of silence.

"You there, Shane?"

"You bastard. You goddamned bastard."

"I just wanna talk," Ross said. "Calm down."

"Calm down?" Shane said, voice rising. "After what you did to me, you want me to calm down?"

"Just hear me out."

"Piss off.

"I need your help."

"Piss off."

"I'm in a jam. Actually, it's Amber. She's injured. Gunshot wound."

"What's this got to do with me?"

"Remember that time I got stabbed and your doctor friend stitched me up? Wondering if you would reach out to him, see if he could help her."

"She can rot in hell for all I care."

"Please, man. This is family. I—"

"Family? Fucking *family*? Don't give me that shit."

"I messed up, with everything that happened at the bank. That's all I can say. You help Amber out, and I'll do anything to make it up to you. Push drugs for you. Let you keep all the profits. Hell, I'll rob another bank. Anything to make it up to you."

"Anything?"

"Anything."

Silence on the other end. Ross grabbed a small paper bag, sprayed some paint into it, and took a long pull, smudging more red around his mouth.

"I made a mistake, man," Ross said into the phone. "One mistake. I don't know what I was thinking. But it can't end everything for us. Our bond is stronger than that."

"Fine," Shane said. "I'll help. But only because I got no cash, no place to go, no nothing right now."

A small smile appeared on Ross's face. "Where you at?"

"Down near Saint Louis," Shane said. "I stole a car after the robbery, barely got away, called up everyone I could think of, asking for help. You remember our old friend Smitty? Owns a bar down here? I'm crashing with him. Only a temporary thing, though. You? Where you at?"

"Over in Iowa. Just outside of Cedar Rapids."

"Got an address?"

"Hold on," Ross said. He left the room and returned a moment later holding an envelope. He read off the address printed on the front of the envelope.

"The hell are you doing there?"

"Long story. I'll give it to you when you get here."

"Fine. Should be there in four hours or so."

"Okay. Thank you, Shane. Never should've turned my back on you. The Blood Brothers—we'll be even better than before."

The call ended. Ross placed the phone back in his pocket. He looked down at Amber. She wanted to say so much. She didn't want Ross to be dragged back into the life they were trying to escape. This plan would only end in disaster.

"D-don't," she said to Ross.

"Yes, babe," Ross said. "This is how it has to be. This is the only way we can get you to a doctor. If this is what I got to do to save you, then it's what I got to do."

"We can't—"

The pain flared up. Like a needle being driven deep into her stomach.

Ross grabbed her hand. "Is it bad?" he asked.

She closed her eyes and winced. Nodded.

"You just gotta try to take your mind off it."

///////////////

Karen pulled her left hand and left foot against the zip ties that secured them to the chair. She bent her body at the waist and leaned as far to the left as she could. By contorting her body like that, she could bring the scalpel in her sock within a few inches of her wrist.

"What are you doing, Mom?" Joshua said.

"I grabbed a scalpel from the hospital. It's in my sock."

"A scalpel?"

"Keep your voice down," she said. Ross and Amber were in the room next to them, only a thin wall between them. Through the walls, she could hear them talking but couldn't quite understand what they were saying. "And, yes," she said to Joshua. "A scalpel."

She tried again: she strained against the zip ties securing her wrist and ankle to the chair, pulling as hard as she could, and leaned her body to that side. The scalpel was still a few inches out of reach.

When she'd grabbed it from the hospital, she didn't have a plan or any real idea of what she was going to do with it. Just seemed like the scalpel was the type of thing that might be useful. If things got out of hand, if something unpredictable happened, it'd be better to have it than not.

"You think you can cut yourself free?" Joshua asked.

"Maybe," she said. "If I can grab it."

She reached once more—still a few inches away—and slumped into her chair. It was no use. She'd been trying to grab the scalpel for the past few minutes, and there was no way she was contorting her forty-two-year-old body enough to reach it. Not unless she tore a muscle or ligament.

Her thoughts drifted to the hospital. She couldn't even imagine how much of a madhouse the hospital was right now. A patient escaping would bring an immediate, urgent response. Alerts and notifications would have been sent out to every department. The entire hospital would be on edge. The police were probably interviewing people, trying to piece together what happened. She wondered if the detective from earlier, Franny, was the one handling the investigation.

Carmella, Karen knew, would be the focus. Police would want to get her story. She could only hope that Carmella would stick to the plan and tell the police that she'd been ambushed at gunpoint by a skinny, scraggly man. If she didn't . . . well, it was only a matter of time before the police stormed her house and the situation got even more out of control than it already was.

//////////////////////

Amber tried to ignore the pain, tried to find some hidden reserve of strength to help her power through the burning, throbbing sensation in her stomach. But nothing helped. The pain persisted.

Ross remained sitting on the side of the bed, stroking her hair, telling her she'd be all right, to just hang on. Amber closed her eyes and focused on Ross's voice. But the only thought on her mind was that this wasn't going to end well. There were a million things that might go wrong. She might not make it. Shane might go crazy when he arrived. Even if they did survive this, where would they be? Back in the same situation as before. No money. Ross teamed up with his brother again, heading on a path that would land him in jail. Or worse.

"You scared, babe?"

She nodded.

"Don't be. I can handle Shane. I can convince him to forgive us. I've always been there for him. Always stuck by his side. One mistake won't change that. Shane, he'll understand."

Had to be the drugs talking. Shane wasn't the type of person who listened. And he certainly wasn't the type of person who forgave. She thought about the endless times she'd seen him lose his temper. The arguments, the fights. The times she'd seen him beat people senseless over something as minor as looking at him the wrong way.

She tried to beg Ross to leave but felt a sharp dagger of pain before she could get a word out. She gritted her teeth and waited for it to dull . . . but it wouldn't.

"You all right?" Ross asked.

She shook her head.

"Hold up," he said. "I'm getting the lady. I'll be right back."

SEVENTEEN

KAREN SAT IN THE CHAIR, CRANING HER HEAD TOWARD THE WALL TO HELP her hear the voices in her bedroom. Through the wall, she could just barely hear Ross's voice. She thought she'd heard Amber speak a few times but she couldn't be sure. She'd also caught bits and pieces of the phone call earlier. It sounded like the person on the other end of the line, whoever it was, knew a doctor, something like that, and was going to help Amber.

"You really think they might just leave?" Joshua asked.

"I don't know."

"If they do, what's going to happen to us?"

She shrugged. She looked down at her sock. The handle of the scalpel was still right there, barely visible. She hadn't even tried grabbing it since giving up earlier. There was no reason to. It was too far out of her reach.

Just then, Ross stormed into the room. In his right hand, he held one of her kitchen knives. He walked over and cut through the zip ties on her wrists and ankles.

"Need you to check on Amber," he said. "Make sure she's okay."

He motioned to the door. Karen walked out to the hallway, Ross following a few steps behind her. In Karen's bedroom, Amber lay in the bed, eyes closed. Her body was shaking lightly and her skin was pale, much paler than before. The front of her hospital gown was stained with splotches of maroon. Karen pulled the gown to the side and looked at the bullet wound. It was a black, jagged hole, the skin around it deeply inflamed.

"How does it look?" Ross said from behind her.

"Bad," Karen said. "Worse than before. It needs to be disinfected, stitched up, looked at by a doctor."

"That's taken care of. She just needs to make it four more hours or so. Can she last 'til then?"

"She should be able to," Karen said.

Ross grabbed the spray paint can and paper sack off a table next to Amber. He sprayed some and took a huff, red spray paint smudging over his chin and lips. He seemed different, mellower; his mood had swung in the opposite direction from the frantic way he'd acted in the forest.

In bed, Amber grunted.

"What was that?" Karen said. She leaned closer to Amber.

"Pain," Amber said. "Hurts."

"Focus on a spot on the ceiling. Inhale deeply, hold the breath, then slowly exhale. Keep doing that. It should help some."

Amber inhaled a ragged breath. As she stared down at her, Karen thought about the scalpel. It would be so easy to bend down and grab it, now that her hands were free.

But what would she do then? She couldn't take Ross on. He had a gun; she had a scalpel with an inch-long blade. It wasn't even a weapon. The scalpel would probably snap in half if she tried to stab him.

Maybe she could take Amber hostage. Hold the scalpel against her throat and force Ross to get rid of his gun. That was a possibility. But who was she kidding? What would she do if Ross refused to drop the gun? Slice open Amber's throat? No matter the circumstances, she wasn't capable of something like that. And even if Ross was acting calmer, she figured it wouldn't take much to send him back into a rage.

"Breathing ain't gonna do much," Ross said to her. "Nothing more you can do? Painkillers, something like that?"

"Not here. She needs antibiotics. Heavy medication. Surgery."

"We're not going back to the hospital—no way," he said. "Walk to that room and I'll tie you up again."

"Hold on," she said. "I heard you talking earlier, through the wall. Something about leaving. What's going on?"

"What'd you hear?"

"Someone said they're on their way."

"Did you hear a name?"

"No. I only heard a word or two. What's going to happen to us when you leave?"

"Haven't thought that far ahead."

Ross motioned her to the door and they walked out of the room, down the hallway, back into the storage room. He zip-tied Karen's hands to the chair armrests.

"Let us live," she said. "We can help you. I'll tell the police whatever you want. Throw them off your trail. If you're going east, I can tell them I heard you say you're going west. If you're going north, I'll say you went south."

Ross didn't respond. He stood up and walked over to the door.

"I mean what I said," Karen said. "We just want to make it out of this alive. If you don't harm us, we'll tell the police whatever you want. You kill us, and we can't help you."

Ross stared at her for a final moment and left the room.

"What would happen then?" Joshua asked after Ross was gone.

"Then?"

"Say he let us live. What would happen after that?"

"I guess we'd stay here. Wait until someone found us. It might take a day, but someone would look eventually."

"I mean after that. Someone finds us. What would we tell the police? Everything?"

"You mean, would we tell them about the accident? The dead body?"

"Yeah."

"I think we'd have to. Be totally honest with them."

She didn't think there was any way around that. It was a little amazing, how the dead body had become almost an afterthought with everything else that had happened. She supposed she would have to tell the police the whole story.

What would happen to Joshua then? Jail? Probably. Things had changed: this was more than a mistake that could potentially be explained away. Joshua killed a man, left the body, then waited for days to pass before reporting it. Even if there was a fight and he was defending his father, she didn't think he'd be able to avoid serious, serious punishment.

Could she really do that, send Joshua to jail? It was such an unbelievable thought.

"We'll figure out what we'll tell the police later, when we get to that point," she said. Then she corrected herself: "If we get to that point."

////////////////

Ross was gone from Amber's room for only a minute. When he returned, he walked over to the window and looked out at the road in front of the house.

"Shouldn't be much longer, babe," he said. "Shane should be here soon."

She was breathing deeply and focusing on the ceiling like Karen had suggested. It wasn't helping much with the pain. Ross leaned over and kissed her forehead.

"How ya feeling?"

"Hurts."

Ross sat down on the edge of the bed and put an arm around her. "Just hang on for a little while longer. You can do this."

She faintly smiled. But she couldn't stop thinking that this was the beginning of the end. Earlier, their plan was simple: screw over Shane, then disappear after the bank robbery. Find some place nice and quiet, some secluded little town, and use the robbery money as a foundation to start over. Begin a new life together, away from Shane, away from drugs, away from it all.

Everything was different now. They had no money. They were wanted criminals with the police looking for them. Shane was entering their lives again, and she didn't even want to imagine what Ross would have to do to repay him. Even if they managed to survive this, then what? They couldn't get jobs or rent an apartment using their real names. She—

The stomach pain flared up suddenly. She yelped and gritted through it. Ross grabbed her hand and squeezed.

"Just hold on, babe. You can do this. Soon it'll be just you and me. Just us, starting over."

ROSS STAYED AT HER SIDE FOR THE NEXT HOUR, HOLDING HER IN HIS arms, stroking her hair. Every few minutes, he sat up from the bed and looked out the window for an approaching car. The pain seemed to intensify as time passed, a steady throbbing that was always present and would suddenly spike at random moments.

After a wait that seemed like an eternity, Ross was staring out the window and his eyes lit up.

"There he is," Ross said. "Shane is pulling into the driveway."

Amber gritted her teeth and slowly sat up in bed so she could see out the nearby window. A black Chevy Tahoe had pulled into the driveway and stopped next to Karen's car.

Ross kept his eyes locked on the Tahoe. He squinted, focused.

"Wait a second," he said. "Who the hell is that?"

Amber stared at the truck. Her vision was cloudy and she had trouble concentrating, but one thing was clear.

It definitely wasn't Shane behind the wheel.

EIGHTEEN

"JESUS CHRIST," ROSS SAID, STILL STARING OUT THE BEDROOM WINDOW. "Who is that?"

The Tahoe stopped and a middle-aged man stepped outside. Heavy coat. Hair so blond it looked white. He was hefty but not really over-weight. He shut the door behind him and hurriedly walked up to the front door.

The doorbell rang. Ross glanced down at Amber. "I don't like this."

"Ignore it," she said.

He shook his head and pulled the gun from the waistband of his pants. "He sees the cars in the driveway. He knows they're home."

Ross left the bedroom. The doorbell rang again.

A moment later, she heard the door open. Ross's voice in the living room: "Hands in the air. Don't move."

"What the—"

"Who are you?"

"Jesus, is that a gun?"

"Yeah, it's a fucking gun. Who are you?"

"What is—"

"Who the hell are you?"

There was some yelling and warbled commotion. The voice that wasn't Ross's yelled out: "My son. Joshua. Where is he?"

"You're the kid's dad?" Ross said.

"Yes. Where—"

"Step inside," Ross said. "Shut the door behind you."

The front door slammed shut.

"Now, answer me," Ross said. "What are you doing here?"

"My son. He's not answering his phone. I—"

"Anybody know you're here?"

"No, I—"

"Walk down the hallway," Ross said. "I'll be right behind you."

///////////////

Karen recognized Teddy's voice in the living room, but she refused to believe he was here. There was yelling in the living room, frantic talking. Teddy's voice, Ross's voice. Then footsteps, coming down the hallway.

Teddy appeared at the door, Ross pointing the gun at the back of his head.

The moment Teddy entered the room and saw her and Joshua tied up, he froze. "Oh my God."

"Shut up," Ross said.

"Are you hurt or—"

"I said shut up," Ross said. "Now, go over to that closet. Grab a chair from inside. Don't do nothing stupid."

Teddy walked across the room. He opened the closet door and grabbed a folding chair from inside.

"Set it over there," Ross said. "Right next to the kid."

Teddy unfolded the chair and placed it beside Joshua.

"Take your coat off. Sit down. Put your arms behind you."

Teddy took off his heavy coat and sat in the chair. Ross grabbed the box of zip ties and secured Teddy's ankles to the chair, just like Karen's.

"Bad time for a drop-in, Pops. You said no one knows you're here? That's not bullshit?"

"No."

"Because I don't want no more surprises. Another surprise, and that's it. I'm sick of pissing around."

"I promise you, no one knows I'm here," Teddy said. "I called Joshua's phone a few times this afternoon."

"Yeah, I know. I had the phone. I heard it ringing."

"I got worried when there was no answer, so I came over."

"Better not be lying."

Ross gave them each a hard glare and left the room.

//////////////

They sat in the room in a triangle, a few feet apart, facing one another, Joshua and Teddy with their hands tied behind them, Karen with her wrists secured to the armrests of her chair, all of them with their feet zip-tied to their chairs.

Teddy looked back and forth between them. "My God," he said. "Who is this guy? What is going on?"

"I went back to the forest," Joshua said. "My glove was missing."

"Your glove? That text you sent—"

"It was a lie. I couldn't find it. I figured I'd go back and grab it quick. And these people, they were out there. The guy you just saw, and a woman. The woman got shot. Mom took her to the hospital, then broke her out."

"We're just waiting for them to leave," Karen said. "She's in the other room, in my bed. She's in bad shape. I think they're leaving soon. Someone's coming to pick them up."

Teddy squirmed in his seat, yanking and pulling his arms against the zip ties behind him.

"It's no use, Teddy," she said to him. "You're not breaking free."

"Then what?" Teddy asked. "What are we supposed to do?"

"We wait," she said. "I wish I had a better answer than that."

////////////

Ross returned to Amber's room. He sat down on the edge of her bed.

"That was the kid's dad," he said. "Looks like a damn party's going on in there."

Ross shook his head. He pulled the baggie of pills from his pocket and popped one.

"The lady, she said if we let them live, they'll tell the cops whatever we want," Ross said. "Could throw the cops off our tail. Help us get a nice head start. Just don't know if we can trust her. Because if she's lying, there ain't no reason to keep them alive."

"D-don't kill them."

"Might have to. Might not have a choice. I—"

Ross's phone rang. He pulled it from his pocket and looked at the screen.

"It's Shane."

He put the call on speaker.

"I'm about forty miles away from the address you gave me," Shane said. "Should be there in, like, half an hour."

NINETEEN

KAREN STARED AT TEDDY AND JOSHUA, A FEW FEET ACROSS FROM HER.
They looked practically identical, sitting in the same positions, side
by side. Same blond hair, jawline, facial features.

Teddy. She had so many questions to ask him. So much she wanted
to say. She felt like screaming at him, demanding answers, demanding
to hear his story of what had happened on the night of the accident.

"So," she said. "Teddy."

He looked up at her.

"What in the . . . what in the *hell* happened?" she said, surprised
by the force behind her voice. "The person dying. Not going to the
police. What . . . just . . . what were you thinking?"

He sighed. Leaned against the back of his chair, collapsing into
it. "You really want to talk about that now?"

"It's either that or silence. And I'm sick of the silence."

"It's complicated."

"We've got time. And nothing else to talk about. So what happened? Why didn't you go to the police?"

"I did it to protect Joshua."

"That's what he said to me earlier. And I'm just having difficulty seeing that. Having difficulty understanding how not going to the police was the right thing to do."

"It wasn't the right thing to do. It was a mistake."

"You think?"

"You just . . . you have no idea how frantic it was, in the heat of the moment. How a situation like that affects your thought process. Not just affects it, make it impossible to think. Everything happened so quickly, and . . . I don't know. . . . I kept thinking about that case from a few years ago. When the politician's son got jail time for the fight he was in. Remember that?"

"Yes. Joshua was talking about it earlier."

"If it would've been a car accident that killed the guy, we would've gone to the police right away. In fact, I was about to call an ambulance right before the guy went crazy and started screaming at us. After Joshua hit the guy with the rock, it just seemed like there was no telling how the police would view something like that. And all I could imagine was what it would be like if Joshua was charged with a crime. Sentenced to the next ten years in jail. Heck, even the next two or three years. Can you imagine? Locked up in jail instead of graduating high school or starting college. On his record forever, following him around for the rest of his life. Eighteen years old, and his life could be ruined."

"But Joshua wasn't at fault. He was protecting you."

"Maybe it'd be viewed differently. Wouldn't take much. An aggressive lawyer. The wrong member of a jury. And if they saw it as something more than him defending me, that would be it. Joshua's life would be over. He's eighteen; he would've been tried as an adult. It just seemed like such a risk. Going to the police wouldn't have brought the guy back to life. It sounds awful to say, but it's the truth. Only thing that would've done was potentially get Joshua in deep, deep trouble. So I told Joshua I thought we should just leave. He was so dazed, I think he would've agreed to anything."

Teddy shrugged his shoulders.

"Like I said, in the heat of the moment, everything was just so . . . overwhelming. I still can't believe any of it. Can't believe Joshua killed the guy. Can't believe we didn't report it. It's haunted me ever since it happened. I came over here to check on Joshua, to see why he wasn't answering his phone. I was starting to get worried. And, believe it or not, I was going to tell you everything when I was over here. Tell you we would go to the police if you thought we should, and just end it."

She looked at Joshua, right next to his father. He had the same dazed look on his face as he'd had when he told her the story of what happened. An empty expression.

She had so many more questions for both of them, so many more things she wanted to say. She wanted to believe that they'd been caught up in an unimaginably horrific situation and had made a bad decision, a terrible mistake—but the situation seemed too complicated to explain away as a mistake.

She just didn't really know what to think.

"It sounds awful, just abandoning the dead body all the way out there," Teddy said. "It *was* awful. Like something a monster would do. I'm not proud of it. I'm sick to my stomach. But I did it for Joshua."

Another weak shrug of his shoulders.

"It sounds heartless, but the opposite was true. The decision came straight from the heart. I was only looking out for him."

///////////////

Almost exactly half an hour after Shane's phone call, a black Dodge Ram pickup pulled into the driveway.

"There he is," Ross said. "Shane."

Amber watched from the bedroom as Ross exited out the front door. He walked across the front lawn and approached the truck. The truck's window was lowered. Ross started to say something to Shane but went silent a moment later. He put his hands in the air and backed away from the car.

Towering over Ross, Shane stepped out of the car, his massive hand wrapped around a gun. Shane yelled something. Ross slowly grabbed the gun from his waistband and threw it down by Shane's feet. Shane grabbed the gun and placed it in the pocket of his hoodie.

He shouted at Ross some more; Amber couldn't quite make out what he was saying. Ross started walking toward the front door, Shane behind him. Once they were close to the house, they disappeared from Amber's line of sight. A moment later, she heard the front door open.

From the living room came Shane's voice, cutting through the tranquil house like a saw blade: "You dirty rat," he said. "You dirty-ass cocksucking rat."

"Put the gun away, Shane. No need for it."

"Like hell there isn't."

The door slammed shut. Then: "Where's she at? Amber."

"Down the hallway," Ross said. "In the bedroom."

A moment later, they appeared at the bedroom door, Ross in front, his mouth a straight line, his eyes wide, a look of total panic on his face. Shane stood behind him like a big, lumbering ogre, pointing the gun at the back of Ross's head. He was wearing the same black hooded sweatshirt and dark jeans he'd worn during the robbery.

"And there she is," Shane said. "Mrs. Fucking Rat."

He scowled down at Amber. His breaths were deep and quick, nostrils flaring like an angry bull's.

"I hear you were shot," he said.

Amber cleared her throat. "Yeah."

"Looks pretty bad." Shane spat out a laugh, a hard, nasty snort. "Karma, sweetie. It's a bitch, ain't it?"

She didn't respond. She couldn't stop staring at the gun, only inches from the back of Ross's head. One squeeze of the trigger was all it'd take to end Ross's life.

"The doctor," Ross said. "You gotta call him up. She needs to get her injury looked at."

"Got some questions first," Shane said. "So, how the hell'd you end up in a place like this?"

"Long story," Ross said.

"Gimme the condensed version."

"Car broke down. Stole a new one from a kid. He tried to take it back and Amber was shot. She got taken to the hospital. She escaped and came here. The kid we took the car from, he lives here."

"This kid, what happened to him?"

"He's still here."

Shane's eyes went wide. He snapped his head around and looked over his shoulder.

"We're not alone? Where's this kid at?"

"Him and his parents are tied up. Other room. Down the hall."

"Take me to them," Shane said. He smacked the back of Ross's head with the hand not holding the gun. It was a light tap, not much behind it, but the impact still made Ross wince and stumble forward. They walked to the door. Before leaving the room, Shane turned and looked back at Amber.

"Don't worry—I'm not done with you," he said. "Not by a long shot."

///////////////

"What is going on?"

All Karen could do was shake her head in response to Joshua's question. She had no idea what was happening. Whoever Ross called had clearly arrived, but it didn't sound like the reunion was a happy one. Over the past few minutes, they'd heard an assortment of noises coming from the other room. Talking. Yelling. Curse words. The name "Shane" mentioned a few times.

Then she heard loud, heavy footsteps trudging down the hall toward the storage room. A moment later, Ross appeared in the doorway. Behind him was a giant, toad-like man holding a gun. He looked like a character from that *Duck Dynasty* show Joshua used to like watching. Bushy beard. Beady eyes. He towered over Ross, a few inches taller and at least twice as wide.

Must be Shane.

"Get in the corner," he said to Ross. Ross walked over to the corner of the room.

Shane looked at the zip ties securing Karen's hands and ankles to the chair, then did the same with Joshua and Teddy.

"Well, look at that," Shane said. "Pretty nice job tying these three up, Ross. Surprised you didn't piss this up like you do everything else you touch."

Shane glared down at her.

"So, you're the kid's mom?" he asked.

Karen nodded.

"And you don't know this asshole?" he said, glancing at Ross. "Never met him before?"

"No, never," she said. "We have nothing to do with any of this."

Shane walked back over to Ross.

"Let's get to it, then. Where's the bread, Ross?"

"The bread?"

"The money from the robbery. Where the hell is it?"

Ross was silent.

"What, you think I came back because of Amber? You honestly think I'm going to help you two after the stunt you pulled at the bank? Hell no. The money, that's what I'm interested in. The money from the robbery. Where is it?"

No response from Ross. Shane took a step closer. They were only inches apart from each other, like two boxers staring each other down before a fight, Shane a grizzled heavyweight, Ross an overmatched amateur.

"I ain't asking again, Ross. Where the hell's the money?"

"It's gone."

"Fuck you, it is. We had a good forty grand from that job. Easy. I cleaned that safe out. No way you could've spent it already. So where's the cash?"

"The cops got it."

Shane tensed up.

"Hold up—cops?" he said. "You didn't say nothing about cops."

"When Amber went to the hospital after she got shot, cops were there. They searched the car she was in. The money was in the backseat."

There was no reaction from Shane at first. He stood there like a statue. Slowly, almost imperceptibly, his hands began to shake. A vein in the middle of his forehead appeared.

"You're lying," Shane said, a whisper.

"No," Ross said. "I'm not."

Shane took another step toward Ross, so close their noses were practically touching. He spoke through clenched teeth. "There's no money?"

"It's gone. But, listen, you get Amber to your doctor friend, and I'll do whatever you want. We can rob another bank, and I'll let you keep everything. I'll sell drugs for you, let you keep the profits. I'll do anything to pay you back. I'll—"

Before he could finish, Shane's hand flashed out and smashed the butt of the gun against Ross's nose. Ross dropped to his knees and cried out, cupping his hands around his nose. Blood poured out between his fingers. Shane pistol-whipped Ross on the back of the skull and Ross collapsed to the ground like a rag doll. His body was completely still, facedown, blood leaking from his nose onto the carpet.

"You idiot!" Shane yelled at Ross. "You goddamned idiot!"

He kicked Ross in the ribs and Ross's body rolled over, crashing against the wall of shelves. Random items fell to the ground. Toys. School projects. The bag of Fisher-Price golf clubs tipped over. A plastic container fell off a shelf and the lid snapped off, a sea of Legos pouring out and covering the floor.

"This is just like you, ain't it?" Shane screamed at Ross's motionless body. His face was turning redder and redder. "That bank job was easy money. A once-in-a-lifetime chance. And you somehow manage to fuck the whole thing up."

Shane kicked Ross in the face, the impact making a sickening crunching noise. More blood gushed from Ross's nose. There was no reaction from Ross; he was unconscious.

Shane stood over Ross, glaring down at him.

He raised the gun and pointed it at the back of Ross's head.

///////////////

"Stop! Don't shoot him!"

Karen yelled the words at the top of her lungs. Everything was happening so quickly; she'd had no time to make sense of any of this. All she knew was that she couldn't let Shane kill Ross. Right now, Ross was a distraction, something for Shane to focus on other than them. If he killed Ross, he'd turn his attention to them. She didn't want that.

"Put the gun away," she said. "Let's talk for a moment."

"Nothing to talk about." Shane took a step closer to Ross, Legos crunching under his heavy work boots. He inched the gun closer to the back of Ross's head.

"I can get you money," she said.

Shane glanced over.

"Everything I have in the bank. Just please, don't kill him."

He glanced at the clock on the wall. "After five on a Saturday. Bank isn't open. Won't be open tomorrow, either."

"We'll go Monday. First thing. I'll withdraw all of my money and give it to you."

"I'm not gonna sit around and wait the entire damn weekend," he said. "Hell no."

He turned back to Ross's motionless body.

"A bullet to the head is letting this bastard off easy for what he did to—"

"Money," Teddy said. "I can get you money. Right now. No waiting."

Shane glanced over.

"I'm serious," Teddy said. "Twenty thousand dollars."

"Cash?"

"Yes."

"Start talking."

"First, put away the gun. Please."

Shane lowered the gun. "This money," he said. "Where is it?"

"Just hear me out," Teddy said. "I work at a car dealership. Sold a car earlier today, and the customer paid cash. We didn't get around to taking the money to the bank, so I locked it up in a safe at the dealership for the weekend. It's still there. I know the combination to the safe and everything."

"There's twenty grand in there?" Shane said, keeping his eyes on Teddy.

"Yeah," Teddy said. "A little more, actually. The sale price was twenty-two thousand."

"Why the hell did the guy pay cash?"

"I don't know. Bad credit? I was just happy to make the sale."

"Twenty-two grand in cash. This isn't bullshit?"

"No. I swear."

"This dealership, where's it at?"

"Far north end of the city. Twenty, thirty minutes from here. This doesn't have to be difficult. You drive me there, I grab the cash from the safe and give it to you. You disappear and let us live."

"Fine, then. Let's go."

"We close at six on Saturdays. We have to wait until no one's there. Only forty-five minutes. That's it."

"Okay. Forty-five minutes."

"Just, please, don't kill anyone," Teddy said. He nodded toward Ross's body—unmoving, facedown, nose still bleeding onto the carpet. "Him included. That's the trade-off, okay? You'll get your money and get away, as long as everyone lives."

Shane glared down at Teddy.

"You got yourself a deal," he said.

SHANE LIFTED UP ROSS BY THE COLLAR OF HIS SHIRT AND DRAGGED HIM over by the radiator in the corner of the room. He grabbed the box of zip ties off the table. He cinched a few zip ties around Ross's left wrist, then a few around his right wrist, then linked them together with a few more, like a pair of handcuffs. He secured the handcuffs to the radiator with a few more zip ties.

He flipped Ross around and set him on his rear. Ross's eyes were closed. His face was a bloody, destroyed mask. His nose was bent at an angle, swelled to twice its normal size.

Shane stared at Ross for a moment, like an artist admiring his handiwork, then turned to Teddy.

"Forty-five minutes," he said. "We're leaving then."

Teddy nodded.

"I'll be back. Got some business with Amber."

"Our deal," Teddy said. "You said you wouldn't kill anyone."

"I'm not gonna kill her."

"Don't hurt her, either."

Shane smirked.

"Can't promise that."

He left the room, trudging heavily down the hallway.

KAREN LEANED BACK IN HER CHAIR AND TOOK IN A DEEP BREATH; SHE couldn't believe everything that had just happened. For a moment, she'd really thought that she was going to see Ross killed, right in front of her. Shane had been ready to blow Ross away; there'd been no hesitation or struggle with what he'd been about to do.

The room looked like a tornado had gone through. The carpet was littered with a sea of Legos. A few plastic containers were upended, lids knocked off. Random items everywhere.

"My God," Karen said. "Is everyone okay?"

Neither Teddy nor Joshua responded, but they didn't have to. Their expressions said everything. They weren't okay. None of them were okay. Not at all.

She looked at Ross, on the other side of the room. He wasn't okay, either. His head was slumped to the side, face bloody and battered, his hands zip-tied to the radiator. The rising and falling of his chest were the only indication that he wasn't dead. He was—

"There's no money," Teddy said, voice flat, barely there.

Karen turned toward him. His head was hung, staring down at the ground.

"What did you say?"

"There's no money at my dealership," Teddy said. "Nothing. I made up the story."

"You lied?"

He nodded.

"My God, why?"

"I had to say something," Teddy said. "Had to buy us some time. That look in his eyes when he was holding the gun—I thought he was going to kill Ross. Kill us after that. I just blurted out the first thing that came to my mind."

She knew that Teddy might be right—he very well might have saved their lives—but she could barely think straight.

"There's nothing?" Joshua said.

"No."

"Nothing at all?"

"Not a dime. Look, the main thing is he can't harm you if he's halfway across the city with me." He turned to Karen. "Can't harm you, either. When I'm gone with him, maybe you can escape. Get free somehow."

"But what about you?" Joshua said. "What are you going to do when you go there and there's no money?"

Teddy shook his head.

"I have absolutely no idea."

TWENTY

AMBER HEARD FOOTSTEPS RUMBLING DOWN THE HALLWAY, APPROACHING her room. A moment later, Shane appeared in the doorway. The gun was in his hand.

"Wh-what did you do?" she asked. "To Ross?"

"He ain't dead, if that's what you're asking. Not yet, at least."

The pain made it difficult to concentrate, but she'd heard enough of the commotion in the other room to know that something bad had happened to Ross. She'd heard some talking, followed by assorted bumps and crashes. Then came a single scream from Ross, brief and bloodcurdling, accompanied by a loud thud.

Shane walked over to her bed and stared down at her, his eyes hard as pebbles.

"Bet you didn't know Ross could scream like that, did ya?" he said. He tucked the gun into the waistband of his pants and sat down on the edge of her bed. "Now, let's see if you can beat him."

Shane reached out so his massive hand was a few inches above her stomach, right over the wound. He slowly balled his fingers into a fist.

Amber's entire body tensed up.

"You're the one to blame for this whole mess, aren't you?" Shane said. "It was you who came up with the plan to screw me over, right?"

Amber was silent. She stared at that fist, suspended over her stomach like a guillotine blade.

"Fine, don't answer," Shane said. "I know it was you. Ross is too damn stupid to come up with something like that. Three weeks I spent, planning out that bank robbery. Had every last detail covered. And then you backstabbing, cocksucking, shit-for-brains *bastards* screw me."

Amber was barely listening. She couldn't look away from his hovering fist.

"Please . . . don't," she said.

"Don't what?"

"Don't . . . don't hit me."

"Don't hit you? You mean, like this?"

Shane smashed his fist down onto her stomach, tearing open the cut, ripping away the dried blood clotted over the wound. The pain was instant and agonizing. The fall at the hospital had been bad; this was a hundred times worse, unlike anything she'd ever felt.

She screamed at the top of her lungs, a primal yell, all of the air leaving her body in a rush.

Shane smashed his fist down on her stomach again, the impact like that of a sledgehammer. Fresh blood splotched onto his fist.

Amber screamed again. Her vision started to cloud. She felt light-headed. Through her haze, she saw Shane raise his fist again. Before he lowered it, she passed out.

Blackness.

////////////////////

There was no money.

Over and over, the phrase repeated in Karen's head. Earlier, she'd held on to a faint bit of hope that they could end this without anyone getting injured or worse. Now that hope had been shattered. It felt like they had nothing. No plan. No next steps. No idea what would happen.

"What are you going to do, Teddy?"

"I don't know," he said, slumped in his chair, lips curled into a frown, eyes empty. "Like I said, I was just trying to buy more time. Trying to stop him from killing us all."

"There has to be something."

"If he's not here, he can't harm Joshua. Can't harm you, either. That's the main thing. If I can get him away from here, once we're on the other side of town, maybe I can escape or—"

The screaming started.

Even from a room away, Amber's screams were so loud that they made Karen cringe. There was pure pain, pure agony, behind the screams. She didn't even want to imagine what could make someone scream like that.

The screams didn't last long—not even a minute—before they abruptly stopped. There was only silence from the other room. Somehow, the sudden silence was worse than the screams.

Karen looked down at the scalpel. Still in her sock. Still out of reach. She pulled her arms and feet against the zip ties, tried to twist and contort her body in the chair. But with her arms secured to the armrests, it was impossible to reach the scalpel. She wasn't even close.

"What are you doing?" Teddy asked.

"There's a scalpel in my sock," she said. "I took it from the hospital earlier. Hid it. It's still there."

"After I leave, keep trying to grab it," Teddy said. "You have to get it and cut yourself free. Do the same for Joshua. And get out of here. Go straight to the police."

"But what about you?" Joshua said.

"I'll try to stall on the way to the dealership. Take up as much time as I can. Maybe one of you can get free before we arrive. Call the police and send them to the dealership."

"But what if we can't get free?" Joshua asked. "What if the police don't make it in time?"

"I don't know," Teddy said. "I wish I had an answer. Let's just hope things work out. Hope and pray."

Shane's heavy footsteps rumbled down the hallway. He entered the room a moment later and looked at them. One of his hands was covered in blood. He slowly ran the hand along the front of his hooded sweatshirt, wiping the blood onto it.

"Did y'all hear those screams?" he asked.

Karen nodded.

"Pretty loud, right?"

She nodded again.

"You remember those screams," Shane said. He looked at Teddy. "If I don't get my money, if this doesn't work out like you say it will, the person screaming is gonna be you."

Shane looked at Karen.

"And you."

He looked at Joshua.

"And you. Think I can make you scream like that, slugger? Trust me, I can."

He looked at Ross, still slumped in the corner, unconscious. Amber's screams hadn't woken him.

"See, that's the difference between me and Ross," Shane said. "He'll run his mouth, act like he's bad and all, but when it comes to it, he's all talk. Not me. I'll get nasty if I got to. Believe me when I say this: if I don't get my money, I will kill everyone in this room. And I will make it hurt."

He wiped his hand on his sweatshirt a final time.

"We leave in an hour," he said to Teddy. "We go into the dealership. You get me the money. And I leave. I don't want no surprises or—"

Shane stopped. Outside, there was a low, crunching noise. Distant, barely audible.

"The hell was that?" he asked.

Karen shook her head. Shane walked over to the only window in the room and glanced outside.

"Shit," he said, spitting out the word. "Shit, shit, shit."

He ran out of the room and thundered down the hallway.

"What's going on?" Joshua said.

"I don't know," Karen said.

But she had an idea. That low sound she'd heard from outside was a familiar one. It sounded like a set of tires driving over the gravel driveway.

A moment later, Shane stormed back into the room. He had a different look on his face, wide-eyed and frantic.

"What is it?" Karen said.

"The cops are here," Shane said.

TWENTY-ONE

SHANE'S EYES DARTED BACK AND FORTH, FROM KAREN TO TEDDY TO Joshua. He grabbed the gun from the waistband of his pants.

"The hell is going on?" he said. He stared at Karen. "Did you call the cops?"

"No," Karen said.

"Did you call them?"

"No, we've been tied up the entire time."

"Why they here?"

"I don't know. I talked to them earlier. Maybe they have more questions."

The doorbell rang. Shane frantically looked around the room.

"Keep quiet," he said to them. "Maybe they'll leave."

"The cars are out front," Karen said. "The house lights are on. They'll know someone is here."

Shane cursed. Looked down at the gun, over at the window, down the hallway, his head on a swivel. He walked over to Karen and leaned in close.

"I'm gonna cut you loose," he said. "See what the cops want, and get rid of them."

She nodded.

"I'm staying back here. My gun's gonna be pointed at the kid the entire time. The cops start looking around the house, they start to suspect something's up, I will kill the kid and take out as many people as I can. If I'm going down, I'm taking everyone with me. Understand?"

"Yes," she said.

"I am not messing around here. This ain't no empty threat. You don't get rid of them, and this will turn into a bloodbath. I got nothing to lose here. Believe me when I say that."

The doorbell rang again. Shane grabbed a Swiss Army knife from his pocket and cut through the zip ties cinched around Karen's wrists and ankles. He pulled her out of the chair and lightly shoved her over to the door.

"Go," Shane said. "Get them to leave."

Karen walked down the hallway. Her mind was racing, her hands trembling as if she had some sort of palsy. Everything felt so chaotic. The police—she couldn't believe the police were here. There were a million possible explanations. Maybe there'd been a security camera she was unaware of at the hospital. Maybe someone had seen her breaking Amber out. Maybe Carmella had decided to confess everything. Maybe Brian had caught a glimpse of her before she locked him in the room.

She reached the door just as the doorbell rang a third time. She looked out the peephole. The same detective she'd talked with at the hospital was outside. Franny.

She took a deep breath and opened the door.

"You're home," Franny said. He wore a button-up tucked into a pair of jeans. Maybe it was in her mind, but his eyes seemed harder than before. More suspicious. Like he knew something was up.

"You're a tough woman to get ahold of," Franny said. "I've been calling you constantly."

"My phone broke, actually," Karen said.

"Glad I caught you."

"Is something the matter?"

"You could say that, yeah," Franny said. "I'd like to discuss a few things with you. Can I come in?"

She couldn't think straight enough to come up with a reason to say no. She led the detective inside and he sat down on the couch. Karen sat on the recliner across from him. She kept her ears tuned for any sort of noise from the other room, just down the hallway. All it would take was any sort of noise for the situation to turn into a disaster.

"I'm sure you've heard about everything that happened," Franny said. "The lady being broken out of the hospital, all that."

"I heard. A few coworkers told me about it."

"Heck of a thing, isn't it?" he said. "We think it was her husband who pulled it off. The nurse who was moving her described the man who attacked her. Lanky, rough. Vague description, but it sounds like her husband."

Karen nodded. So Carmella had stuck to the story.

"Now that she's disappeared, this has turned into a big deal," Franny continued. "Much more than some random shooting. And that brings me to why I'm here. I have a few more questions about the story you told me earlier."

///////////////

Joshua sat in the storage room, still reeling from the past five minutes. It had been a roller coaster of emotions. There'd been a brief glimmer of hope when he heard that the police were here, then anxiety and unease as his mom left the storage room. And now, as he sat in his chair, just barely able to hear his mom talking to the police in the living room, he didn't really know what to feel. He had no idea what was going to happen next.

Shane stood only a few feet away, clenching his gun, holding it like he was just waiting for a reason to start shooting.

Joshua looked at his dad. He gave Joshua a weak smile. Was there any chance they would survive this? Any chance at all?

Maybe he should do something. He thought about yelling out. Making some sort of commotion. The police were only a few feet away—this was a chance to end this. It might be the only opportunity they'd get.

It all boiled down to one question.

Should he take a risk?

///////////////

Should she take a risk?

Karen thought about alerting Franny somehow. A hand gesture. Lowering her voice to a whisper. Or maybe writing a note and passing it to him. *A man is in the other room, holding us hostage. He has a gun. Please help.*

But then what? She had no idea. She might save them all. Or she might make the biggest, costliest mistake of her life.

"Easiest thing to do would be to get your story again," Franny said. "So go ahead. Walk me through it."

"Walk you through what?"

"Finding her on the side of the road. I need to make sure I have all my details straight. So tell me your story again. Step by step. I know you did earlier, but maybe I missed a detail. Maybe you forgot to mention something."

"Sure," Karen said. "I was driving along and—"

"What time was this, again?" Franny said.

She thought back. "Early. Four in the morning—around that time."

"And where were you going?" Franny said.

She paused. Thought back to the first time she'd talked to Franny. *What explanation had she given him?*

"Where was I heading? Nowhere, really. I couldn't sleep. Just decided to drive around."

"Do you do this a lot, drive around in the early morning with no destination in mind?"

"Sometimes. It's calming. It helps when I'm stressed-out."

"Okay, so you're driving along. Then what?"

"I saw something on the side of the road. The closer I got, the more I realized it was a body. A woman. She was moving. After that, everything is kind of hazy. I remember pulling over. Realizing she was hurt. I applied pressure to the wound. Helped her into my car."

"And you're sure the area you took me to earlier was where you found her?"

"Yes. Positive."

His eyes stayed on her for a second; then he pulled out a notebook and wrote something in it. He looked back up and stared at her with cold, hard authority.

"When you found her, did she have the backpack with her?" Franny asked. "The bag full of money?"

Karen shifted in her chair. Her eyes skittered away from Franny, around the room, down the hallway. "She did, yes. It was strapped on her back."

"So she's just lying there on the side of the road, shot, with a backpack full of money?"

"Yes. Exactly. I had no idea what was in the backpack, though. I barely even paid attention to it."

"What happened after you put her in your car?"

"I drove straight to the hospital. I asked her a few questions to distract her. Nothing important."

"I know I asked you earlier, but why didn't you call nine-one-one?" Franny spoke in such a direct, focused way. She got the impression he was trying to make her uncomfortable. It was working.

"All I cared about was saving her," she said. "Once I was halfway to the hospital, I thought about calling nine-one-one. By that time, I figured it'd be quicker to keep driving and take her myself."

Franny slowly nodded. Her eyes flashed around the room, down the hallway again. *Stop it.* If she kept nervously looking down the hallway like that, Franny would start to wonder why.

"And you're sure you didn't see anyone else in the area when you found her? No one running from the scene or anything like that?"

"No. Not at all."

"Think back. Take your time. You never know what might be relevant."

"There was nothing," Karen said. "She was all alone out there."

He silently stared at her for a few moments after she answered. He knew she was lying to her. She could just tell it. She was positive he was going to ask why she wasn't being honest, ask her what she was hiding . . . or ask to see around the house.

Instead, he put his notebook away and stood up from the couch.

"One final thing to say, and I'll be on my way," he said. "I just want you to know, you need to be totally honest with me. You could be in a lot of trouble if you don't give me the whole story. If you're worried or scared, there's no need to be. We can protect you."

"Protect me?"

"Sometimes, people see things and they're reluctant to tell the police the entire story. Maybe they're worried they might make an enemy out of some bad people if they get involved, put themselves in danger, so they figure it's safer to keep their mouths shut. I've seen it happen plenty of times. Or maybe they were threatened. 'Don't say anything to the police or we'll find you and harm your family,' that sort of thing. If that's the case here, let me know. There's no need to be scared. I can make sure you're safe."

"No. I've told you everything."

"You're sure?"

"Of course. I wish I could help you. Believe me."

"I'll be on my way, then. If you think of anything at all, contact me."

Franny kept his eyes locked on her for a second longer, then walked over to the front door. Karen followed him. For a second, she allowed herself to relax. It was over. He was leaving.

And then it happened.

From down the hall, Amber yelled out.

///////////////

The ringing doorbell woke Amber. She blinked a few times and looked around the room. She had no idea how long she'd been passed out. Her skin felt blisteringly hot, scorching everywhere. Her throat was so dry that it felt as if it had been rubbed raw with sandpaper.

Water—she needed water.

The doorbell rang again.

She looked out the window and saw something that nearly floored her: a car was in the driveway. A black Crown Vic. Even through her blurry vision, she could see the government license plate and the three long antennas mounted to the trunk.

An unmarked cop car. She was positive of it.

Her heart hiccupped in her chest.

The doorbell rang a third time and she heard the front door open in the living room. There was talking. A voice she didn't recognize. A man. She waited for the police to come storming in and save her. Waited to hear the sounds of Shane getting blown away in a shoot-out. Waited for . . . something to happen.

But all she heard was talking. It went on for a while. She couldn't understand what the people in the living room were saying, but they kept talking, on and on.

More time passed. And then she heard the voice she didn't recognize mention something about leaving.

Leaving? No. That couldn't happen.

She opened her mouth. Tried to push out a scream. Nothing. Her throat was too dry.

She heard movement in the living room. A noise that sounded like the front door creaking open.

She tried to yell again. "Help" came out, but it was barely more than a low croak, like a dying engine.

She took a deep breath and pushed it out from the pit of her stomach. There was a stabbing, excruciating pain. She gritted through it and kept pushing, harder, harder.

And finally, she yelled.

/////////////////////

Franny stared at Karen. "What in the world . . . ?"

She froze. Amber's yell wasn't as loud as her screams from earlier—this noise wasn't even really a scream; it was more of a groan, a hoarse, guttural sound—but the noise was still clearly audible in the living room.

"Who was that?" Franny said.

Karen cleared her throat, tried to keep her expression calm and composed. "My son," she said. "He's sick. In bed."

"Is he all right? He sounds terrible."

"Sounds worse than it is," she said. "Bad sore throat. He's been like that all day."

Franny stared back at her. He believed her—at least, she thought he did. The noise had clearly come from a person, but it didn't sound female. There was no cry for help or anything like that. More than anything it sounded like a grunt, like something from a caveman.

Just then, there was the sound of a few quick, heavy footsteps from down the hallway. Franny glanced over but most of the hallway wasn't visible from where they were standing.

"Was that him?" Franny asked her.

"Yes. He's been in and out of the bathroom all day." She yelled toward the hallway, "You all right, sweetie?"

No response.

"Check on him," Franny said. "See if he's all right."

"I can check later. Once you've left."

"Go ahead," Franny said. "I can wait here. Better safe than sorry."

She nodded and walked across the living room, down the hallway. Hurrying without running. She had to get to Amber before she yelled out again.

In the bedroom, Shane was already standing over the bed, his hand clamped over Amber's mouth. The footsteps she'd heard earlier. In bed, Amber weakly writhed, trying to slip free, but she was no match for Shane.

"Go back," Shane said, whispering, staring at Karen in the doorway. "Get rid of him."

She nodded.

"I can hear everything. Don't try to tip him off. Trust me, I can make it to the other room before he can."

She walked back out to the living room. Franny stood in the same spot, right in front of the door. A calm, focused look on his face.

"Everything okay?" Franny asked her.

"He's fine," she said.

"You're sure? He sounded terrible."

"Nothing some NyQuil and bed rest can't cure."

Franny motioned out to the driveway.

"All these cars out here, who do they belong to?"

She looked outside. Her car and Joshua's were parked next to each other. Teddy's Tahoe was parked behind them. In the grass a few feet from the driveway was a dusty Ram pickup—must be Shane's car.

"My car, my son's car, and he does bodywork in his free time. Those other two are cars he's working on."

It wasn't the best explanation, but it was as good as she could do. She waited for Franny to ask her more questions; instead, he thanked her for her time. He opened the door, exited the house, and walked to his car. She watched him through the window. When he passed Joshua's car, he paused and stared down at the crack in the windshield. Studied it. He looked at the busted grille. Karen tensed up and held her breath . . . and then Franny walked on and entered his cruiser.

Once his car had disappeared down the road, she finally let herself take in a long, deep breath.

SHE GLANCED BEHIND HER, OVER AT THE HALLWAY. IT WAS EMPTY. SHE reached down around her ankle and pulled up the cuff of her pant leg. She grabbed the scalpel and slipped it under the wristband of her watch. Checked to make sure it was securely in place. She pulled her shirtsleeve down to conceal it.

"He's gone?"

She tensed up and turned around. Shane stood in the hallway, gun in hand, pointed at her.

"Yeah," she said. "He's gone."

Shane walked over to the window and looked outside. He was panting heavily, his chest rising and falling with his breaths.

"Christ, I can't believe this," he said.

"I did everything you asked," she said. "I promise you, I didn't say anything to him. I don't want him coming back here. I just want this to be over."

Shane motioned to the hallway with his gun. "Back to the room. Let's go."

She walked back down the hallway, Shane behind her. She could feel the tip of the scalpel poking her skin under the watchband.

As she passed her bedroom, there was a noise: "Help."

Amber. Her voice was low and barely there, not nearly as loud as her yell from earlier.

Shane ignored her and they entered the storage room. Teddy and Joshua were in their chairs—unharmed, thankfully. Ross was still slumped, unconscious, in the corner on the other side of the room.

Shane grabbed a few zip ties and secured her wrists to the chair armrests. She held her breath as his hands passed within an inch of the scalpel, but he didn't see it. He secured her ankles to the chair legs.

"We are out of here," he said to Teddy once he'd finished. "Now. No more messing around. No more—"

"Help." Amber, again. Her voice was still weak, but it was a little louder than before.

Shane glared at the wall, then stormed out of the room, footsteps thudding down the hallway. Karen looked at Joshua.

"You're all right?" she said. "Not harmed?"

"I'm fine," he said. "I should've yelled out. Screamed for help. I almost did . . . but I just couldn't do it."

"No," she said. "Would've been too risky."

"What now?"

"I moved the scalpel," she said. "I think I can cut myself free."

She twisted her wrist and looked down at it, right under her watchband.

"I need time, though," she said. "It's going to take a while."

"How long?"

"Twenty minutes? Maybe longer? I don't know. I can barely move my hands. I'll have to cut through, little by little."

"I'll stall," Teddy said. "I'll drive slow on the way to the dealership. Give you some time. When you get free, leave with Joshua. Go to the police."

She nodded. So that was their plan. There was a chance it might work. Teddy would leave with Shane. She would cut herself free. Cut Joshua free. And they would escape.

"Once you're safe, send the police to the dealership," Teddy said. "And hope, pray, they get there in time. Because this guy isn't going to be too happy when he finds out there's no money."

///////////////

Amber was shivering and sweating, felt cold one moment, hot the next. Everything around her was out of focus, blurry and faded, like she was looking at the room through a filter.

She croaked out a "help." She didn't know if anyone could hear her, but she didn't think it'd matter if they could, anyway. The cop was gone; even with her weakening vision, she'd seen the car pull away. She'd tried to yell out to him, scream so loudly he could hear her through the walls, but it was no use, not with Shane's hand clamped over her mouth.

She moved her hospital gown to the side and looked at her stomach wound. It was covered in blood and puss, the skin swollen and puffy.

She let the gown fall back into place and closed her eyes. Croaked out another plea for help.

She could hear voices from the other room but couldn't understand what was being said. She couldn't even tell who was speaking. All she knew was that it wasn't Ross. No matter how groggy she was, she'd recognize his voice.

She hadn't heard him in a while. There'd been the commotion earlier, that loud thud. Nothing since then. She hoped he was okay. If he wasn't—

"Would you shut the hell up?"

Shane stood in the doorway. He walked into the room and, towering over her, looked down at her stomach. He moved his hand so it was a few inches above her wound and extended his index finger like the tip of a dagger, pointing it directly down.

She opened her mouth to tell him no but didn't get a sound out before Shane shoved his finger directly into the wound. There was a disgusting wet moan and a paralyzing jolt of pain. She retched a few times, like she was choking, then turned her head to the side and vomited. Not much came up, mostly mucus with a little blood mixed in.

Shane pushed his finger in deeper, burying it up to the knuckle.

Black spots flashed in front of her eyes. Her stomach was on fire. She screamed as loudly as she could, her throat burning.

Shane took his finger out of her stomach, but it brought no relief.

She retched again. Vomited. A thin strand of blood dabbled onto her chin.

Pain. Everywhere. It was like a blanket, covering her.

She tried to scream again, but she couldn't find her voice. She lay in bed, eyes closed, jaw clenched, as she moaned and tried to ignore the pain.

///////////////

Karen heard screams from the other room. A retching noise. More screams. The noise petered out to a light whimpering she could barely hear through the walls. A moment later, Shane appeared at the door and walked over to Teddy.

"So, this dealership—how far is it?" he said.

"Twenty miles. Around that."

"How long's it gonna take you to grab the money?"

"Not long. We'll park outside. I'll grab the money and bring it out to you and—"

"I'm coming in with you. You're not going in alone."

"Okay. Fine. The whole thing won't take long. But I told you, we have to wait for six o'clock, until everyone has left for the day."

"We'll drive now. I'm getting the hell out of here."

"Let's wait here for a few minutes. Just to make sure everyone will be gone."

"No, dammit. If people are still there, we'll wait at the car place."

Shane walked over to Joshua and cut the zip ties around his hands and feet.

"Stand up."

Karen froze. Locked eyes with Joshua. She'd misunderstood Shane. Had to have. "Wait, what—"

"The kid's coming, too," Shane said. "My insurance policy. To make sure things happen like they're supposed to."

"No," Teddy said. "Just you and me."

Shane glared at Teddy. "You calling the shots now?"

"We had a plan. We—"

"Listen, I'm no fool. I don't trust you. The kid's coming. If I don't have him, you'll try something."

"Take me instead," Karen said. She could barely force the words out.

Shane shook his head. "No. Look, the plan don't change. Pops grabs the money from the safe. Gives it to me. And I leave. Everything happens like that, and we're all happy. It doesn't happen like that, and the kid'll pay."

There's no money, Karen thought. She opened her mouth to yell, plead, say something, anything, but no words came out.

Shane walked over to Teddy and cut his zip ties with his pocket-knife. Teddy and Joshua walked over to the door, Shane following them with the gun pointed at their backs.

Before leaving the room, Joshua turned around and looked back at Karen. His eyes were wide, mouth slightly open. He looked so helpless. So scared.

She wanted to say something, do something, somehow fix this.

Instead, all she could do was watch them leave, a scream trapped in her throat.

TWENTY-TWO

KAREN HEARD THE FRONT DOOR SLAM SHUT. A MOMENT LATER, THE FAINT sound of a car starting up outside.

Her mind raced, a million thoughts, a million miles an hour. That look Joshua had given her before he left had broken her heart, shattered her.

No more wasting time. She slid the scalpel from behind her watch. Her fingers pinched around the handle, she started methodically sawing away at the zip tie on her wrist.

It was slow going. It was impossible to put a lot of force behind each cut. She couldn't move her arms, so flipping her wrist back and forth was the only way to saw through.

She bit her lip and concentrated. Kept slowly moving the blade along the zip tie, sawing back and forth.

And then, a grunting noise.

On the other side of the room, Ross opened his eyes. His gaze was spacey and distant. The blood on his face had dried. One cheek was bruised. His nose was swollen and mangled from Shane's earlier kick.

"God, my head," he said.

He blinked a few times, looked around the room.

"What . . ."

He looked at the zip ties fastening his hands to the radiator and pulled at them. It was no use. The zip ties held.

"Shane," he said to Karen. "Where is he?"

"He's gone," Karen said.

"How is she?" he asked her. "Amber."

"She's still in the other room," Karen said. No point in telling him about Amber's screams earlier.

Ross kicked out and banged one of his feet against the wall, making a loud, echoing sound.

"You doing all right in there, babe?"

There might've been a response, might not. Karen couldn't tell.

"What are you doing?" Ross said to her.

"Cutting myself free. I have a scalpel."

Ross slammed his foot against the wall again.

"We're coming, babe! We will be there soon."

Karen bit her lip and concentrated as she continued cutting. She looked at the zip tie. No progress yet. It wasn't even slightly frayed.

Still a long way to go.

Joshua sat in the passenger seat of Shane's pickup. His dad was next to him, both hands on the steering wheel, staring straight ahead, his expression blank. Shane was crammed into the truck's small backseat, the gun pointed at them.

The truck was dusty and ratty, had a musty smell to it. Some of the upholstering was torn. A crumpled McDonald's bag rested on the floor mat.

"So, this car dealership—how much further is it?" Shane asked.

"Ten minutes."

"You're sure this time? No more games, Pops. You try to stall again, I'm gonna start getting pissed."

Teddy had gotten off at a wrong exit and driven around for a while until Shane got impatient. He'd looked the dealership address up on his phone, realized they'd taken a detour, and yelled to get back on the highway.

They drove on. It was too dark to see Shane in the backseat, but Joshua could hear him behind them, feel his eyes locked on them, sense the gun pointed at their backs.

There was no money. He had no idea what would happen when they showed up at the dealership and Shane found out. He hoped his mom could get free and alert the police before they arrived. That was their best, probably only, chance at surviving this. Hope that the police could save the day. Or at the very least distract Shane, even if it was for only a second or two. That might be enough of a window of opportunity to get away.

After driving down the highway seemingly forever, they pulled into a roadside parking stall near the car dealership. The lights in the dealership were on. A few people stood near the entrance. Outside the dealership were rows and rows of cars for sale, stretching on forever.

His dad killed the engine.

"We'll have to wait a few minutes until everyone leaves," he said. The truck's dashboard clock read 5:56.

"Then we'll sit here," Shane said from the backseat. "Neither of you move."

///////////////

The scalpel between her fingers, Karen moved her wrist back and forth, pulling the edge of the blade against the zip tie. Still barely any progress. It was nearly impossible to put any force behind each movement using only her wrist. She'd been sawing for at least ten minutes already and the zip tie was still barely frayed.

"Hurry it up," Ross said.

"I'm trying," she said.

"You gotta keep sawing at the same place. Over and over again."

"That's what I'm doing."

She stopped cutting for a second and strained her wrist against the zip tie, pulling as hard as she could, hoping to snap free from the restraints. No luck; the zip tie held.

She resumed cutting. Already, she was thinking about what she would do once she was free. Call the police. That was her first step. Right away. She hadn't involved the police earlier when she'd had a chance, but there was no alternative any longer. She had to call them. Send them straight to the dealership and hope for the best.

"Try pulling again," Ross said to her.

"I just did."

"Try again."

She gritted her teeth and pulled against the zip tie as hard as she could. She let out a low grunt. Hands balled into fists, she pulled, yanked, strained against the zip ties. She jerked and—

The scalpel fell out of her fingers. She grasped to snag it but she was too late. It fell to the floor.

"Dammit," she said.

"What?" Ross said.

"I dropped the scalpel."

She looked at it, a few inches away on the carpet. She extended her foot as far out from her body as she could, pulling against the zip tie. The tip of her shoe could just barely graze the handle of the scalpel.

"Can you reach it?" Ross asked.

"Yeah. I think so."

With the scalpel trapped under her shoe, she slid it back closer to her body. She stared at it on the ground. She'd have to kick off her shoe, pick up the scalpel with her toes, and fling it back up toward her body, from where she could transfer it back to her hand and continue cutting. It'd be nearly impossible. She couldn't move her foot more than a few inches in any direction because of the zip tie. Flinging the scalpel back up to her body and moving it to her hands would take a miracle to pull off, a one-in-a-million shot.

"Kick it over here," Ross said.

"What?"

"I'm serious," he said. "Kick it over to me. I can cut out of my zip ties, easy. Then cut you loose."

He was right, she knew. Kicking the scalpel to Ross would be much easier than picking it up with her toes and hurling it back toward her body to attempt to somehow get it back into her hand.

She'd have to trust him.

"Okay," she said. "I'm going to send it over to you."

She cocked her foot back as far as the zip ties would allow and kicked the scalpel toward Ross. It slid on the ground and came to a stop a few feet from him. He stretched out his leg and moved the scalpel closer with his foot. When it was right next to the radiator, he pulled his hands hard against the zip ties, stretched out his fingers, and grabbed the scalpel.

"Got it!" he said.

He started sawing away, occasionally stopping to pull and yank at the zip ties. It took him only a few minutes to free his hands. Once he was unbound, he stood up from the ground, stumbled a little, and caught himself.

"Cut me loose," Karen said.

Ross didn't even look at her. He ran past her, out of the room. She heard his steps thundering as he sprinted down the hallway.

///////////////////

A few minutes after they arrived, the lights inside the dealership all went out. A group of six people exited the building and walked across the parking lot to several cars parked in a small lot off to the side. They each entered a different car and drove away.

"They're gone," Shane said. "Let's get to it. Let's grab the cash."

"Just don't do anything stupid," Teddy said.

"That's up to you, whether I do something stupid or not. You try something, I'll start doing plenty of stupid shit. Now, let's go. Drive up to the entrance."

Teddy started the truck and drove across the parking lot, up to the entrance, past endless rows of cars, price stickers in the windows.

The three of them were silent as they drove. The silence was unnerving and eerie. Joshua wanted to say something to break it, but what was there to say? Ask Shane how his day was going? Ask him how he'd react if, hypothetically speaking, there was no money?

No need to ask—he'd find out soon enough.

"No one's still inside, right?" Shane said. "There's no night security guy or anything?"

"No. It'll just be us."

"Better be. No surprises. I don't want no surprises."

Joshua tried to think of a way to escape. He glanced at the door handle, right next to his hand. Could he grab it, throw the door open, and escape before Shane had a chance to shoot him? He doubted it. The gun was right on him. Shane would have time to squeeze off at least a few shots. They wouldn't all miss. And he'd have to somehow communicate to his dad to leave at the same time or else he'd be a sitting duck.

His dad pulled to a stop a few feet from the dealership entrance and killed the engine. They stepped out of the truck and started walking up to the entrance, Joshua and his dad in front, Shane behind them with the gun.

They reached the entrance door. The front of the building was solid glass, looking into a lobby area that was vacant and dark.

"I'm grabbing my keys from my pocket," his dad said. "I need to unlock this door."

"Okay," Shane said from behind them. "The gun's pointed right at the kid. You try anything, he gets it."

His dad grabbed the set of keys from his pocket.

"Now open up the door," Shane said. "Hurry it up."

/////////////////////

Through the wall, Karen heard Ross talking in the other room. Couldn't understand exactly what he was saying. There was some movement, other indiscernible noises. More talking. After a minute, his footsteps rumbled back down the hallway. He appeared at the door and hurried over to her. Cut through the zip tie around her left wrist, the one around her other wrist, then the zip ties around her feet.

"Go check on her," he said. "Amber. Tell me what to do."

He helped Karen stand up from the chair. They hurried down the hallway, into her bedroom. She stepped past the entrance and froze, staring down at Amber in bed. Amber's gown was pulled to the side, revealing her stomach wound. The bed sheets and her gown were splattered with blood. There were a few smudges of red on the carpet and walls.

Amber's body was pale, her mouth slightly open. She was alive but in bad shape.

"Go!" Ross said. "Help her."

"I might have something in the bathroom," Karen said.

"Go. Get it."

She ran out of the bedroom. Down the hallway. Past the bathroom—there was nothing in there strong enough to help Amber. A phone was what Karen needed. She'd given Ross her cell after she arrived home from the hospital and hadn't seen it since, so she sprinted over to the landline phone in the living room. Picked it up. Dialed 911.

A ring. Then a voice.

"Nine-one-one. What is your emergency?"

"Send police to Franklin Auto Dealership."

"Ma'am, could you—"

"Send the police. Right now. There is a man there with a gun. He has my teenage son."

"Are you—"

"Just send them," she said and slammed the phone down. She patted down her pockets. Couldn't find her keys. Glanced around the kitchen, tried to remember where she'd put them. She looked out the window and saw her car. She ran outside and there they were, in the ignition. She'd left the keys there after she broke Amber out of the hospital and, unbelievably, they were still there.

She jumped into her car and fired up the engine.

She reversed out of the driveway and headed toward the car dealership.

///////////////

Amber's head felt as if it were coated in cotton. She was shivering and sweating. Felt cold and hot. Weak—she felt so weak.

"You're gonna be fine, baby."

She turned her head. Ross stood at her side. His nose was crooked and bloody. One eye was bloodshot.

"The lady, she's getting something for you. Medicine or something."

Amber nodded. "What happened?" she said, her voice little more than a whisper.

"Happened? Shane. He was back here for the money. Went crazy when he found out there was none. But that's all right. We don't need him. This lady, she's going to help you. Get you good enough to travel and we'll get out of here. We'll drive far away and—"

A noise came from outside: a car starting.

"What the . . ." Ross glanced out the window. "Shit, she's leaving!"

///////////////

Joshua watched as his dad selected a key from the key chain and tried to fit it into the entrance door keyhole. The key wouldn't fit. His dad tried another. There were at least twenty keys on the key chain. He'd tried four already. None had fit.

"Goddammit, I said no more games," Shane said. "Hurry it up."

"Too dark to see which key I need."

It was barely six, but darkness surrounded them. The dead of winter, when night arrived early. Occasionally, a car would pass by on the road in front of the dealership, but none stopped; they were too far away for anyone to see what was happening.

His dad tried another key. It didn't fit. Joshua glanced over his shoulder, hoped to see a police cruiser on the road or pulling into the dealership. But there was nothing.

His dad selected another key. Dropped the key chain before he could try it.

"Christ," Shane said. "This door isn't open in the next minute, things are gonna get ugly."

///////////////

Karen focused on the road as she sped down the highway, headlights cutting through the night, passing cars like they weren't even moving. The speedometer needle was past ninety. She pressed her foot down on the accelerator and the needle climbed a few notches higher.

She didn't even know what she'd do once she arrived at the dealership. Didn't know what scene would greet her, didn't even know if Joshua and Teddy would be there. A million questions raced in her mind. Had the police arrived? Had they even taken her call seriously? Had something already happened to Joshua and Teddy?

She continued on, down the interstate, fingers white-knuckling the steering wheel. The car's interior had a coppery smell from Amber's blood still smudged in the backseat. Karen almost rear-ended a car and swerved to avoid it.

In the distance, the dealership's large roadside sign was just visible.

Just past the sign, she could see something else, too: pulsing red and blue police lights, flashing into the sky.

///////////////

Joshua watched as his dad grabbed another key. Before he had a chance to fit it into the keyhole, Joshua heard a noise to the left of them.

Police sirens.

They all snapped their heads over and looked in the direction of the sirens. A police cruiser was a couple of hundred feet away, racing past the rows of cars toward them, lights flashing.

The cop car screeched to a stop a few feet away from them. The driver's-side door flew open and a uniformed officer jumped out, gun in hand. A moment later, the passenger door opened and a second officer jumped outside. They both began yelling but got only a few words out before the gunshots began.

Shane started shooting. The gunshots were right behind Joshua, like cannon blasts. He fell to the ground, hands over his head, ears ringing, every muscle in his body clenched.

The officers yelled some more. There was a barrage of gunshots from Shane. Joshua curled into a ball on the ground and closed his eyes as gunshots continued to ring out.

"Joshua . . ."

He opened his eyes. His dad was only a few feet away, on his knees. Right in front of the dealership entrance door . . . which was open, keys dangling from the keyhole.

He reached out and grabbed Joshua's arm. They stood up and sprinted past the open door, into the dealership.

Behind them, more gunshots. Then a yell: "Shit!" It didn't sound like Shane, but it was impossible to tell. Too much was happening.

Joshua kept running, right beside his dad, into the lobby. It was so dark Joshua could barely see a few feet in front of him.

Another yell from behind them: "Dammit!" That one vaguely sounded like Shane.

They reached the middle of the lobby, one hallway leading off to the left, one off to the right. He followed his dad down the one to the left. They ran down the darkened hallway, closed doors on either side of them.

From behind them, Joshua heard loud panting, heavy breathing. He glanced over his shoulder and saw a thick, bulky silhouette lumbering down the hallway, heading straight toward them.

Shane.

Then came the flash of a muzzle and the crack of a gunshot, the noise echoing in the empty hallway.

A gunshot. Then another one.

Beside Joshua, his dad yelled out and collapsed to the ground, grabbing his thigh. Even in the near total darkness of the hallway, Joshua could see the blood on the leg of his dad's pants.

"Are you shot?" Joshua asked.

His dad nodded. He tried to stand up but his leg buckled under him and he fell back down to the ground.

Behind them, Shane's shadowy figure made its way down the hallway, closer and closer.

TWENTY-THREE

KAREN ARRIVED AT THE DEALERSHIP AND PULLED INTO THE PARKING LOT. Heart racing, she drove across the parking lot, heading toward the red and blue flashing lights near the building.

When she was closer, she saw a police cruiser. Two officers were right outside of it, one lying on the ground, one huddled over him. The one on the ground held a bloody hand to his shoulder. Next to the cruiser was a dusty Dodge Ram pickup. The driver's door was open, interior light on.

No Teddy in sight. No Joshua. No Shane.

As she neared the building, three cruisers with their sirens blaring pulled into the parking lot from a side entrance. The cars parked next to the scene and officers jumped out. They ran over to the two officers on the ground. There was some yelling. A few of the officers ran toward the dealership, guns drawn.

She parked her car fifty feet from the pickup. Jumped out. An officer yelled at her to get back in her car.

"I called this in," she said. "I'm the one who called nine-one-one. My son. Where is he?"

"Back in your car!" he yelled. He turned and ran toward the entrance.

Police officers ran around. More yelling. Sirens wailed. Lights flashed. Two more police cruisers roared across the parking lot toward them.

Chaos. Everything was chaos.

//////////////

Joshua leaned over his dad in the hallway. The leg of his pants was soaked in blood. Blood continued to gush from his thigh.

"Run!" his dad said. "Get out of here."

"No."

He draped his arm around his dad's shoulders. Attempted to help him stand up. He lifted and—

"Don't move, kid."

He turned around. Shane was directly behind him, chest rising and falling. His shoulder was bloody, his shirt soaked in red—he must've been hit during the shoot-out. He squeezed the shoulder with one hand and held the gun in his other hand. He pointed it at Joshua.

Outside the building, a group of police cruisers arrived at the scene, sirens blaring.

"Fuck!" Shane mumbled, staring out at them. "Fuck!"

Shane looked at the closed hallway doors on their left, on their right. He ran over to the closest door and tried to open it. Locked. He raised his leg and smashed his foot against the door. The door splintered around the handle and flew open.

"Over there. Go!"

Shane ran back over to Joshua. He grabbed Joshua and dragged him over to the door, one hand gripping his arm like a vise, the other pressing the gun into his back. Before they entered, Joshua looked back and saw a final image of his dad on the ground, holding his leg, the white tile around him covered in blood.

Through the door was a garage. A white car was in the middle of the room; it was too dark to see what model it was. Power tools and other items lined the wall. The garage door was pulled down behind the car.

In the hallway, there were footsteps, yelling. Sounded like an army storming the scene.

"Shit," Shane said. "Shit."

Shane frantically looked around the room. Right past the door was a board with at least ten different sets of keys dangling from pegs. Shane swiped them all off the board and started pounding the remote unlock button on each, throwing the keys to the side when they didn't unlock the car.

In the hallway, the yelling was getting louder, closer.

Shane hit the button on a set of keys and threw them to the side. Another. Another—and the car in front of them honked once. The headlights flashed and the interior lights turned on.

Shane grabbed Joshua's arm again and dragged him over to the passenger door, the gun pushing into his back. He threw open the passenger door and shoved Joshua into the car.

"Don't move."

Shane ran around the car and jumped into the driver's seat. He fired up the engine.

A police officer appeared at the door.

Shane shifted the car into reverse and floored it.

The officer fired a shot at the car.

The rear of the car smashed into the garage door and ripped a hole in it. One hand holding the steering wheel, the other on the armrest pointing the gun at Joshua, Shane kept the accelerator floored. They were in a parking lot, smaller and not crowded with cars—the rear of the dealership. On the opposite side of the building, Joshua could see red and blue police lights flashing into the night sky.

Shane slammed on the brakes. Joshua rocked forward in his seat. Shane shifted the car into drive and sped forward. Behind them, an officer appeared in the hole in the garage door. He yelled something at the car and fired his gun in the air.

Ahead of them, the parking lot stretched out for a couple of hundred yards. Beside the dealership was a flat grassy field with a LOT FOR SALE billboard at the edge. Shane drove over and jumped the curb that divided the parking lot from the field, the car rocking forward. They started driving through the field, the car tires kicking up grass and dirt.

//////////////

More cop cars arrived, their lights flashing, sirens blaring. A few more officers sprinted into the dealership. An ambulance arrived and paramedics ran over to the injured officer, loaded him onto a stretcher. A few cars on the highway had pulled to the side of the road to let the emergency vehicles pass, bottlenecking the traffic. Car horns were honking. Noise and commotion were everywhere.

Karen wanted to scream. Yell out. Do something, anything. She felt so helpless; she needed answers. Where was Joshua? Teddy? Were they in the dealership? Had they escaped somewhere else? She recognized the pickup from her driveway—they must've taken it here . . . so they had to be here somewhere, didn't they?

A uniformed officer walked over and stood next to her. The radio clipped to his shoulder was broadcasting a jumble of noises and voices. He turned the volume down low. "You're the one who called in the emergency?" he asked.

She nodded. "Yes. . . . My son . . ."

The word trailed off.

"Everything will be fine," he said. "We've got over twenty officers in there. We'll find him. We—"

At the dealership entrance, two officers stumbled out of the building, their arms draped around a man, helping him walk.

It was Teddy.

She watched them move from the entrance across the parking lot. Once they were close enough, she could see that Teddy's leg was covered in blood. She ran over. She looked at his bloody pants, looked at the officers on either side.

"My God, my God," she said.

"I'm fine," he said.

A paramedic with a gurney appeared and helped Teddy onto it.

"Joshua," she said. "Where is he?"

"I don't know. He shot me, took Joshua."

The paramedics rolled the gurney toward an ambulance. Karen watched as they loaded Teddy inside. Her mind was swimming. An officer appeared and stood beside her. He might've been the same officer she'd just spoken to, might've been a different one. She couldn't remember.

"We'll find your son," he said to her. "If they are in there, we will find them. And we will make sure he's safe."

He kept talking to her, the words not even registering, until he was interrupted by a loud crashing noise from behind the dealership. Like a wall falling down. Tires squealed. There was a popping noise: a gunshot. The dealership building blocked Karen's view and prevented her from seeing what was going on. She ran over to the side of the building and saw a white car reversing through an open lot behind the dealership. It came to an abrupt stop and started moving forward. The car sped through the lot, jumped a curb, and drove across a large empty field next to the dealership. A few officers standing beside her ran over to their cars and jumped inside. They drove in the direction of the car, pursuing it; the white car had at least a half-mile head start.

Karen watched the car disappear across the field—was Joshua inside? All around her was a scene of total madness—police cruisers speeding toward the white car, officers running around. The ambulance carrying Teddy pulled away, lights flashing, just as two more ambulances arrived on the scene.

It was all too much. She couldn't hold back. She lowered her head and started crying.

TWENTY-FOUR

THE CAR MOVED ACROSS THE EMPTY FIELD, ROCKING UP AND DOWN.
Joshua was frozen in the passenger seat. Shane still had the gun resting on the center console, pointed at him. Every time the car rocked, Joshua flinched, bracing himself, certain the bumping would cause Shane to inadvertently pull the trigger.

He glanced over at the passenger door. Right there. The door handle inches away.

"Don't open that door, kid," Shane said. "Don't even think about it. You move an inch and I'll blow you away."

Shane sped across the open grassy lot. In the rearview mirror, Joshua saw a few police cruisers pulling away from the dealership and trailing them. But they were so far back there, not even close.

Ahead of them, a residential neighborhood bordered the park. Shane sped toward it. The car rocked forward as they drove over another curb, onto a residential street. Most of the houses in the neighborhood still had lights on. They sped down a street. Down another. Ran a stop sign. Houses flew past. It felt like they were going a million miles an hour.

They turned and the tires squealed. The group of police cars was still behind them but barely even visible.

They took another turn. Sped down a few blocks. Another turn. A few more blocks.

Right in front of them was an on-ramp for a highway. Shane pulled up to it and slammed on the brakes.

"Hey, kid, look at me."

Joshua looked over at Shane. He saw Shane's face for a split second, then the blur of his fist. Before he could brace himself, a punch smashed against his nose.

There was an intense, shooting pain.

And then Joshua was unconscious.

THE OFFICER LED KAREN OVER TO ONE OF THE POLICE CRUISERS AND helped her onto the front bumper. She sat there, head buried in her hands, crying. She was close to completely breaking down and turning into a slobbering, blubbering, inconsolable mess.

Helpless. She felt so helpless.

Someone draped a blanket over her shoulders. Asked her if she wanted anything to drink. She didn't even respond, just kept her head lowered, staring at the ground as she cried.

Time passed. Five minutes. Ten. Fifteen. She looked at the dealership entrance. She hoped, prayed, that the doors would open and Joshua would walk out, unharmed, safely guarded by police officers.

Another officer appeared at her side. As before, she had no idea whether he was someone she'd already spoken to. She couldn't remember anything from earlier.

"We're still searching," he said. "We haven't found your son inside yet."

"They've been searching for twenty minutes now," she said, her voice barely there.

"There's a lot of ground to cover. We'll find him."

"That car that disappeared. The one that drove away."

"He might've been in there. We don't know. We're looking for it now."

She kept her eyes on the dealership entrance.

"He was in the car, wasn't he? He's not in the dealership. He's gone."

"We'll find him."

THE CHAOS BEGAN TO SLOW DOWN. POLICE CARS STOPPED ARRIVING. ALL the ambulances were gone. The bottlenecked traffic on the shoulder of the nearby highway had disappeared.

A few officers stood, talking, in front of Shane's black pickup. Yellow crime scene tape had been strung up on the periphery of the parking lot. A few news vans were parked on the other side of the tape.

At one point, Detective Franny arrived. He came over to Karen, asked if she was all right. She shook her head. Of course she wasn't all right. She had a million questions but no strength to ask any of them. Maybe the answers to her questions were what she was truly afraid of.

Getting the news that they'd found Joshua and he was hurt or shot or even worse. It was all she could think about. Teddy had been shot. What would stop Shane from doing the same to Joshua?

Time passed. It felt like an hour, but when she glanced at her watch she saw it had been only ten minutes since that white car had disappeared across the nearby lot. She felt her hope slowly fading, fading away.

And then it happened. An officer walked out of the dealership and approached Franny. He said something. Franny said something back. They both looked over at her. Her heart skipped a beat. The officer said something else to Franny, who nodded and walked over to her, his face completely blank.

He shook his head. Every muscle in her body froze.

"What is it?" she asked.

"They're gone," he said. "The general manager of the dealership arrived a few minutes ago and gave us access to the security footage. Shane forced Joshua into the car and left with him."

Franny placed his hand on her shoulder.

"We'll do all we can," he said. "The pursuing officers lost the trail, but we have the car's license plate. Every officer in the city is looking for it. They can't be far. We'll find them."

"He's gone?" Karen said. Watching the car disappear, she'd been positive that Joshua was in there, but she'd held on to a faint bit of hope that she'd been wrong. No longer. Joshua was gone. Ten minutes didn't seem like much time, but it was. If they got to the interstate, they could be outside the city already, headed anywhere.

"Right now, we need to take you in to the station," Franny said. "Get your story. Learn everything we can from you to help us find them. And we will find them. Trust me on that. Is there anything we need to know before we leave?"

Even with her mind jumbled and barely able to function, she thought of something. A bit of information that might come in handy.

"There's someone at my house right now," she said. "Two people. They've been holding us hostage."

Franny kept his eyes on her. "Hostage?"

"Yes. This whole thing . . . It's complicated. But the people at my house, they're involved in this, too."

"We'll send a team over right away," Franny said.

TWENTY-FIVE

AMBER WALKED FROM THE BEDROOM TO THE LIVING ROOM, THOUGH SHE wasn't walking so much as she was being dragged along by Ross. His arm was draped around her shoulders as he helped her move. Her legs were wobbly. Head spinning. Her stomach throbbed. Not as bad as when she'd been lying in bed, but she didn't know if it was a good thing or not that the pain wasn't as intense.

She felt Ross's arm dig into her back and pull her along.

"Slower," she said. "Slow down."

"No. Gotta hurry. Gotta get out of here."

They walked on. She just couldn't keep pace with Ross. He was moving so fast. Quick steps, jumpy movements. Earlier, right after the woman had taken her car and driven away, he'd paced around the room and mumbled to himself. He'd asked her a few questions about what to do next. He'd then taken three pills, smashed them into a powder on the table, and snorted them.

The effect had been instant. Like a switch had been flipped. He'd grabbed a phone from his pocket and looked at a few things. A moment later, he tore a sheet out of a *Better Homes & Gardens* magazine beside the bed, quickly scrawled something on it, and threw the phone back into his pocket. He helped her out of bed and they walked down the hallway.

She didn't know where they were going.

"Come on, come on," Ross said, pulling her down the hallway.

"I'm trying."

They reached the living room, grunting and groaning the entire way. He set her down in a recliner and hurried over to the window. Two cars were outside. The kid's car with the cracked windshield and a Tahoe.

Ross moved away from the window and threw open a few cupboard doors. He picked up a stack of letters on the table and tossed them to the side. His head was on a swivel as he scanned the living room.

"Keys," he said. "Need to find the keys."

She watched him run around the room, trying to find the keys. He looked genuinely frightening, his face mangled, his movements sped up. One eye was starting to swell shut.

"Dammit, dammit!"

He hurried out of the room. Into the kitchen. She heard him opening drawers, rummaging around, slamming them shut. Silverware clanked. A few dishes shattered.

He ran back into the living room. Grabbed a few coats resting near the door and went through the pockets, tossing the coats to the side after he'd gone through them. He ran over to the couch and threw the cushions off, flinging them across the room.

"Nothing," he said. "Nothing, dammit."

He looked out the window. Back over at her.

"Let's go."

"Where—"

"Come on."

He helped her up out of the chair and they walked outside. It was dark, not pitch-black but close to it. He dragged her over to the Tahoe and sat her down in the passenger seat. He balled his hand into a fist and pounded the plastic covering around the ignition, the impact so hard she thought he might break his hand. The covering loosened after a few blows and he ripped it off. Some wires and other metal pieces were exposed.

"What are you doing?"

"Hot-wiring it," he said. "If I fuck around enough, might be able to jump it."

He yanked out a few wires. Touched the ends together. When that did nothing, he yanked out a few more. Tried the same thing. Nothing.

He threw the wires down and pounded his fist against the dashboard. "Come on, you piece of shit! You stupid piece of—"

There was a noise behind them. Distant. Ross snapped his head toward it. Amber slowly turned her head and saw a pair of headlights approaching on the gravel road. A couple of hundred feet away.

Ross threw open the car door and ran down the driveway. He stopped in the middle of the road and waved his hands in the air. The headlights slowed and came to a stop a few feet in front of him. A truck. Beat down and rusty.

An old man stepped out. He wore a red-and-black-checkered flannel shirt. Skinny. Gray hair. Lined face.

He stared at Ross's bloody face. From this distance Amber could just hear his voice.

"What happened?" he said. "Are you injured—"

Before he got another word out, Ross charged forward and tackled him. The old man stumbled backward and fell to the ground. Ross pounced on him and started throwing punches. One after another. His fists were like blurs, rising and falling, pummeling the old man.

The old man screamed. Yelled.

Amber watched the beating, stunned. It had happened so quickly that it had barely registered.

The beating continued, more punches, brutal, savage. If Ross continued, he would kill the old man.

She pushed open the door and yelled at him to stop. Her voice wasn't much, and Ross didn't even hear her. He continued pummeling away.

Amber reached across the center console and pressed the car horn. It sounded, and Ross stopped punching the old man. He looked over at the Tahoe. Looked back down at the motionless old man. She thought he was going to start beating him again. Instead, Ross walked back over to the car.

"Come on." He picked her up out of the Tahoe and carried her over to the truck in the road. His breaths were short and quick. The truck was still running, and the headlights illuminated the old man on the ground. As they passed him, he grunted. Ross looked down at him and delivered a final, brutal kick to the old man's ribs. The old man yelled, briefly and piercingly, then went silent.

She cringed and looked away. Ross set her down in the passenger seat and buckled the seat belt. She winced as the strap pulled tightly over her injured stomach. Ross walked around the car and sat in the driver's seat. He shifted the truck into drive and sped away.

TEN MINUTES LATER, THEY WERE DRIVING DOWN THE HIGHWAY. ROSS'S hand on the wheel was shaking. Every few seconds, the truck would sway a little on the road and veer a few inches in and out of their lane until Ross jerked the wheel back.

"Where . . ." Amber began. The word trailed off. She swallowed, tried to clear her throat. "Where are we going?" she croaked.

Ross wasn't listening to her. He was focused on the road, his one good eye staring out from the bloody mask of his face. He constantly ground his teeth, the muscles in his jaw flexing.

"W-where are—"

"Somewhere I wanna go," he said. "Quick stop. I—"

A horn blared from beside them. Their pickup had coasted into the path of a passing car. Ross jerked the wheel to the right.

"Screw off, asshole!" he yelled as the car passed him.

They drove on, Ross's unsteady hand on the wheel, the truck continuing to sway. She felt like she was on a rickety roller coaster. Ross reached into his pocket and pulled out the magazine sheet he'd scrawled on earlier. Looked at it.

"Almost there," he said.

Her eyes stayed on Ross. His image kept going in and out of focus. A leering smile was on his face. He looked mad—his smile, his face bloody and battered, one eye swollen shut.

Seeing him beat the old man earlier had disturbed her. The beating had been so savage. Ross had continued even after the man was helpless to fight back. She'd honestly thought he was going to beat him to death. Almost as bad as the beating was the final kick he gave the man, that heartless, brutal kick he'd given the old man as they'd passed. He was as out of control as she'd ever seen him.

Ross slowed down and pulled off the highway. He took a few turns. The hand holding the steering wheel continued to shake, the car tottering back and forth. He kept gritting his teeth.

He finally stopped on the side of a road. No other cars were around. An empty, darkened parking lot was nearby, in front of a few businesses in a run-down brick building. A vacant storefront. A dingy restaurant with a Closed sign in the window. And in the middle, a shop with a dark sign, just visible in the shadows. GUN SHOP, it read.

"That's the place," Ross said.

"A gun shop?"

"Can't do anything without firepower," Ross said. "Figure we'll get some guns and rob a bank. Or a bunch of gas stations. A thousand bucks at each of them. We rob a few, it adds up."

The plan was ridiculous; it wasn't even a plan. It was just a random, crazy idea. He gritted his teeth again. Looked at his reflection in the rearview mirror.

"And then, Shane—I want revenge," Ross said. He was talking so quickly, the words sounded like one big jumble. "Look at what he did to my face, the bastard. I want him dead."

He slammed his fist against the steering wheel.

"He's down in Saint Louis, I bet," he said. "Returned to his buddy Smitty. We'll show up and give him a big ol' surprise."

"N-no."

Ross wasn't listening. He floored the accelerator. The tires squealed. The truck sped forward, heading straight toward the gun shop.

Amber tried to brace herself for the collision.

////////////////////////

Karen sat in the interrogation room, barely able to keep her eyes open. A cup of coffee was on the table in front of her, steam rising from the cup. An empty chair was on the other side of the table. A few minutes ago, Franny had sat her in the room and left her by herself.

She stared at the cup on the table and thought about Joshua. It was impossible to think about anything else. On the way there, the officer driving the cruiser she was riding in had told her how confident he was they would find him. She wanted to believe, but it was tough. Almost an hour had passed now. All she could do was pray. Pray that they would find him. And that he'd be unharmed once they did.

Franny opened the room door and walked over. He sat down in the chair across from her.

"Officers went to your house," he said. "No one was there. But we did find something. Someone, actually. A man was outside, very badly beaten. Your neighbor. Bob Chamberlain."

"What?"

"He said he was driving home. A lanky guy ran out into the road. All bloody. He thought the guy was injured and stopped. The old man took a beating. The lanky guy took his truck. Loaded a woman inside and left. Chamberlain saw them head north. Into the city. Even if they're passing through, we're looking for the truck."

"Is Mr. Chamberlain okay?"

"Got roughed up pretty badly. He's being taken to the hospital."

She couldn't believe it. Mr. Chamberlain was her neighbor dating back to when she was a child growing up in the house. About the sweetest old man alive. He would always bring them strawberries in the summer. Would clear their driveway of snow in the winter with the snowplow attachment on his tractor. She felt physically ill, thinking of him suffering a beating.

"So, that's where we are currently," Franny said. "Now I have some questions for you. A lot of them, actually."

"I'm sorry. I haven't been honest with you."

"Didn't take me long to figure that out. I've thought you were hiding something since we talked first. The breakout at the hospital, you had something to do with that, didn't you?"

"They forced me to break her out. Well, he did. Ross. Her husband. They were at the house when you were there."

"That yell."

She nodded. "It was her. Amber. My son had a gun pointed at him. He would've been killed if I said anything to you. It was Shane. Ross's brother. He showed up later, right before you did. He was furious because the money from the bank robbery was gone. I thought he was going to kill us all."

"This is getting confusing," Franny said. "Easiest thing to do would be to tell me everything from the start. And I mean everything. No detail is too small."

She nodded. Yes, that would be easiest. Total honesty. It was time to tell him everything: the accident that started everything, the fight afterward when Joshua hit the man with the rock, Joshua and Teddy not reporting the crime, the events that happened since then.

"This all began with my son," she said. "He was out driving and—"

There was a knock at the door. An officer with a thick mustache stuck his head inside.

"Need to talk with you," he said to Franny.

"Can it wait?"

"No."

The tone of his voice made her heart catch in her chest. Something was clearly up.

"What is it?" she said. "Is it my son? Tell me."

"Just give us a second."

Franny walked out of the room. Karen sat in her chair, her mind racing, hoping there would be good news, praying that her world wasn't about to be crushed.

All she could do was wait for answers.

TWENTY-SIX

THE TRUCK SPED ACROSS THE PARKING LOT, HEADING STRAIGHT FOR THE gun shop. Amber looked down at her seat belt to check it; it was fastened. She opened her mouth. She tried to scream but she just couldn't push any noise out.

The truck bounced up and down as they raced forward. Pain flared up in her stomach as the truck jostled her around. She closed her eyes.

There was a thundering, crashing noise and an impact that rocked her forward in her seat. A piercing, intense stinging in her stomach. The wind was knocked out of her; she couldn't breathe for a moment.

An alarm started ringing. She opened her eyes. The truck had knocked off the metal gate covering the gun shop entrance and crashed through the shop's front windows. Dust and smoke lingered in the air.

Ross threw the car door open and stepped out into the shop. Amber stayed in the car, wincing through the pain. She watched as

Ross ran over to the front counter and jumped over. A large metal locker had been knocked on its side during the crash, the door on the locker partially torn away. Ross pulled and yanked at the door and eventually pried it completely off. He pulled two shotguns out of the locker.

He ran to a glass display case on the other side of the shop. He swung one of the shotguns like a bat and shattered the glass. He reached past shards of broken glass and grabbed a few handguns. He took a plastic bag from behind the counter and threw the guns inside. The alarm continued to wail.

Seated in the car, Amber watched Ross run around the gun shop like a madman, the truck's headlights illuminating the shop interior. She glanced over and saw the keys dangling from the truck's ignition. If she dug deep down, she thought she could find the strength to power past the pain and drag her body over to the driver's seat. She could drive away. Leave Ross behind. End this right now.

It was an unbelievable thought, abandoning Ross—but she didn't know what else to do. This was not going to end well. Whatever came next, it would not be good. Ross was completely out of control. He was going to hurt someone else, probably kill someone. All these guns combined with the way he was acting would only equal disaster.

She was scared of Ross—she couldn't believe it, but she was. That had never happened before. She'd seen him do plenty of crazy things over the years but she'd never reached a point where she was frightened of him. But the way he'd beaten the old man earlier had rattled her; it had been vicious. And now Ross seemed so angry and determined. The look in his eyes was wild, completely out of control.

Outside the car, Ross threw open a drawer behind the counter. He picked up boxes of bullets and shells and threw them to the ground until he found what he was looking for. He tossed a few boxes into the bag with the guns. Grabbed another shotgun and set it inside.

So many guns.

She sat in the truck, thinking about what she should do next, trying to focus her muddled thoughts, as the alarm continued to scream out. It was so loud that she didn't hear the sirens as the police cars pulled up outside.

SHE SAW THE FLASHING RED AND BLUE LIGHTS OUT OF THE CORNER OF her eye. Amber snapped her head toward them.

Two cop cars were parked out front of the gun shop.

The moment she saw them, she knew: it was over. This was going to be the end. They were trapped. Cornered. Nowhere to go.

"Shit!"

Ross screamed the word, staring at the police cruisers out front. He ran across the shop floor to the truck.

"Shit, shit, shit," he said.

He threw the bag of guns on the front seat. Reached inside and pulled out a shotgun. Grabbed a box of shells. Dropped it. Shells spilled onto the truck floor. He cursed and fumbled around on the floor until he found two of the shells. He loaded them into the shotgun.

He aimed the gun toward the store's shattered front window and fired two booming shots out toward the parking lot. She heard yelling from out front but couldn't understand what was being said. Another police cruiser arrived. Three cars out front now.

Ross grabbed one of the handguns and loaded it with bullets, hands shaking, breathing heavy. He set the handgun on the front seat.

"I can take them," he said.

She shook her head weakly.

"I'm serious," Ross said as he loaded the shotgun with more shells. "Take them out and leave."

"N-no—"

"I got this!"

Outside, two more police cruisers arrived, lights flashing. An officer emerged from one and peeked out from behind the open car door. He was baby-faced, looked like a teenager.

She glanced at Ross. His eyes burned with intensity. He fired two blasts from the shotgun. Seemed like he wasn't really aiming at anything, just firing randomly in the direction of the police cars.

He leaned back into the front seat. Grabbed more shells off the floor and reloaded the shotgun.

"Let's give up," she said.

"Surrender?" Ross said. "Fuck that."

"P-please," she said.

She watched him clenching his jaw as he forced more shells into the chamber, breathing heavily. There was no use in trying to convince him to leave. No point in trying to make him stop. His mind was made up.

This was where it would end. Ever since they'd double-crossed Shane, she'd held on to a faint bit of hope that they could have a happy ending. No matter how long the odds or how hopeless things seemed, she believed. But no longer. Ross was just too out of control. There was no way they were getting out of this.

She tried to force out a few words but Ross wasn't paying attention to her. He fired two booming shots from the shotgun, then grabbed the handgun off the front seat and fired more shots out at the police cars. He threw the handgun back onto the front seat. He leaned over the front seat, looking on the floor mat for more of the shotgun shells he'd dropped earlier. The handgun he'd set on the front seat was still there, only a few feet away. She grabbed it and lifted it up. It was a struggle; the gun felt as if it weighed a hundred pounds.

She didn't want any innocent people to die. Didn't want to see anyone else get injured. All she'd wanted was a life with Ross. The Ross she loved. If that wasn't possible, then there was no point.

In the second that passed before she ended his life, she thought of the good times. The happy memories. There'd been a lot of them. The good times before the drugs, back when she toured with Ross and Shane and life was nothing but fun. She remembered how empty she'd felt without him when he was locked up. She remembered those perfect few months in Nebraska after Ross was released. He'd vowed that he was a changed man, and he had been. He'd been free—free of drugs and free of Shane. All she'd wanted was to have that life again. That was it. Just the two of them, together. She'd been so positive that she could save Ross, but she wouldn't even have a chance to try. They would never even reach that point.

Maybe this was for the best. She'd given it a shot. Had they stayed with Shane, it was only a matter of time before Ross's life would've ended, anyway. The drugs would've claimed him, or he and Shane would've continued on a path that would've led only to self-destruction. At least this way, she'd tried to save him. She'd failed—but she'd given it a shot.

Beside her, Ross continued fumbling around on the floor, searching for the shotgun shells.

She loved him. Even more than that, she loved the man she knew he could be. And she owed it to herself—more important, owed it to him—to try to help him become that person. But it just wasn't going to happen. It was over. He wasn't going to go down without a fight, but she wasn't going to let him go down with a fight and harm anyone else. It was time to end it.

"I'm sorry, baby," she whispered.

Her hand trembling, she moved the gun so it was only inches away from the top of his head. She mustered every ounce of strength she had left to clench her fist and pull the trigger. There was a gunshot, loud but still drowned out by the alarm, then an explosion of red that spurted out of his head, splattering onto the truck's dashboard. The recoil of the gunshot sent her arm flailing to the side. Ross's body slumped down to the seat, then fell to the ground outside the truck. He lay there, motionless, blood pouring from the gunshot wound and covering the floor of the gun shop.

TWENTY-SEVEN

AMBER FELT LIKE SHE WAS HAVING AN OUT-OF-BODY EXPERIENCE AS SHE sat in the truck and stared out at the gun shop, her head floating, her mind detached. Nothing seemed real. She didn't seem alive.

Ross was dead. She'd killed him. She couldn't believe it had happened.

In the rearview mirror, she saw more police cars arriving. A few officers crept up to the destroyed shop entrance, their guns drawn. They approached her. Another group of officers walked up to Ross's body on the ground and looked at it.

The officers near her started yelling. She loosened her grip on the gun and it clattered to the floor. She weakly raised her hands in the air.

The next few minutes passed in a blur. Two of the officers lifted her from the front seat and carried her outside the shop. They set her on her back on the concrete. She stared up at the dark night sky as more police cars arrived. The officers leaned over and started talking to her, but she couldn't understand what they were saying. Their lips were moving but she could barely even hear their voices.

The next thing she knew, she was lying in the back of an ambulance. A technician was huddled over her, looking at her stomach wound. Two uniformed police officers stood next to him.

They were talking. First to her. Then to each other. Jumbled words, incoherent phrases.

Then she recognized a word. A name, actually: *Shane*.

One of the officers had spoken his name. The officer was looking down at her. She concentrated on his words. She understood another one: *Joshua*. The kid from the house.

She was slowly able to understand what he was saying. Shane was missing. He had Joshua with him. They were asking her if she knew where they were.

Her mind was a mess, but there was something in there. A thought. An idea. A bit of information.

She tried to speak. A sound like a gurgle came out. The officers looked down at her.

"I-I know."

The officer on her left spoke. "What was that?"

"Shane. I know . . . where he is." At least, she thought she might. And if nothing else, she could help them find him. Do something good. Prevent Shane from causing any more tragedy.

"Where?" the officer asked her.

In a low voice, she forced out a few words and told him.

/////////////

Joshua slowly opened his eyes and blinked a few times to attempt to clear his clouded vision. His head ached. Nose throbbed. Throat was on fire. As his eyesight cleared, he looked at his surroundings. He was in a room. Looked like a cabin or something. The floors were made up of long wooden planks. An unlit fireplace in the corner. A mirror, scuffed with dirt and grime, on one wall. Under that was a small table with a plastic Walmart bag resting on top. There was a single window in the room, closed blinds covering it.

He was seated on the ground in the corner of the room, hands tied behind him, identical to the pose he'd been in all day at the house. There was no chair now, just the cold, hard floor. He pulled against the restraints with what little strength he could muster. The restraints held.

He thought back to the scene at the car dealership. His dad—was he all right? He could only hope the gunshot wasn't serious.

He remembered hardly anything after Shane punched him and knocked him out. He'd drifted awake in the car a few times but had lasted only a few seconds before slipping back to sleep. He had no idea how long Shane had driven, no idea which direction he'd headed in.

Now he was here. Wherever here was.

He heard movement, sounded like it was coming from just outside the only door in the room. He thought about calling out. Decided not to.

Instead, he sat there. Continued pulling against his restraints, trying to break free. He knew it was pointless, but he kept doing it, anyway.

The floor creaked with the sound of heavy footsteps approaching the room. A moment later, Shane appeared in the doorway. His shirt was off—not a pretty sight. Flabby chest, hair everywhere, enormous gut. There was dried blood covering his left arm, a deep maroon. A small bullet hole was ripped in his shoulder.

He looked at Joshua and walked over to the table with the plastic Walmart sack on top. Pulled out a box of Lucky Charms and tore it open. He dug his hand inside and grabbed a handful. Threw them into his mouth. He pulled a Mountain Dew bottle from the bag and took a swig to wash them down.

Joshua watched him eat. Thought about asking a few questions but remained silent.

Shane took a final handful of cereal and threw down the box. It landed on its side and some of the cereal spilled out onto the floor. He looked at the shoulder bullet wound in the mirror and uttered a curse word.

He pulled a cell phone from his pocket. He pounded away at the screen.

"Shit," he grumbled after a while.

He walked over to Joshua and turned the screen toward him.

"Looks like we're famous."

Displayed was an Internet browser showing a news article.

The headline: SHOOT-OUT AT CAR DEALERSHIP, GUNMAN STILL AT LARGE.

Right under the headline was an article with a variety of pictures.

A group of police cars outside the dealership, their lights on.

A picture of the white car Shane had stolen from the dealership. Under the picture was a graphic with the car's license plate.

A mug shot of Shane.

A school picture of Joshua.

Joshua scanned the article and caught two words that stuck with him: *no fatalities.*

The significance of that phrase sank in. No fatalities.

His dad wasn't dead.

Shane put the phone away and walked across the room. Pulled back the blind and stared out the window. It was dark outside. All Joshua could see were bare tree branches and ground covered with dead grass and a light sprinkling of snow.

Looking out the window, he tried to figure out where they were. The frozen ground and trees were the only clue, but they weren't much help. They weren't too far south; that was about all he knew.

They could be anywhere.

///////////////////

Shane stared out the window for a long moment, then turned to Joshua.

"I'm in one hell of a pickle, kid," he said. "No money. Cops after me. My damn picture's on the news. I got two plans right now. Two ways I might get out of this. Plan A and Plan B."

He pulled his phone from his pocket.

"I'm hoping like hell that Plan A works. You should be, too."

He tapped the phone screen a few times. Set it on the table in front of him and put the phone on speaker. He sat down, the chair creaking under his weight, and buried his head in his hands.

The phone rang a few times; then an answer. A thick Southern voice: "Shane?"

"Yo, Smitty."

"I just saw your ugly mug on the Internet. The fuck, man? What's going on?"

"Some shit went down."

"I'll say. A shoot-out. A manhunt. And you got a kid with you? A hostage?"

"Yeah. Like I said, things got a little crazy. Listen, I'm coming back to Saint Louis. Need to stay with you for a few more days while I figure some shit out. Lay low."

"Hell of an ask," the voice said. "But we might be able to work something out. It'll cost you, though."

"Cost me?"

"Yeah. Before you left here, you said you were getting some money from your brother. Money from a bank robbery. Forty grand, you said. Gimme a nice cut of that—say, ten grand or so—and we can work something out. Happy to let you lay low for a bit."

"Turns out he didn't have the cash. The money's gone. The dumbass got it taken by the cops."

"Then I'm not helping. Stay the hell away from me."

Shane clenched his jaw.

"Shit, come on, man. You let me stay with you earlier."

"Your picture wasn't all over the news then. It is now. Big risk, taking you in now. If there was serious money involved, I'd consider it. But if there ain't, you're on your own."

Shane balled his hand into a fist.

"Listen, I'll—"

"Drop it. Don't waste your breath. I'm not letting you stay with me. Want my advice? Turn yourself in. On the run like this, you don't stand a chance."

"Shove your advice up your ass."

A hearty laugh from the other end of the line. "Take it or leave it. Just trying to help you out. Only a matter of time before they find you."

The call ended. Shane banged his fist down on the table a few times.

"Fuck!"

He closed his eyes. Breathed deeply and slowly. He put his phone in his pocket and looked at Joshua.

"So much for that," he said. "Guess it's time for Plan B."

////////////////////

Karen sat in the interrogation room and waited for Franny to return. The wait felt like a year. She prayed that he'd have good news when he came back. She wanted to pace around the room just to do something but didn't think she'd be able to stand up, let alone walk, without falling to the ground.

The more time passed, the more certain she became that there would be no good news. Something had happened to Joshua. He was harmed, injured, something even worse. This winding, nonstop nightmare would finally end in the worst way possible.

Finally, the door opened and Franny walked back into the room.

"What is it?" she asked. "Has something happened?"

He nodded. Told her to calm down. Then slowly relayed everything he'd just learned.

A gun shop had been broken into. Two officers patrolling in the area arrived at the scene and found a truck crashed into the entrance.

It was Mr. Chamberlain's truck. The truck Ross and Amber had stolen.

There'd been a shoot-out that ended with Ross dead and Amber being rushed to the hospital.

"On the way to the hospital, she mentioned something," Franny said. "There was someone Shane was staying with before he showed up to your house. A friend of his. A guy named Smitty. He met up with this guy after he was left behind at the bank robbery."

"Where?"

"Saint Louis. Owns a bar down there, apparently. Amber said Shane mentioned it to them earlier. Said that's where he was hiding. She thinks he might've returned."

"With Joshua?"

"Maybe. We don't know. They wouldn't have had time to make it to Saint Louis yet, but we alerted the local police department, anyway. They did a search and think they found the guy."

He pulled a sheet of paper from his pocket and looked at it.

"Ronald Smith is the name," he said. "Owns a bar down near Saint Louis. Involved in some pretty bad things. Officers are on their way to this guy's house now to ask him a few questions."

She silently stared off. It wasn't bad news, but it wasn't really good news, either. Nothing had changed. They still had no idea where Joshua was or if he was harmed.

"We're hoping Shane has tried contacting this Smitty," he said. "Maybe he knows where they are. Right now, just be cautiously optimistic. It might be nothing, or it might be something. We'll know more soon, once officers have arrived and talked with him."

"How soon?"

"Soon. That's as much as I can tell you now."

TWENTY-EIGHT

SHANE SAT AT A DESK IN THE CORNER OF THE ROOM OPPOSITE JOSHUA.
He frantically scribbled onto a sheet of paper. A few crumpled wads
of paper littered the floor around the desk.

His phone was propped up on the desk, an image displayed. His
eyes went back and forth from the phone to the paper, back to the
phone, as he drew.

Even though he was on the other side of the room, Joshua had
briefly seen what was displayed on the phone screen. It was an image
of a bank lobby. Shane was sketching out a crude drawing of the image onto the sheet of paper, adding in stick figures and a squiggly line
marking a path around the lobby.

He was working out a plan to rob the bank. That much was obvious. But there was plenty else that wasn't obvious.

Joshua struggled against the restraints behind him. Pulled, yanked, contorted his arms. Nothing. Shane glanced over at him and smirked.

"Don't even try getting free, kid," he said. He spoke quickly. "You ain't exactly the first person I've tied up. You break free from that, you deserve a damn medal."

Shane returned to scribbling on the piece of paper. Earlier, he'd grabbed a baggie full of pills from his pants pocket and popped a few. He'd been moving quicker since then. Had a frantic, desperate look in his eyes.

"What . . . what's going to happen?" Joshua asked.

Shane turned from the desk and looked at him.

"I'm working on a plan over here," Shane said. "See what I'm drawing?"

"I think so."

"What is it?"

"A bank."

"Yep. A bank. Gonna rob it. You and me both, actually. Your role'll be a hell of a lot easier than mine, though."

"What do you mean?"

Shane smirked at him. He gave a brief, mad chuckle.

"No reason I can't tell you," he said. He grabbed another sheet of paper off the desk. "Let's say the bank I want to rob is right here."

He made an *X* on the right side of the paper.

"And then, let's say your dead body is found all the way over here."

He made an *X* on the left side of the paper.

"Now, if that happens, where do you think every single cop in the area is gonna be?" He tapped the left side of the paper. "Over here. At the body of the kid who was missing. A long-ass ways away from the bank. Which means I'll have time to grab a lot of money and get the hell out of Dodge before the cops even know what happened."

Shane crumpled up the sheet of paper and threw it on the floor.

"You're a distraction, kid. That's your role. And I have a feeling you'll be damn good at it."

Shane chuckled again. He turned back around and continued sketching on the sheet of paper.

///////////////

Franny had been in the room for only a moment when the mustached officer from earlier appeared at the door again. Same drill as before. Franny left the room to talk with him, leaving Karen alone.

She sat and waited. She just wanted to hear something. An update. Just wanted to know what was going on.

There was a small window in the door, and she could see people running by out in the hallway. A commotion outside. Something was going on.

Franny reentered the room.

"Okay," he said. "Officers in Saint Louis went to the house of Ronald Smith. Sure enough, he was the Smitty we're looking for. He denied everything at first, but they had leverage on him and he spilled the beans. He said he'd just spoken with Shane. Claims that Shane wanted to come down. He said no. And he says that was the extent of their conversation."

"Did he say anything about Joshua?"

"No. Nothing."

She felt like she'd been kicked in the gut.

"We got Shane's phone number and contacted the cell phone

provider," Franny said. "They traced the cell towers the call was placed through and were able to narrow down an area close to here. A campsite about twenty miles outside of town. Not used in the winter. We've got people on their way there right now. The call was placed fifteen, twenty minutes ago. So they could've left since then. We'll know soon."

"What if they're there?" Karen asked. "What will happen?"

"Saving Joshua, that's our priority. We won't put him in danger. We'll do whatever it takes to bring him home safe."

Karen leaned forward in her chair. They needed a miracle. She knew they probably didn't deserve one, not with the awful things that had happened to bring them to this point. But she prayed for a miracle nonetheless, prayed that a miracle would occur and this would have a happy ending.

///////////////

Shane put his T-shirt back on, cursing as he worked his injured shoulder through the armhole. The front of the shirt was splotched with dried blood. He threw on his black sweatshirt over it, then crumpled up the bank drawing and put it in his pants pocket.

"It's showtime."

He walked over to Joshua and bent down. He hooked his good arm under Joshua's armpit and lifted him off the ground like he weighed nothing. They walked across the room, Joshua with his arms still bound behind him.

"My mom will pay you," he said. "Just call her."

"I'm through with that," Shane said from behind him. "I'm sticking to what I know. Getting cash the hard, old-fashioned way."

Joshua walked up to the front door. The wood around the door handle was splintered, a large chunk of it resting on the floor. Like the door had been kicked in. Outside, there were trees everywhere. Some sort of wooded area. Even though it was dark, Joshua could see a few buildings that looked identical to the one they'd just left. Small log cabins. The place was some sort of campground. Empty, probably closed for the winter.

Parked right next to the cabin was the white car Shane had taken from the dealership. He set Joshua down in the front seat.

"Just sit there," he said. "Don't move. Don't try to be a hero, okay?"

Shane slammed the passenger door shut and walked around the car. He sat down in the driver's seat and started driving away. They passed through a wooded area that looked similar to Hawkeye Wildlife Management Area, where everything had begun. Maybe there was something fitting in that. The whole thing coming full circle.

They drove down a few worn paths. After five minutes, they reached a darkened sign that read CAMP GREGORY. Next to it was a large cabin with REGISTER HERE written on an arrow sign pointing toward the cabin entrance. Past the sign was a highway. Shane drove up to the highway and came to a stop. Just as he turned onto the highway, a police cruiser appeared over the crest of the hill, half a mile away.

THE POLICE CAR'S FLASHING LIGHTS WEREN'T ON AND IT WAS DARK, BUT there was no mistaking what the car was.

Shane saw it first. He screamed a few curse words. He floored the accelerator and turned onto the highway, but the midsize sedan was no match for the police cruiser. The cruiser caught up with them in less than a minute. Once it was a couple of hundred feet behind them, the flashing lights came on.

Shane kept the accelerator floored. Their speed kept increasing, up to eighty miles an hour. The police cruiser stayed directly behind them, lights flashing. Past it, Joshua could see a second car, a couple of miles back, heading in their direction.

Shane was panting. Cursing. He scanned the road, looking for something, but Joshua didn't know what he could be looking for. There was nothing out here. Just a flat, straight highway with flat, straight land on either side. Some trees, that was about it.

The police cruiser remained behind them, following at a steady pace, not losing or gaining ground. The second police cruiser had reached them and was right behind the first one. Their car and the two cruisers were in a straight row.

"Christ!" Shane yelled. "Dammit!"

Joshua sat in the passenger seat. With his arms bound behind him, he felt so helpless. Exposed. Shane's foot was still pressed down on the accelerator. They were going so fast that the car dashboard and body had started to shake. They were—

Shane took his foot off the accelerator and slammed it down on the brake. The tires squealed. The car fishtailed. Joshua rocked forward in his seat, his chest hitting the dashboard. The police cruiser behind them swerved to avoid their car but clipped the rear left side of their bumper. The police cruiser veered onto the highway shoulder, tires squealing, then sharply turned back onto the highway, where it slammed into the second cruiser. Both cars swerved onto the highway shoulder and crashed into the highway ditch, next to each other. The fronts of both cars crumpled with the impact. One of the cruisers flipped onto its side and skidded to a stop. Steam started rising from the car hoods.

Shane screamed. "Ha! Hell yes!"

The rocking and swaying of the car had tossed Joshua around in his seat; it had been impossible to hold on to anything or brace himself. He was sitting sideways in his seat now, shoulder resting against the dashboard, hands still behind him. One of his feet was down near the floor. The other was sprawled out from his body, on top of the center console between him and Shane.

Shane had a crazed smile on his face, was practically shaking with excitement from the car chase. They left the scene, the police cruisers crashed on the side of the road disappearing as they drove away from them. Up ahead was a turnoff for a road that ran perpendicular to the highway. Shane slowed to take the turnoff.

Joshua looked at his foot, resting on the center console, just a few inches from the steering wheel.

The car approached the turn. To the side of the intersection was a small drop-off to lower ground, around twenty feet.

Shane turned the wheel to the right to take the turn.

This was it, Joshua decided. His chance. He had to take it. If he didn't do anything, there'd be nothing to do but wait for this to end. Whenever that would come, however that would be, this wasn't going to end well. There was no doubt about that.

He had to take a chance. Had to take matters into his own hands.

He kicked his foot out and hit the steering wheel. The car sharply veered as they took the turn. They weren't going nearly as fast as they'd been going on the interstate during the chase, but they were still going fast. Thirty miles an hour, probably. Shane tried to correct the wheel before the car fell down the drop-off beside the road, but he was too late.

The car tumbled down and slammed into the ground. It flipped onto its roof.

Either the car didn't have airbags or they were faulty, because they didn't inflate.

Joshua fell against the windshield.

Shane's face smashed against the steering wheel.

The car rolled onto its side, fell back on its wheels, and skidded to a stop.

EVERYTHING HAD HAPPENED SO QUICKLY, IT TOOK A MOMENT FOR IT ALL to register. Joshua felt a shooting pain in his arm. He smelled something—gas? The car headlights were still on, shining out onto the flatland surrounding them.

Shane was beside him. Slumped in his seat. Eyes closed. Head lolled to the side. Blood pouring from his nose, down into his beard.

Joshua tried to move his legs. Couldn't. They were wedged under the dashboard at an awkward angle. He shifted his body in his seat, wincing at the pain in his arm. He gritted his teeth and leaned forward. Moved his body so his back was to the car door. He felt around behind him and ran his hands along the door until he found the handle. Pulled on it. The door opened and he tumbled outside. He landed on his back, and the pain in his arm roared to life again.

He tried to stand up but it was impossible with his hands behind his back. Instead, he rolled away from the car, wincing every time he rolled onto his injured arm. He stopped after a few seconds; he was making himself dizzy.

He heard a noise and glanced over at the car. Shane was conscious. He opened the door and stepped outside. Blood kept pouring from his nose down into his beard.

He tried to walk, stumbled. Fell to the ground.

He glanced over. Saw Joshua. Their eyes locked.

"You bastard," he said.

SHANE REACHED INTO HIS HOODIE POCKET. HIS HAND EMERGED HOLDING the gun. He kept his eyes on Joshua and smiled. One of his front teeth had been knocked out and his mouth was covered in blood.

He stood up shakily and took a step toward Joshua. Fell down again. Stood up again and lumbered over. Joshua tried to roll away, but he just couldn't move fast enough to escape.

"Kid . . ." Shane said. "You damn fool."

He took another step. Fifteen feet away. Joshua kept rolling away, but everything was spinning. The pain in his arm was screaming.

Shane took a few more lumbering steps. He fell to the ground. Dropped the gun. Felt around on the darkened ground until he found it.

He stood up and continued to approach, stumbling and swaying but remaining on his feet. When he finally reached Joshua, Shane stuck his leg out to stop him from rolling any farther. Shane was right on top of him. Just a foot or two away. Everything was spinning. In the distance, about a mile away, he saw the flashing red and blue lights from the police cruisers, crashed on the side of the road, immobile.

Shane raised the gun. Joshua kicked out. His foot connected with Shane's leg but Shane didn't even flinch. Joshua yelled for help, screamed as loudly as he could. It was his only defense; it was useless.

Shane opened his mouth, like he was going to say something, final words before the kill. Blood dripped out of his mouth from the gap where his front tooth had been.

Shane's hand holding the gun was shaking. He pointed it at Joshua, right at his chest. Point-blank range.

Joshua closed his eyes.

Braced himself.

And heard the loud explosion of a gunshot.

SUNDAY

TWENTY-NINE

KAREN OPENED HER EYES. STARED UP AT THE CEILING. FOR A MOMENT, she was positive that yesterday had been a nightmare. It hadn't happened. But the thought passed instantly. Of course it had been real. That's why she was here in the hospital and not at home, in her bed.

She still couldn't believe how close everything had been. Last night, she'd gotten the entire story of what had happened. Officers had arrived at the campsite they'd traced Shane's phone to just as Shane and Joshua were leaving. A minute later, and they would've missed them. There was a car chase, the officers crashed, and Joshua had caused Shane's car to flip before they could get away. Shane had chased Joshua down and was about to shoot him . . . and then an officer from one of the crashed cars had arrived. He'd sprinted more than a mile after he saw their car go off the side of the road. The officer started firing just as Shane was about to shoot Joshua. He didn't stop firing until Shane was dead.

Joshua had been taken to Mercy Hospital. He had a concussion and a dislocated shoulder . . . but he was alive. They'd gotten the miracle she'd hoped for.

One second, one mistake, and the ending could have been far different. Had the police arrived a few minutes later, had the car crashed at a different angle, had the officer's aim been slightly off . . . things would have been far, far different.

After arriving at the hospital, she'd kissed Joshua. Hugged him like she'd never hugged him before. He'd undergone tests to determine what injuries he'd suffered in the crash, and she'd waited for him. By the time everything ended, it was nearly four in the morning. The doctor who treated him decided to keep Joshua overnight as a precaution. A nurse let Karen into a patient room that wasn't in use and she slept at the hospital. Not that she'd had much of a choice. Their house was still a crime scene. At least, it had been last night. Her bed was still soaked in Amber's blood.

"You're awake already, I see."

She looked up. One of the floor nurses she'd spoken to briefly last night was standing at the edge of the room.

"Yeah," Karen said. "I'm awake. Not sure how alert I am, though."

She glanced at a bedside clock. Six thirty a.m. Only a few hours had passed since everything ended.

"You have visitors here," the nurse said. "Wanted to see if you're up for guests."

The nurse gave her some names. Karen recognized them all. Her coworkers.

"Send them in," she said.

The nurse smiled and disappeared. A moment later, a group of her coworkers entered the room. Ten of them in all. Carmella was with them—Karen hadn't seen her since the breakout at the hospital.

There was barely enough space for all of them in the patient room. Some sat down on the edge of the bed; most remained standing. They all walked over and hugged her.

"How'd you know I was here?" she asked.

"Word travels quickly around the hospital," her coworker Dan said. "We heard what happened. At least, parts of it."

"Like what?"

"Three people took you and Joshua hostage. The woman being broken out of the hospital, that was you who did that. There was a shoot-out at a car dealership. A car crash. Two people are dead—two of the people who took you hostage."

"Yeah. That's the story. Some of it, at least."

"How's Joshua?"

"Concussion, separated shoulder," Karen said. "He won't be swinging a golf club for a while. Not that that really matters."

"What can we do? Anything?"

She shook her head. "Not really. I'm still in shock, to be honest."

"We've all been calling your phone."

"My phone is . . ." What had happened to her phone? She remembered when she returned from the hospital, Ross had taken it from her. She had no idea what he'd done with it. "My phone's gone. Can't imagine how many messages I have."

They talked some more. Every few seconds, she'd hear the same phrases: *So sorry . . . We're here for you. . . . Everything will be fine. . . .*

She did her best to answer their questions and hold up her end of the discussion, but she felt so gloomy. Considering the circumstances, things could have ended far worse than they had. That was little consolation, though. She'd meant what she said earlier; she really felt like she was in shock from it all. But as down as she felt, it was good to see her coworkers. Good to be around them. It was nice to have the support.

"We should get going," Dan said after a few minutes. "We just wanted to stop by. Tell you we're here for you. We'll talk later, once things have died down."

They each hugged her on the way out. After everyone else left her room, Carmella stayed behind.

"Hey," she said to Karen.

"Hey."

"I'm glad things are fine. I'm probably the five millionth person to tell you that, but it's true."

"Thanks."

"I keep wondering if there was something I should've done," she said. "When you came to me. I didn't mention you to the police when I spoke to them after the breakout, and I keep thinking things would be different if I'd said something to them."

"No. You did what I told you. I thought it was the right thing to do. Maybe it was. Maybe it wasn't. In the end, I guess everything worked out."

"I finally came clean this morning. A police detective called me and wanted to get my story again. And I told him everything this time. I told him I lied earlier, and that you forced me to help you break the woman out. I gave the detective the truth. I couldn't keep lying."

"That's fine. You're not in trouble, are you?"

"I don't think so. I'm supposed to talk to some hospital administrators later on."

"I'll tell them the story. Tell them I forced you to help me."

"Don't worry about it," Carmella said. "At least, not now. You have more important things to focus on."

KAREN STOPPED BY JOSHUA'S ROOM. HE WAS SLEEPING, SO SHE WENT down a floor and visited Teddy. She hadn't forgotten about him, even with everything that had happened. She'd briefly spoken with him last night after she talked with Joshua. The surgery to stitch up the bullet wound in his leg had gone well. There was some muscle damage but nothing serious.

The door to Teddy's room was open, and she walked in. He lay in the patient bed, head turned to the side, staring out the window, his blond hair a little disheveled.

"Feeling better?" she asked.

He looked over at her. A brief smile. "Yeah. Don't think I could feel worse than last night if I tried."

She sat down in a chair at his bedside.

"Joshua?" Teddy asked.

"Still sleeping. Unless something changes, we'll go home later."

"Sounds like they're kicking me out, too."

They sat in silence for a long time, both of them staring off and avoiding eye contact. Just sitting there, a million unspoken words between them.

"So, what happens next?" Teddy eventually said.

"I still have to talk with the police. Give them my full statement. That's supposed to happen today."

"You haven't talked with them yet?"

"I did earlier. When Joshua was missing. I told them everything

I could about Shane. But I didn't tell them about the accident. The hit-and-run that started this all. We were so focused on finding Joshua that there wasn't time to tell them everything. And then last night, it was nearly four in the morning by the time they brought Joshua in and finished with him. By then, the detective was gone. He said he'd get my statement tomorrow. Today."

"Guess it's time to come clean, then," Teddy said. "Admit everything. Do what we should have from the start. Tell the police everything. We don't really have a choice."

"We might."

"How so?"

"Earlier, I was thinking. I was thinking about the body."

In fact, she'd been thinking about it constantly. That had been the main reason she'd gotten hardly any sleep last night: she was thinking about the body. Now that everything had slowed down, she'd had time to truly consider their situation and the events that had led them here. The accident. The body. And now, the punishment.

If she told the police about the dead body and the cover-up, Joshua would be looking at jail time. She didn't see any way he would avoid it. He was eighteen. In the eyes of the law, he was an adult. Some people might have compassion because of everything they'd been through, but the facts were the facts: he'd killed someone and left the scene without reporting it.

She couldn't even imagine how crushing it would be, if Joshua was locked up in jail. After all they'd been through, not just over the past few days but over the past eighteen years, she didn't think she could handle him being taken away from her.

She recalled what Teddy had said earlier. If they told the police everything and Joshua was convicted of manslaughter or a similar crime, he could be looking at years in jail, maybe many years. Locked up in jail instead of graduating high school or starting college. Still locked away as his friends finished college and moved away to different cities, maybe started families of their own. The conviction would be on his record forever, following him around for the rest of his life. Eighteen years old, and his life could be ruined.

"The body, it's still out there in the forest," Karen said to Teddy. "No one's found it yet."

"I know. I've been looking at the news. There's been no mention of it."

"We might not have to tell the police about it."

"What do you mean?"

"I think you know exactly what I mean. I know this is a person's life. I know it's terrible and wrong to even think about not telling the police what happened. But I just can't get it out of my head, Joshua going to jail. His life being ruined."

She shook her head. "I just don't know."

But she did know. She'd already thought about it last night. Thought about it endlessly. And no matter which angle she looked at it from, there was just no way she could convince herself that telling the police about the body was the right thing to do. She couldn't turn Joshua in.

That was her decision. There'd been so many paths and choices that led to this point, and now this was the final decision to make. She couldn't believe she was even considering such a thing, but she was. Actually, no, she wasn't considering it—her mind was made up.

"I'm not going to say anything to the police," she said. Teddy stared at her. Not much of a reaction on his face. It was like he expected her to say exactly that.

"You're sure you want to do this?" he asked.

"No," she said. "I'm not sure about anything. But this is my decision."

She stood up from her chair.

"I have to go," she said. "The police will be back soon to talk with Joshua and me. I want to make sure our stories are straight. Just wanted to come here and let you know what I decided."

She walked toward the door.

"Karen?" Teddy said.

She turned back to him.

"I'm sorry," he said. "This whole thing, it's all my fault. But I did it for Joshua. You have to believe me."

She believed him, but it was impossible not to feel some anger toward Teddy. The feeling wasn't much, though. Here she was, faced with the same situation, and making the same decision. Covering up what had happened to protect Joshua.

There was plenty she wanted to say to Teddy, but it would have to remain unspoken for now. Too much else to focus on.

THIRTY

KAREN GLANCED AT A CLOCK AS SHE WALKED BACK THROUGH THE HOS-pital. Almost seven a.m. Franny would be returning to the hospital soon. Stop by Joshua's room, get their stories straight; then there was one more thing she needed to do before the police returned.

In his room, Joshua was still sleeping. Shoulder bandaged up. A few bruises on his face. There were specks of dirt in his blond hair. Maybe it was blood. She leaned over his bed and shook his arm. His eyes fluttered open.

"Hey, you," she said.

"Hey, Mom."

"Feeling okay? How's your head?"

He shrugged. "Better. I guess."

"I need to talk with you," she said.

She looked over her shoulder, out at the hallway. Just to be safe. It was empty.

"I still haven't given my statement to the police, but they'll be talking to me soon," she said. "You, too. I want to talk about what we're going to say to them."

"What do you mean?"

"The accident. The dead body. I was talking with your father. We're not going to mention what happened in the forest to the police. It just . . . it seems too risky. I don't want this to end with you going to jail. I can't stand that thought. But I want to leave it up to you. The decision is yours. If you'd rather come clean and tell them everything, we will."

Joshua shook his head. He turned away from her. His lip started quivering. He turned and buried his head in his shoulder, the one that hadn't been dislocated. His eyes became watery.

"Don't do that," she said, reaching over and stroking his hair. But maybe it was for the best. Just let it all out. Cry it away.

Joshua wiped his eyes and turned to her.

"Do you really think it's the right thing to do? Not tell them?"

"No. It's not right. Definitely not. But it's what I think we should do."

Joshua sniffled. "Okay."

"We'll begin our story the night we were ambushed, out in the woods. Like nothing happened before that. We'll say we were out looking at the stars. Ross and Amber confronted us, a fight broke out, and Amber was shot. Just like what happened. He forced me to take Amber to the hospital by holding you at gunpoint. Told me if I said anything about him, he'd hurt you. Sound good to you?"

Joshua nodded.

"Okay. That's our story. We'll stick to that."

"The clothes I wore on the night of the accident," he said. "They're still at the house. Under the deck. They're all bloody."

"Why are they there?"

"When I got home that night, there wasn't time to get rid of them," he said. "I pulled back that loose board and threw them under the deck. Figured I'd do something about them later."

Karen stood up from her chair.

"I'll grab them from the house, get rid of them," she said. "Then there's one final thing to do."

She leaned over, kissed Joshua on the top of his head, and left the room.

SHE HURRIED THROUGH THE HOSPITAL, OUT TO HER CAR IN THE PARKING garage. Left the hospital and drove away. She stared out the windshield, solemn-faced, as she drove through the city. A mixture of nerves and dread in her stomach. The smell of blood in the car's backseat had only gotten stronger overnight.

Her first stop was their house. She parked out front and walked around the back. Pulled the loose board on the side of the deck and there it was: a plastic garbage bag. She grabbed it and opened it up. A charred, burned smell rose from inside. She could see a pair of pants, what looked like two deformed shoes. And the coat. The coat she'd bought Joshua for Christmas.

She carried the bag out to the car and pulled away. She drove on the interstate, turned onto a few gravel roads, and eventually reached Hawkeye Wildlife Management Area.

Trees everywhere. The sheet of paper she'd printed off showing

Joshua's cell phone location was still in her car cup holder. She referenced it as she drove on.

She did her best to avoid thinking about what she was preparing to do. Tried to clear her mind and remain calm—but that was impossible. She drove on, deeper and deeper into the forest. The morning sun was rising in the distance; it was actually a pleasant sight. The forest wasn't nearly as creepy as it had been in the middle of the night, when darkness surrounded her.

As she drove, she thought about backing out. Reconsidering. She knew this was wrong, but she kept driving, her car bumping and jostling on the uneven road.

She looked at the sheet of paper.

Getting close.

More driving.

Closer.

A few more minutes of driving and she arrived. The body was right there, on the edge of the road. A huddled mass. Black coat. Dark pants.

She slowed her car and pulled just past the body, so it was near her trunk. She stayed in her car and stared out the windshield, her expression blank, all business. She had to do something about the body. It was the final loose end. Right now, the police didn't even know the body was there, but once Amber was healthy enough to give her statement, she'd surely mention the dead body that was out in the forest when she and Ross had encountered Karen and Joshua the first time. After the police came and found the body, there was no telling what would happen. They'd have questions for Joshua and her. What had happened? How had the person died? Why was the body out in the middle of nowhere? Maybe they'd even find something on the body linking it to Joshua—his DNA or some sort of trace evidence that had gotten on it during the scuffle after the accident. A million things could potentially go wrong once the police found the body.

No, if she wanted to end this for good, she had to get rid of the body.

She gave herself a final chance to turn around and drive back. Instead, she opened the car door. Stepped outside. Took a deep breath. She popped the trunk with the button on her key fob and walked around to the rear of the car.

The body was faceup in the same location it had been in the first time she'd seen it. It hadn't started to smell much, just a musty odor like wet sneakers: a scent of rot and decay. The smell wasn't overpowering, but it was enough to make her gag.

She stared down at the man's ghost white face. Open mouth. Unblinking eyes. A large gash on the side of his head, near his temple. Blood covering his face, splattered onto his coat.

She still had no idea who this man was or what he'd been doing all the way out there. Seemed like an odd place to go for a stroll, but that was about the only explanation she could come up with.

She doubted they would ever know.

She took a few steps and stood directly over the body. She clenched her jaw, braced herself, then leaned down and grabbed the arms. She dragged the body over to her open trunk. She clenched her jaw even harder, ground her teeth together, and bent over. She closed her eyes as she worked her arms around the body—she couldn't handle such an up-close view of the dead man's face. She picked up the body and tried to hoist it into her open trunk, but the body kept slipping out of her hands. It was heavy—even worse, it was awkward. Hard to get a good grip.

After a few failed attempts, she was able to work her arms around the back of the body and get the torso into the trunk. Then the legs. The head. The arms.

She slammed the trunk shut and walked around to the driver's seat. She sat down and exhaled so deeply she thought she would pull a muscle in her back. A few more deep breaths. She nearly started crying.

After she'd calmed herself, she pulled back onto the road and drove away.

THIRTY-ONE

AMBER LAY IN BED. STARED AT THE CEILING. SHE WAS IN A HOSPITAL ROOM that looked nearly identical to the one she'd been in after she was shot.

She had no idea how long she'd been here. She could recall only bits and pieces of everything that had happened since she'd arrived. Her clearest memory was of meeting with a doctor after her surgery. He'd told her she was lucky to be alive.

She didn't feel lucky. Didn't really feel alive, either. Whatever medication she was on made her feel dazed and tired. Like she was in a dreamworld. She vaguely recalled speaking to a police detective at some point. He'd asked her a number of questions but she couldn't remember what he'd asked or whether she'd actually been able to form responses. She was just too tired to remember much of anything.

In a way, her grogginess was a positive: she was so exhausted that nothing that happened yesterday truly seemed real. Ross was dead. She'd shot him. She remembered that much, but it just wouldn't register that he was gone. Everything would sink in at some point, she figured. Just not now. Once the drugs wore off, she'd probably be able to recall with total clarity everything that had happened, and the full weight of it all would come crashing down on her. After that happened, maybe she'd be able to numb the pain. Convince herself that the man she'd killed wasn't the real Ross, the Ross she loved. That he was someone different. Someone who was out of control. The way he was acting, it was inevitable that he would get himself killed. She'd only prevented him from hurting anyone else on the way out.

Not only was Ross gone, but her life was over, too, she knew. There'd be no happy ending for her. Ross was dead and she was looking at years in jail for the bank robbery. No way she was getting out of that. If she was convicted of murdering Ross on top of the robbery, she might spend the rest of her life behind bars, though she figured a jury might view it as self-defense.

There was a pinprick of pain in her stomach. Not too intense, but even through the haze of the medication, she felt it. She winced. Closed her eyes. Tried to ignore the pain. An image suddenly came to her. The face of the woman involved in all this. Karen. And her son. Couldn't remember his name right now. Amber wondered what had happened to them. Wondered if they were safe. Wondered if they'd survived. She hoped so.

If nothing else, she hoped that at least someone would have a happy ending.

//////////////

Karen drove out of Hawkeye Wildlife Management Area. Back onto the gravel roads. It'd be faster to get to her destination via the highway, but she wanted to avoid any and all major roads. Something bad could happen on a major road. A distracted driver, an accident, the police arriving to look at the damage and wondering about the smell coming from the trunk.

She drove on, tires crunching over gravel and kicking up rocks. She occasionally encountered a truck heading in the opposite direction but she was mostly by herself. She constantly looked back at the car trunk in the rearview mirror. A dead body was back there. A dead body she was about to dispose of. It was all so unbelievable.

Driving on the gravel roads was slow going, but after what felt like an hour, she arrived at an area that was perfect for what she needed to do. She parked on the side of the road. All around her was farmland. No cars, no houses. Cedar Rapids was just visible in the distance, ten miles away at least. Just a few feet off the road was the Cedar River, the biggest river in the area. Even with the cold temperatures, it wasn't frozen over. Just a few chunks of ice floating in it.

Isolated and right next to the river—the spot was ideal. She grabbed the bag of clothes and walked over to the grassy marsh beside the river. This close, she could hear the noises of the river, the flowing, the movement. She threw Joshua's clothes, one by one, into the river, then wadded the garbage bag into a ball and threw it in. She watched the current carry everything away. There was no telling how far they'd go. The river eventually met up with the Iowa River, then the Mississippi River. From there, they could end up anywhere.

She walked back to her car and stood outside the trunk. She scanned the area around her, looked back and forth. Nothing. Still no one and nothing nearby.

It was time.

Her heart was hammering. She hit a button on her key fob and the trunk popped open a few inches. She opened it all the way and was hit with a musty smell that was a little more intense than it had been earlier. She turned her head to the side and held her breath as she reached into the trunk. She wrapped her arms around the body and lifted it out. Flopped it onto the ground.

A final quick look around. Nothing. No one.

She grabbed the body's arms and dragged it off the road. Down into the roadside ditch. Across a few feet of land that separated the road from the river. There was no time to waste. She felt as though she should say something, some final apology, but she remained silent. It seemed so cold and heartless, what she was about to do, but she just didn't have a choice. She just couldn't leave the body in the forest, just waiting to be discovered, like a ticking clock, counting down.

She bent down and shoved the body out into the water. The river was shallow at the edges and the current wasn't strong. The body just stayed there, barely submerged in water. She took off her shoes and socks and walked out into the river, submerging her feet in the icy-cold water, and pushed the body toward the center of the river.

Eventually, the current picked up the body and it started floating away, down the river, away from her.

THIRTY-TWO

KAREN RETURNED TO THE HOSPITAL. THE NEXT FEW HOURS WERE A BLUR.
She talked with Franny. Told him her story, from the start.

She and Joshua had been out looking at stars.

They encountered Ross and Amber.

Ross had accidentally shot Amber and had forced Karen to take
her to the hospital, threatening to harm Joshua if she mentioned him,
then forced her to break Amber out of the hospital.

Then Shane showed up and things got out of control.

Franny had asked her questions. She'd answered them. From what
she could tell, he believed her. At least, she thought he did. She thought
he believed Joshua, too. As Franny talked to him she'd waited outside
his hospital room, holding her breath, hoping that this was almost
over and there'd be no more surprises. When Franny opened the door
to Joshua's room and told her he was leaving, she felt such a sense of
relief that it nearly knocked her to the ground. It felt wrong to be

relieved, like she didn't deserve to feel anything positive right now, not after so much horror had occurred. But she couldn't help it.

Once Franny was gone, she felt exhausted all of a sudden, so tired she could barely keep her eyes open. It was all finally catching up with her. She'd felt worn-out at times over the weekend, but that was nothing like the total exhaustion she felt now. Before, there'd always been her adrenaline to combat the sleepiness and keep her alert. But now, it was as though her body knew that it was all over and there was nothing left to keep her going.

She felt like she could sleep for days.

KAREN HESITATED FOR JUST A MOMENT AS SHE TURNED HER HOUSE KEY and pushed open the front door. She knew she was being paranoid, but she had a brief, momentary feeling that someone was waiting on the other side, just waiting for an opportunity to snag her and Joshua, whisk them away, and begin everything all over again.

But there was no one behind the door. Just silence. The living room looked as it always had. There was no indication that anything out of the ordinary had recently happened.

She waved out to the police cruiser in which she and Joshua had been driven home from the hospital. The officer behind the wheel waved back and reversed down the driveway. He drove away on the road out front.

Finally, she let herself breathe.

She kicked off her shoes. Joshua did the same. She turned and looked at him. His arm was in a sling and his eyes were half-open. He looked so weary.

"Doing all right?" she asked him. A foolish question, but she felt like she should say something. It was the first question that came to mind.

"I think I'm going to lie down," Joshua said.

"Yeah," she said. "I almost dozed off a couple times on the drive home."

Joshua walked across the living room and over to the hallway. It felt like something more meaningful should happen after all they'd been through, like they should sit down with each other. Discuss their feelings. Talk about everything that had occurred. But she didn't think she'd be able to string together more than a few coherent sentences. Her mind was like a computer that had overheated—the only way to continue on was to rest and reboot.

Before Joshua disappeared into his room, she called out to him.

"Hey," she said.

He turned to her.

"Wait a sec," she said. "Come here."

He walked back over to her. She reached out and hugged him. There was so much to say, but she didn't have the energy to say any of it. She'd hugged him at the police station and the hospital, but this hug seemed as though it had more significance than those had. Like now that it was just the two of them and they were safely back home, everything truly was over.

She held him in her embrace. She felt one of his arms close around her back and squeeze tight. When she finally let go, she saw that he had tears in his eyes.

"Thanks," he said.

He walked away from her. She watched him disappear down the hall. A moment later she heard the door to his room close.

She stayed in the living room for a moment after he'd gone, then walked to her bedroom. If she listened closely, she felt like she'd be able to hear the echoes of Shane's footsteps thundering down the hallway.

She stopped outside her room. Paused for a moment and opened the door.

The cleaners were finished, she noticed. Franny had given her the number of a professional service to clean and disinfect her house once the police were done with the crime scene, and she'd called them from the hospital. They'd come to the hospital to get a key from her and told her they'd start on the house immediately.

The room had a faint smell of disinfectant. The carpet had been scrubbed clean—somewhat clean, at least. Splotches and stains were still visible. The bloody bedsheets had been taken by the police as evidence, but the mattress was left behind; it was stained with dried blood. She'd have to throw it out, get a new one.

She didn't know how she would ever be able to sleep in this room. Would this room ever feel like her bedroom again, or would it simply serve as a reminder of everything that had happened?

It wasn't just her bedroom, either—would she ever be able to look at the house in the same way again? She doubted it. There was something sad about that. The house where she'd lived for nearly all her life might never feel like home again.

It seemed like such a small thing, like something totally irrelevant in light of everything that had happened. And it was—there was so much else to be sad about—but it still left her feeling disappointed.

She shook her head. She'd have plenty of time to think about things like this later on, tomorrow, for the rest of the week, for the rest of her life, even. But not now.

She walked out to the living room and found a nice warm blanket in the closet. She lay down on the couch.

And she fell asleep instantly.

THE
NEXT WEEK

THE
NEXT WEEK

THIRTY-THREE

ON MONDAY, THE STORY WAS COVERED CONSTANTLY ON LOCAL NEWS broadcasts and in the papers. Karen watched all the reports, read all the articles. The full story that eventually came out was that a bank robbery had happened in Nebraska. Amber and Ross had ditched Shane after the robbery. Their car had died outside of Cedar Rapids. They'd found Karen in the forest and tried to steal her car. Amber had been shot during the scuffle. Ross forced Karen to drive Amber to the hospital. Took Joshua as a prisoner to ensure she didn't go to the police, then forced Karen to break Amber out. The shoot-out at the car dealership happened after Shane tracked them down and tried to get money from Teddy before leaving.

As with any good lie, some parts of the story were true, and some weren't.

It felt weird, giving interviews and telling her sanitized version of the story as if it were the truth, as if she had nothing to hide. Felt even weirder seeing the published articles, reading them and knowing there was so much more that wasn't being told.

She did her best to keep the details to a bare minimum during interviews. She was worried that she might let something slip that would contradict the official narrative. Say something that would start a chain reaction that would end with the police getting suspicious that she was hiding something.

That was, if they weren't already suspicious. As far as she knew, the investigation was ongoing. Franny had called her earlier, told her that Amber had mentioned that a dead body was already in the forest when she and Ross had arrived. When he'd gone to the forest to search, he hadn't found anything.

Karen said she had no idea what Amber was talking about. Franny told her he figured she was making it up, probably trying to complicate the investigation and confuse them, maybe even avoid punishment.

TUESDAY AFTERNOON, A FEW OF KAREN'S COWORKERS VISITED. SHE'D politely turned away most people who stopped by the house to chat—she didn't feel like talking or repeating her lies—but she decided to let her coworkers in. She missed them. She wanted to talk with them. Wanted to be around them. They'd briefly seen each other at the hospital, but the interaction had been so rushed.

There were hugs, greetings, relieved smiles. And of course questions. Her nurse manager told her to take off as much time as she needed, but she told him she'd be back to work for her Friday shift. She honestly thought about going back sooner. It would offer a distraction. Give her something to do. Already, even after just a day, she'd grown tired of being boxed up in the house. The memory of what had happened in there was still too fresh. By Friday, she figured the story would be old(er) news and there wouldn't be as much attention to deal with.

They treated her as if it were a badge of honor to go through what she had, almost like she was a celebrity. In a way, she was; it was surreal to see herself and Joshua on the front page of the local newspaper and featured on the evening news. But it was also a false celebrity. They treated her like that because they thought she was a helpless victim. An innocent bystander who'd been in the wrong place at the wrong time.

They talked some more, but something about the visit was off. It was in the way they looked at her, the way they reacted to her statements. When talking with her, they all seemed a little reluctant and tentative, not their normal selves. She figured they knew her well enough to be able to tell that she was hiding something, but she knew they couldn't have suspected the entire story.

After they'd left, she realized Carmella hadn't been with them. Karen figured she must've been working.

ON WEDNESDAY, JOSHUA RETURNED TO SCHOOL. HE PUT IN ONLY A HALF day, and when it ended, they spent the afternoon together. They went to the theater to watch a movie. Grabbed a bite from the mall food court. Went for a walk. She hoped it would be therapeutic, but they were both so sad and distracted.

That night, they ate dinner together, just the two of them. It was the first night they'd been able to sit down and eat together like they normally did.

"So, what was it?" Karen asked. "What was the highlight of your day?"

Joshua shook his head. "Really, Mom? You want to play this game?"

"Yeah. Let's go. We have to start getting back to normal little by little. Or at least attempt to. So go ahead. Answer the question."

"A lot of people came up to me at school, told me they were happy I was okay," Joshua said. "That was kinda cool."

"That's nice."

"What about you?"

The highlight of her day—what was it? Tough question. She'd moped around the house when Joshua was at school. Distracted herself by looking for bargain mattresses online to replace her old one. Tried to take a nap on the couch but had given up after lying there with her eyes open for almost an hour.

"It was nice spending the afternoon with you," she eventually said to Joshua.

That was the obvious answer. Really the only answer. But even as pleasant as their afternoon together had been, it had felt off. Just a tad uncomfortable.

They ate in silence for a while. She tried to think of a few questions that could spark conversation, but she couldn't come up with anything.

"Okay, be honest with me," she finally said. "How are you doing?"

He shrugged.

"I don't know. It's tough."

"What's tough?"

"Everything. I keep thinking about all the stuff that happened. The dead guy. Being held hostage. All that. I can't focus on anything else."

Focus. Yes, she was having trouble focusing, too. It was like there was a part of her that just wouldn't let go of the memory of everything that had happened. A part of her that just wouldn't let her move on with her life.

"I wish I knew what to tell you," she said. "It's only been a few days. Things will get better."

Advice-wise, that was as good as she could do right now. It was still early, probably too early, to start to cope with it all. At least, that's what she told herself. Both she and Joshua would begin trauma counseling at some point, but not yet. It seemed too soon.

TEDDY CAME OVER TO THEIR HOUSE AFTER DINNER. HE SAT ACROSS FROM Karen at their kitchen table, a cup of coffee resting in front of him. He wore a polo with his car dealership logo on the chest.

"How are things?" she asked him.

"Let me put it this way," he said. "I feel worse than I look."

"You don't look that bad," she said.

In truth, he did. Bags under his eyes. His expression distant. Looked like he'd gained a few pounds around his waist, but his face was thin and gaunt.

"I just can't sleep," he said. "I'll lie in bed at night. Close my eyes. And nothing happens. I just lie there as the minutes tick away."

"You're not the only one," she said. "Just being in this house creeps me out. Too much happened here. And the body . . . I can still picture the body. How . . . dead it was. The image of it floating away in the river."

Teddy took a sip of coffee. Stared down at the table. Earlier, when Teddy was still in the hospital, she'd told him how she got rid of the body in the river. The story had floored him.

"Everything just feels so weird," she said. "Seeing how people look at me with compassion. Admiration, even, for everything we went through. If they knew the entire story . . . I can only imagine how they'd look at me then."

"I know what you mean," Teddy said. "My coworkers at the dealership have asked me to repeat my story of what happened about a million times. And every time, they always believe it. They don't suspect I'm lying at all."

Teddy looked down the hallway. Joshua's door was shut.

"How's he doing?"

"Down. Sad. Not much different from me. The golf, I think that hurts him. Not having that. Big part of his life."

She'd taken Joshua for a checkup yesterday. His brain scans looked fine but his dislocated shoulder was worse than doctors had initially thought. They'd decided it would require surgery. With recovery time, he wouldn't be able to swing a golf club for at least six months.

"He's bummed he'll miss his senior year of golf," she said. "He's been looking forward to it. Pretty minor in the grand scheme of things, but it's got him down."

"I've texted him a few times," Teddy said. "To check in. I can just tell by his texts that he's down. His responses are short. Terse. No emotion."

She stared down at his closed bedroom door. She just wanted to see him happy. That was it. She could handle her own gloominess. She just didn't want to see Joshua so down.

She and Teddy sat there for a moment, in silence. Any anger she'd felt toward him had disappeared. It'd be hypocritical to be angry with him. She could've gone to the police at any point. She'd had plenty of opportunities to do so. And every time, she'd lied, lied, lied.

"The body's still missing," Teddy said. "No one has found it yet."

"Yeah. I know."

"Hard to believe it's been out there for three days and no one has found it."

"It might be an even longer wait. It could be carried anywhere. There's no telling how long it'll be until it's found."

NOT LONG, IT TURNED OUT.

The next day, an article ran in the local newspaper. Buried in the back pages. Few people probably even paid attention to it. The article stated that a body had been found in Missouri, washed up on the banks of the Mississippi River. The body was identified as that of William Scanlon, a resident of the Cedar Rapids area. Forty-two years old. No immediate family. Part-time carpenter.

Karen searched online to learn more about him. There wasn't much.

A Facebook page. Thirty-one friends. Hardly any activity. Two messages of consolation were posted.

She found an amateurish Web site showing a few photographs he'd taken, most of abandoned barns and wildlife. A few of the photos were actually pretty good.

An arrest record online. A few counts of assault. Public intoxication.

And that was mostly it. No LinkedIn page or other social media. There was no record of marriage. No children.

The article mentioned foul play was suspected in his death but gave no details beyond that.

ON FRIDAY, KAREN FOUND OUT THAT SHE'D LOST HER JOB.

She showed up for her morning shift feeling a little excited. A bit of a jump in her step. She was looking forward to doing something more than sitting around the house. It'd be good to be around her coworkers again.

When she arrived in the ICU bay, the nurse manager on duty told her she needed to go to the administration office. She was taken to a room and she waited until two women and one man, all wearing suits, entered.

"We have a few questions for you," one of the women said.

She'd expected as much. She'd figured that she'd have to answer questions about when she'd broken Amber out of the hospital. Instead, the questions were focused on what had happened when she saw Carmella steal medication earlier in the year. She answered them honestly, told them the entire story: she'd seen Carmella steal the medication but had decided not to turn her in since it was for her mother.

When they were finished with their questions, they sent her home for the day. Told her not to return to the hospital until she heard back from them.

The call came two hours later. Her employment contract with the hospital was terminated, effective immediately. Her nursing license was suspended, pending further investigation by the state nursing board.

She hung up the phone and stood in the living room for a long time, staring at the ground. Her hands were lightly trembling. Her head was floating.

She was blindsided, barely able to stand. It had happened so suddenly. There had to be some way to fix this, but she could barely think straight.

She moped around the house for the rest of the afternoon. Cried some. A coworker reached out to tell her how sorry she was and told her that Carmella's contract had been terminated, too. Her license was suspended, possibly revoked, for stealing medication. She might face criminal charges.

Strangely, the news about Carmella affected Karen even more than losing her own job.

Carmella was so sweet; she'd only wanted to help her mother. She didn't have anything to do with any of this. The only reason she was involved was because Karen dragged her into it. Blackmailed her. And now her life was close to ruined.

"YOU STARTING TO SLEEP BETTER?" KAREN ASKED TEDDY, LOOKING across the kitchen table at him.

"Sleep?" he said. "What's that?"

"If you find out, let me know."

A brief smile from Teddy. He'd continued to come to the house every evening. She didn't have anyone else to talk to about everything that had happened, no one she could relay her feelings to. There was Joshua, but she didn't want to burden him. She was happy to listen to him, but she didn't want him worrying about her. He had his own problems.

And so Teddy had become her confidant. Her sounding board.

The person she talked to. Every night, he'd come over to the house and they'd spend an hour or two talking. In a weird way, everything that had happened had brought them closer than they'd ever been, even when they'd dated when they were younger.

"The answer to your question is no," Teddy said. "I still can't sleep. It's starting to really affect me. I'm slow all day at work. Can barely form a coherent sentence. The other day, I drifted to sleep at my desk. Almost got caught by my boss."

It was surprising how comfortable she felt around him. How smoothly the conversation flowed. Even when there were silences, they weren't awkward or uncomfortable. Neither of them felt the need to fill them with talk.

Teddy looked down at Joshua's room. Door closed, again. They could just barely hear the low beeping sound effects of some video game he was playing.

"What about him? How is he?"

"Still down."

"I was starting to wonder if it was me. I was worried that he blamed me."

"It's not just you. It's everything. Dealing with it all."

Teddy shook his head.

"I thought that when they found the body, it would bring closure," he said. "Or start to, at least. Like that was the one thing that would tie everything up. But it did nothing. I still can't sleep."

"Closure," she said. "I don't know if there's anything that can bring it."

"I started looking online. Looking at tips about moving on after a traumatic event. Time, they always say. Time heals all wounds. Time has passed; it hasn't done much yet."

"It's still early."

They sat in silence for a while. She was still reeling from being fired. Nursing was such a big part of her life. Far more than just a job. It was how she defined herself in a lot of ways.

She hadn't started looking for a new job yet. Eventually she would. Not in nursing—she was still waiting to hear whether her license would be revoked. But she'd eventually need some sort of job, something to do. Just not right now. Starting a job and dealing with everything else seemed like too much to happen at once.

She'd reached out to Carmella and apologized profusely. Carmella had insisted that it wasn't Karen's fault and said she took full responsibility for stealing the medication, but her words sounded so insincere. Like something she was saying to avoid what she truly wanted to say. The exchange was more awkward than anything else.

Karen got up from the table. Filled a glass with water. Sat back down across from Teddy. Silence.

The door to Joshua's room opened. He slowly walked down the hallway and appeared in the kitchen.

"How ya doing?" Teddy asked.

"Okay."

He walked over to a cupboard and looked inside. Grabbed a few Slim Jims.

The doorbell rang. Joshua walked into the living room to answer it. They watched him slouch by the table and disappear.

"I'm worried about him," she said.

"He has plenty to look forward to. I hope he realizes that. College. Everything after that. His whole life. Hopefully he can move on and—"

"Mom." Joshua's voice. From the living room.

"Yes?"

"Come here."

The tone of his voice worried her. She glanced at Teddy. He shrugged. She stood up from her chair and walked out of the kitchen, Teddy following. He walked with a slight limp from the bullet wound in his leg.

In the living room, Joshua stood next to the front door.

Beside him, standing just outside the open door, were Detective Franny and a man she'd never seen in her life.

THIRTY-FOUR

"HAD A FEW QUESTIONS FOR YOU," FRANNY SAID. THEY'D SAT DOWN IN the living room. She, Teddy, and Joshua sat on the couch. Detective Franny was in the chair. The person he was with stood at the edge of the room. He'd identified himself as Detective Rodriguez. Older, dark-skinned. Hadn't said much beyond a greeting yet.

"Sure," Karen said. "About what?"

"Actually, I was speaking to Joshua." Franny turned toward him. "Can you answer a few questions for us?"

Karen looked over at Joshua. He slowly nodded, eyes wide, mouth slightly open.

"There was a news article from a few days ago about a dead body that was found," Franny said. "Did you happen to see the article?"

"No," Joshua said.

"A friend didn't mention it to you, anything like that?"

Joshua shook his head.

"The body was found down in Missouri, washed up on the banks of the Mississippi. The local police identified him as someone from around here and alerted us. William Scanlon. That name ring a bell?"

"No," Joshua said, his voice cracking.

Franny looked at her and Teddy. "Either of you recognize the name?"

They shook their heads. Karen felt like her heart was going to explode from her chest.

"The case was a weird one," Franny said. "Best as we can tell, he was missing for about a week. The guy didn't have many friends. No job at the moment. Hardly anyone even noticed he was missing."

Franny opened a notebook and looked inside.

"The case is being viewed as a homicide," he said. "Not an accidental drowning. No water in his lungs, so he was dead before he was thrown in the river. Plus, he had a number of suspicious injuries. One of his knees was pretty busted up. Traumatic injury to the side of his head."

"Why are you asking us about him?" Karen said. She had no idea why she was playing dumb. Franny was clearly here for a reason. He knew something.

"A few reasons," Franny said. "Last week, we got a call about him. Turns out Mr. Scanlon was a bit of a hothead, had some trouble with the law in the past, and had been getting anger-management treatment for a few years. His psychiatrist called and told us that Scanlon hadn't shown up to his weekly appointment. The shrink was worried. We looked into his disappearance but nothing came of our search.

"A couple days passed, and we learned why we couldn't find him: he was floating in the Mississippi. Dead as a doornail. After his body washed up onshore in Missouri, the local police found something interesting. There was a camera and some film in the pocket of his coat. His shrink told us he liked taking photos in his free time—sounds like the hobby calmed him, helped him with his anger. Now, the camera was ruined from the water, but the film was stored in a waterproof case. It survived, and we developed the photos."

Karen's stomach rose. She was going to be sick. She was sure of it.

"Most of the photos were of trees and wildlife. A bunch of pictures taken in some sort of forest. We did some searching around, some comparisons, and we think the photos were taken in Hawkeye Wildlife Management Area. Ever been?"

His eyes were locked on Joshua. Joshua stared down at the ground, unblinking. Looked like he was frozen.

"A few times," Joshua said.

"Recently?"

"I don't know. Like a month or two ago."

Franny reached into his briefcase and pulled out an eight-by-ten photograph. He set it on the coffee table.

"This is one of the photos we recovered."

It was a wide shot of the sun setting in the distance behind a group of pine trees. There was a cluster of bushes to the left of the trees. Nothing much stood out about the photograph—

"Look in the lower left corner."

Karen did. There was a small, blurry white mark about half an inch wide.

"Can you see what that is?" Franny asked.

No one responded.

"We had our guys tinker around with the photo. Enlarge it. Sharpen it. And this is what it looks like."

Franny set another picture on the coffee table. It was a blown-up shot of the white dot. The photo was blurry but clear enough for Karen to see it was of a car.

The six digits on the car's license plate were barely visible. They were the six digits of Joshua's license plate.

"That's your car, right?" Franny said.

Joshua nodded. Karen was having difficulty breathing.

"So your car was out there, the night this guy was," Franny said. "Did you happen to see him?"

"No," Joshua said.

"Sure?"

Joshua shook his head.

"I started doing some thinking," Franny said. "I remembered your car. I noticed the windshield when I was here. It was bashed in. The grille was a little busted up, too. What caused that?"

"My friend knocked over a shelf. The shelf fell onto it."

"This friend have a name?"

Joshua gave them Aaron's name. The detective standing on the edge of the room, Rodriguez, wrote down the name in his notebook.

"Can I take a look at the car?" Franny asked.

Joshua glanced at Karen. Back at Franny. He nodded.

They all stood up and walked out to the garage.

JOSHUA WAS CERTAIN HE WAS GOING TO COLLAPSE AS HE WALKED OVER to the garage. This was going to be it. The end.

In the garage, Detective Rodriguez looked at the spiderweb crack in the windshield. He leaned in close.

Joshua held his breath. There'd been some blood on the windshield the night of the accident. He'd wiped as much as he could away with the sleeve of his coat, then poured a bottle of water over the windshield to wash away the remaining blood.

Had he gotten all of it? He had no idea. He'd been in such a hurry. Rushed and hasty. He'd meant to clean it again to make sure there was nothing left, but so much had happened and he hadn't gotten around to it.

Franny stood to the side, staring at them. Not even attempting to hide the fact that he was looking at them.

Joshua looked at his dad and mom. They stared straight ahead, focused on Detective Rodriguez as he examined the windshield.

"Looks like something here," Rodriguez said.

Franny walked over. Rodriguez pointed at an area next to the crack in the windshield. There was a small, barely visible red smudge on the glass.

"Look like blood to you?"

Franny nodded. "It does."

Franny turned to Joshua. "Is that what it is? Blood?"

"No. I don't know."

"Which is it? No? Or you don't know?"

"I don't know." But of course he knew. It was blood. No doubt about it. The police would do testing, link it to the dead man, and there'd be no talking his way out of it. There was nothing he could say to save himself.

"You don't have to play dumb," Franny said. "I've seen enough blood in my career to know what it looks like. And that right there is blood. So, what is going on here? Earlier, Amber told us that the two of you were standing over a dead body in the forest when she and Ross arrived. Not out looking at stars. We thought she was crazy. But now I'm starting to wonder."

Joshua looked at his mom, his dad. He stared down at the ground.

"Look, the pictures prove that this Scanlon guy was out in Hawkeye Wildlife Management Area right before he died," Franny said. "You were, too—at least, your car was. And when we test this blood, we'll find out if it belongs to Scanlon or not. So if you're hiding something, the smart thing to do is to be honest."

It was time to confess. Time to do what he should've done from the start. Come clean. Admit to everything and deal with the consequences. He would—

"I have something to tell you."

His dad's voice. Joshua looked over at him. Teddy was staring at the two detectives, his expression solemn and serious.

"What is it?" Franny said.

"A confession," Teddy said. "I was out there that night. I was driving Joshua's car. And the man whose body you found . . . I'm the one who killed him."

KAREN STARED AT TEDDY, BARELY ABLE TO BELIEVE WHAT SHE'D JUST heard.

"What are you talking about?" Franny said.

"Joshua and I, we were out in the forest a week ago," Teddy said, speaking slowly. "Late at night. I was driving his car and hit a man. Injured him. When we went over to check on the guy, he was furious. He was big, much stronger than either of us. All of a sudden, he went crazy, pushing and shoving us. At one point, he had Joshua pinned to the ground. I thought he was going to seriously hurt him, so I grabbed a rock. Hit him in the head with it. Everything was so frantic. It happened in an instant. Right after I hit him, he stopped moving. I didn't mean to kill him."

"You didn't report this?"

"I was worried. I dumped the body in the river. Told my son to keep it a secret. It was a mistake. That's all I'll say."

Karen listened to it all, stunned, in total shock. There was a part of her that wanted to tell the police that Teddy was lying. Just come clean and tell the truth. But she couldn't. This was how it was going to end. With Teddy ending it for good. Making a sacrifice for Joshua.

"We'll need to bring you down to the station and get your full statement," Franny said.

Teddy nodded. "That's fine."

SO MUCH HAPPENED OVER THE NEXT FEW DAYS THAT IT WAS DIFFICULT to keep track of it all.

Teddy gave his statement and took the blame for everything that had happened. The story was heavily covered in the news. Karen had so many questions for him, so many things she wanted to say, but he was locked up in jail and there was no way to talk to him without the conversation being recorded. She wanted to ask him why he'd done it. Wanted to ask him what he'd been thinking. And, she supposed, she wanted to thank him, too. Thank him for sacrificing himself for their son.

The last she'd heard, it sounded as though he might get off with only a few years. It wasn't really the crime he'd get in trouble for. It was the cover-up.

Teddy had insisted that he'd pressured Joshua into not reporting the crime. Even so, Joshua would face some sort of punishment. He hadn't reported the car accident or the dead body. But his punishment would be nowhere near as severe as Teddy's. His lawyer seemed confident he could keep him out of jail.

In the meantime, Joshua was allowed to return home. He seemed so down. He truly loved his dad, and she could tell his absence pained him deeply. Karen talked a lot with Joshua in the days that followed. They cried a lot, too. Joshua told her he wasn't going to Clemson, that he didn't want to be so far from home with everything going on. She said to think about it, give it some time, but she could tell his mind was made up. He couldn't leave.

The days kept passing, but even so, she couldn't begin to move past everything that had happened. Mostly because so much had taken place in their house. Every single day was a reminder of it all. When she slept at night, it was in the same room Amber had almost died in. When they grabbed something from the storage room, it was the same room where they had been tied up and nearly lost their lives. Even seeing Joshua's car in the garage was a reminder of the accident that had started everything.

Reminders everywhere. Every feeling still lingered.

She held out hope that maybe all she needed was time. She'd never be able to forget about everything, but she hoped that, with time, she might be able to start to move on. Maybe eventually details would be difficult to remember and her sadness would start to disappear.

Time. That was all she needed. That was all Joshua needed, too. She hoped so, at least. There was no magic potion or cure. Just time.

With the passing of time, she hoped they could both eventually start to move on.

They might not get a happy ending, but they would at least get an ending.

And maybe that was all they could hope for.

ACKNOWLEDGMENTS

Many thanks to my agent, Laney Katz Becker. Both books I've written have been improved tremendously through her expert advice, and I truly owe her everything.

I'm so fortunate to work with an amazing editor, Danielle Perez at Berkley. Her knowledge and insight helped this book become the best book it could possibly be. Plus, she's a genuinely great person who's just plain fun to work with.

I also want to give a special thank-you to my publicist, Lauren Burnstein, and marketer, Fareeda Bullert, who are both incredible. And a huge thank-you to Ivan Held and the entire team at Berkley.

Thank you to my copy editor, Eileen Chetti, who did an amazing job making sure the book's details were consistent and accurate.

A majority of this book, like my first novel, was written at Y Café at Twelfth Street and Avenue B in New York City. Thanks to Tommy and Gigi and the rest of the staff for the countless great meals and drinks they served me while I wrote.

ENJOYED *ONE FATAL MISTAKE*?

DON'T MISS TOM HUNT'S THRILLING DEBUT:

A KILLER CHOICE.

'Unputdownable and highly recommended'

LEE CHILD